GW00693700

Rosemary Friedman's first novel *No White Coat* was an immediate success. Since then she has published 21 fiction and non-fiction titles which have been widely translated and serialised by the BBC. She has also published many short stories. *The Writing Game*, an inspirational memoir for writers and readers, was published in 1999.

She has written commissioned screenplays for film and TV in the UK and US, and her play *Home Truths* toured successfully in major venues throughout the UK. Rosemary has judged many distinguished literary prizes, contributed book reviews to the TLS and major national newspapers and is an active member of English PEN. She is married to a psychiatrist and lives in London.

INTENSIVE CARE

BY THE SAME AUTHOR
ALL PUBLISHED BY HOUSE OF STRATUS

No White Coat
Love on My List
We All Fall Down
Patients of a Saint
The Fraternity
The Commonplace Day
The General Practice
Practice Makes Perfect
The Life Situation
The Long Hot Summer
Proofs of Affection
A Loving Mistress
Rose of Jericho
A Second Wife
To Live in Peace
An Eligible Man
Golden Boy
Vintage

INTENSIVE CARE

ROSEMARY FRIEDMAN

For Pam and Philip
with love.

Rosemary Friedman

26/4/01

HOUSE OF
STRATUS

Copyright © 2001 Rosemary Friedman

All rights reserved. No part of this publication may be reproduced, stored in a
retrieval system, or transmitted, in any form, or by any means (electronic,
mechanical, photocopying, recording, or otherwise), without the prior permission of
the publisher.
Any person who does any unauthorised act in relation to this publication may be
liable to criminal prosecution and civil claims for damages.

The right of Rosemary Friedman to be identified as the author of this work has been
asserted in accordance with sections 77 and 78 of the Copyright, Designs and Patents
Act 1988.

This edition published in 2001 by House of Stratus, an imprint of
Stratus Holdings plc, 24c Old Burlington Street, London, W1X 1RL, UK.

www.houseofstratus.com

Typeset, printed and bound by House of Stratus.

A catalogue record for this book is available from the British Library.

ISBN 0-7551-0012-3

This book is sold subject to the condition that it shall not be lent, resold, hired out, or
otherwise circulated without the publisher's express prior consent in any form of
binding, or cover, other than the original as herein published and without a similar
condition being imposed on any subsequent purchaser, or bona fide possessor.

This is a fictional work and all characters are drawn from the author's imagination.
Any resemblances or similarities to persons either living or dead
are entirely coincidental.

For Julia Polak

ACKNOWLEDGMENTS

I am grateful for the help and support of Professor Julia Polak, Dr Anne Bishop, Dr Emma Friedman, Jo Hatton (in memoriam), Professor K K Adour, Mr Said Habib, Richard Lawson, Dr David Springal (in memoriam), Brian Spiro, Dr Emma Birk and Sandra Lock.

PROLOGUE

According to the Audemars Piguet Fletcher had given her for her birthday, the minuscule face of which she found increasingly hard to read, it was getting on for six o'clock and Harrods had promised to deliver the ice-cream bombe by half-past five at the latest.

At the age of seventy-two, Clarice Goddard entertained at her Knightsbridge home increasingly rarely. She and Fletcher had made a conscious decision to ignore Jung's admonition to spend the afternoon of their lives differently from the morning, and had decided to march to the rhythm of their psychic rather than their corporeal ages. While at weekends they were comfortably tucked up in bed by ten with their reading specs, the newspapers and the TV, there were few nights in the week, which they spent in town, that they did not put in appearance at one function or another: charity concerts, Save the Children or Friends of the Tate, appropriately kitted out for the part. Socialising was a full-time job; at her time of life, just keeping the ancient monument that was her well-preserved body in working order was a full-time job. A glance at the *Harpers & Queen* diary with its gold tooled initials – for which she surreptitiously removed the coupon from the magazine in one waiting-room or other each November – revealed a series of appointments which lined the pockets of various dental and medical practitioners in the environs of Harley Street. She was waited upon in addition by a hairdresser, who not only ensured that she never went grey, but who cut her thinning hair with the kind of attention bestowed on the topiary, privet swans and eagles which graced the lawns of Meadowlands, their Norfolk home, plus a chiropodist (podiatrists they called themselves now), a beauty therapist (depilation and eyelash tint), a diet counsellor (Fletcher had already had one coronary bypass operation and she was determined he should not have another), a masseuse, and sundry reflexologists, acupuncturists, thallaso-, aroma-,

i

and whichever other therapists happened to be in vogue. Add to that the dressmaker she shared with Her Majesty the Queen, the milliner who ensured she was suitably (though not ostentatiously) hatted for Ascot and the Royal Garden Party (where she was always amazed to discover that Her Majesty neglected to provide paper napkins because of the consequent litter), the *corsetière* where they kept her vital statistics on file, the old Greek where she had her shoes hand-made for a sum which made her wince, and the smiling manicurist who came from Hong Kong and attended her at the flat.

Clarice was proud of her hands with their long fingers, the knuckles only negligibly thickened by arthritic changes, their tapering almond-shaped nails with a smooth coating of creamy varnish, the flattering circles of platinum and diamonds and the handsome square-cut emerald which matched exactly the *poule de soie* of the figure-hugging top she wore over her black taffeta skirt, and which reflected, in the purest of translucent greens, the dancing light from the newly-cleaned crystal chandelier. She had a thing about hands. In a man it was the first thing she looked at. It was one of the reasons she had married Fletcher, possibly the only reason. They had little in common. She had thrown in her lot with the fledgling banker on her return from her Swiss finishing school largely to avoid having to make a decision about what to do with her life from the unexciting choices on offer, and to escape from the paternalistic constraints of a home where a good marriage, for the three girls at any rate, was, in accordance with the precepts of Jane Austen and the post-war years, the quintessence of achievement.

She had met Fletcher at a ball – where else? – and the solid warmth of his unambiguous response to her body as he steered her clumsily round the dance floor excited her far less than his immaculate hands, proficient and strong, on the steering wheel of the family Bentley as he drove her home to Groom Place.

They had been married at Meadowlands and the honeymoon, paid for by Fletcher's father who was chairman of the bank, had been spent at the Hotel Scribe in Paris and the Negresco in Nice. As far as sex was concerned, Clarice, who had been a virgin at the time both in body and mind, could take it or leave it, and while Fletcher took it, at opportunities both available and unavailable, she left the mechanics of it to him and was happy to let him get on with it while, neither liking nor disliking what seemed to her a grossly overrated pastime, her mind was elsewhere. He was a good husband. Of that there was no doubt. While he had kept his marriage vows to love and to cherish her, about which there was not the slightest degree of dissimulation, once the children began to arrive reservations started to infiltrate her preoccupied mind about his promise to remain faithful to her, but as things turned out she was hardly the one to talk. After fifteen years of a relatively harmonious marriage in which both she and Fletcher settled down into their respective places, Clarice, in a belated sexual awakening which concealed itself in a bout of unaccustomed depression, became uncomfortably aware that there was something lacking in her life and that what she desperately needed was the touch of a stranger: the exploration of another body and another mind. She found herself, for a moment too long, holding the gaze of unknown men, blushing, like a young girl, at the attentions of the least likely of them.

In an attempt to accommodate Fletcher, who spent his weekends, when it was not the season for shooting, on the golf course, she had agreed, whilst he was in Japan on business, to take lessons from the pro at his club so that they might enjoy golfing holidays together. The pro, whose name was Mike Beasley, had found it necessary to stand behind her and put his muscular arms around her body in order to demonstrate the correct back swing, and it neither surprised nor disgusted his pupil when she swivelled in his grasp one day to find a passionate tongue in her mouth. Mike had accepted a position as golf pro on a new Robert Trent golf course near Marbella. Their short-lived affair had astonished Clarice only in so far as her own responses were concerned. In an anonymous hotel room above a Surrey pub, she had flung off her accustomed modesty together with her underwear and kneeled to take his powerful penis in her mouth, giving it the attention and regard she had refused, point-blank, no matter what inducements he offered, to bestow upon Fletcher's no less accomplished organ. Oblivious to the fact that her cries of pleasure could be heard through the afternoon window which was pulled hastily shut by her erect Adonis, she had screamed and begged in a crescendo of delight, which afterwards she was amazed to find had come from her own vocal chords.

If she shut her eyes now, even after all these years, she could have drawn a map of her lover's lean body – with its carpet of curled hair that met the long line extending from his penis to his deep navel in the front and petered out at the base of his spine at the sharp divide of his trim buttocks – which she had been unable to resist smothering with uninhibited kisses. All that had been long ago. Back safely in Fletcher's bed, while her body had been willing to abandon itself to an experience she had found quite mind-blowing, to coin a phrase, her authoritarian mindset was not, and both had shrivelled back into apathetic acceptance, neither welcoming nor complaining of his advances. It was some years now since they had settled comfortably into the more undemanding routines of companionship. She neither knew nor cared what Fletcher did with his undiminished sex drive. Since that time the mutual dependency which couples in their advancing years mistook for love had developed between them. Each cared when the other was ill, mentally out of sorts, or unable to cope with what had become an increasingly alien and often hostile world apparently run by children. The unspoken fear that, sooner or later one of them was bound to lose the other as a result of age, illness, or a combination of both, strengthened the bond between them. Next year – it was hard to believe – they would celebrate half a century of marriage to each other, an aberration in this day and age, and they were already discussing how to celebrate the momentous occasion that coincided neatly (she liked everything to be neat) with the millennium. Clarice, in a rush of unrealistic benevolence, had suggested that they took their entire tribe, children and grandchildren, on a family holiday to some exotic location. Fletcher, who had been shaving at the time, almost cut his chin with the old-fashioned razor by which he still swore. He raised his bushy eyebrows in the bathroom mirror and said how could you live for a day, let alone a week, in the midst of a brood which included the four warring siblings that were their own children and a diverse assortment of infants and teenagers, some of whom had embraced one or other of the prevalent weird cults, pierced and adorned their bodies in the most bizarre and primitive fashion, were slaves to impossible feeding regimes, were in many instances attached to undesirable partners, and in any event were more than likely to be in the midst of examinations or in an alternative hemisphere. Fletcher was right of course. It had been a romantic dream on Clarice's part as she imagined them all on a deserted island skipping scantily clad round some tropical beach, as in a Boucher painting, in an excess of love and goodwill. In the event they had settled for a cocktail party at Claridge's and were preparing the guest list, already reduced by natural wastage.

When the front doorbell rang, breaking into her reverie, Clarice guessed it must be the ice-cream bombe she had ordered to accompany the tropical fruit salad prepared by Milly, the Filipina maid who had been in her employ for more than twenty years and was more of a friend than a servant. The dessert would satisfy the taste of those of her six dinner guests – the table would only accommodate eight – who had a sweet tooth. With the small heels of her black satin pumps sinking into the deep velvet pile of the carpet, she made her way along the hall, hurrying in case the delivery boy, although it was usually quite an elderly man these days possessed of old-fashioned courtesy, assumed there was no one at home and took the dessert away again.

Opening the front door with the spyhole and several locks with which they safeguarded themselves against intruders at night, Clarice was ready to register her complaint about the tardiness of the delivery (which she would insist be passed on to the manager of the Food Hall). But it was not the bombe.

Two youths, balaclavas over their heads, pushed their way roughly past her, pausing only to turn the Banham in the lock and remove it from the keyhole. In the space of a few seconds a dialogue took place in Clarice's mind: there had been a number of 'incidents' in the vicinity recently. She should not have opened the door. Murphy the doorman, a constant vigilante, should not have let the two into the building. She never opened the door without looking first through the spyhole – Fletcher had warned her often enough. Fletcher would be back any minute to put on his black tie and organise the drinks. So would Milly, who had gone home to change before she waited at table. The police, she must telephone the police… The two were there before her, ripping the instrument (which sat on the satinwood console table and matched the dove-grey Brussels weave carpet) from its socket. One of them wore blue jeans, a brown leather jacket and heavy walking boots, the other a track-suit, with a white stripe down the leg, and trainers.

'Safe keys.' The taller of the two held out a brown hand, as if she kept the key of the safe about her person. Hesitating for only a moment, she realised that the other young man, the one who had ripped the telephone from the wall and wound the severed flex neatly round his pale fingers, had whipped agilely behind her and was holding what felt suspiciously like the blade of a knife to her throat. She grasped, for the first time, although even now it did not really sink in, that she was in serious trouble.

'Hand over the fucking keys, Grandma.' The voice was menacing but paradoxically it was the appellation which offended her. Although she was indeed a grandmother several times over, she hated to be categorised as such, preferring to regard herself as a still youngish woman who just happened to have grandchildren, rather than as a stereotypical grandmother, which according to her children for whom she refused to babysit, she was not. The knife was pressing uncomfortably hard against her Adam's apple.

'I don't have the key...' She admired the fact that she had kept her cool and not allowed herself to be intimidated, but did not recognise the quavering sound of her own voice.

'Bullshit!'

'My husband has the key...'

'Don't give me that crap.'

'He'll be here any minute.' She looked involuntarily at the Audemars Piguet before it was snatched roughly from her wrist, burning the skin and bringing tears to her eyes. She sobbed with self-pity as the emerald solitaire and the diamond eternity rings were torn from her fingers, bruising and scraping the knuckles and making them bleed. This was getting decidedly unfunny. She wished fervently that she had allowed Fletcher to connect them to Red Alert as he had suggested, the advertisements for which depicted an elderly, grey-haired woman with whom she had no wish to identify, sprawled unconscious on the floor.

'Move!' The coarse voice, which clearly belonged to someone of the lower denominations, was tense. Mention of Fletcher's imminent return had made him uncertain. Deciding that it was preferable to lose her jewellery and whatever valuables Fletcher had in the safe rather than her life, Clarice led her careful way to the bedroom, terrified that the knife blade, which was still at her throat, would slip. Opening a cupboard she removed the safe key from beneath a pile of Fletcher's impeccably ironed and neatly folded shirts. As she turned to hand it to her captors she realised with shock that the smaller man of the two was unzipping his jeans. Oh God, surely not that. This was turning into a real nightmare. Surely that was not what they wanted from a woman of her age? She tried to remember whether one was supposed to struggle or submit when threatened with sexual assault and prayed that it would not be what they referred to in the newspapers as an 'indecent' one, as if any of it were decent. She tried not to stare as the man, who had a missing tip to his finger, extracted his purple penis and proceeded in full view of her to urinate on the ivory carpet, a deed to which she reacted with almost as much disgust as if she had in fact been raped. Pulling herself together (a carpet was, after all, only a carpet when all was said and done) Clarice decided to try reason.

'Listen you two, why don't we try to sort this out between us…?'

'Shut your fuckin' gob.' The urinating man had now jumped up on to the bed and was in the process of defecating on her quilt. This was going too far. She thought that she would faint. That she was going to be sick. Aware of the knife, pressed harder now to her throat, she decided that the entire episode, which seemed to have lasted for ever but which had taken no more than a few moments, was not happening to her and that she was dreaming it. She led the way into the dining-room where, on the drawn-thread tablecloth, translucent slices of smoked salmon were tastefully arranged on blue glass plates, each with its lemon half, to await her guests. As she moved towards the portrait of herself, for which she had worn a *guipure* lace dress to emphasise her tiny waist and which had been painted at the time of her marriage, an outstretched hand removed the cling-film and helped itself to a grubby fistful of smoked salmon which disappeared rapidly beneath the balaclava. Reverting to dinner party mode, she thought irrationally – what strange tricks the mind played! – that as the hostess she would have to make do with half an avocado and pretend that she did not care for salmon.

As she struggled to remove the portrait concealing the wall safe, she realised that she had been half expecting some flattering comment on the likeness, which had been captured in pastel colours by quite a well-known artist.

'Get the fuck on with it.' The words were accompanied by an unexpectedly sharp blow to her ear, making her dizzy. The key was snatched preremptorily from her hand and inserted into the lock. This left the tumbler with its arrow and its dedicated code, which she had used only a short while ago to get her emerald ring from the safe. Both the six digits, and the number of turns of the marked wheel which must be executed in specified directions with each entry, refused to come. She knew that the first two numbers had to do with their eldest daughter's birthday, which was on the 22nd of March, unless it was the youngest's on August the 15th. Either 22 or 15 followed by 99 – which was what the doctor used to make you say when he wanted to look down your throat and which they had decided was easy to remember – then the year in which Fletcher had been born or was it the date of his birthday? She tried 22, turning the tumbler four times to the left and trying to get her shaking hand to stop the dial precisely on the line, then three turns to the right and 99, two more to the left and 23, the 23rd of May. She pulled the handle. Nothing happened. It must have been 24, 1924, the year Fletcher had been born...

There was another blow, this time to the other ear. It was no good, her mind had seized up. A fist in her back brought her to her knees as a frantic hand wrenched at the unyielding handle to the safe.

'I'm sorry,' she heard herself apologising. 'I can't remember the combination.'

'She's 'aving us on.'

''Aving us on are you, Grandma?' A kick from the heavy boot flattened her on to her back on the narrow stretch of parquet between the chairs and the wall, which smelled of the liquid wax Milly had applied that morning.

'Leave it. The silly bitch 'as lost 'er marbles.'

There was a crash from above as the crisp tablecloth was pulled from beneath the place settings, sending shards of blue glass, slivers of smoked salmon and halves of muslin-wrapped lemon scudding over the floor. Clarice thought how concerned her grandfather would have been at the decimation of the set of plates which he had brought back from Murano as a present for her grandmother and which had been in the family for so long. The tablecloth was used as a container to hold what she assumed (she was unable to see) were her silver candlesticks and cutlery, the wine coasters and anything else that was of value from the table, while her captor hastened to bind her hands and feet with the telephone flex, which he slashed into two and tied in cruelly tight knots. Slipping the knife into his waistband, he aimed a series of vicious kicks at her body.

'Cut it out, Wayne!'

'Wayne! Wayne? Fucking fuckhead!' Taking his anger at his companion's indiscretion out on Clarice, her assailant kicked her sharply, several times, in the region of her kidneys. Although the pain was worse than that of childbirth and made her want to vomit, the chandelier on the ceiling was revolving and she was soon past feeling it. She no longer thought, no longer cared. 'Fucking Paki!' Using his full force, the youth brought his foot down, again and again until he heard the satisfactory crack of bone.

*   *   *   *   *

Fletcher's first intimation that all was not well was that Murphy, a proud Janus, was not at his usual post in the pillared foyer, sitting at his desk near the lift from which he vetted all comers to the building. Assuming that the porter had been summoned by one of the tenants to replace an out-of-reach light bulb, or that he was delivering a parcel, Fletcher took the lift to the second floor as usual, where he was surprised to find a square package from Harrods (leaking slightly at the corners) left on the outside mat. Neither of these two anomalies prepared him for the tribulation that was to come.

Picking up the sodden box and letting himself into the flat, the fact that the telephone on the console table had been disconnected did not register; neither did the observation that a salt cellar had been dropped, spilling its contents on the hall floor. Clarice, he surmised, had gone into the kitchen to fetch a dustpan and brush. 'Clarice!' He called her name.

The silence puzzled him. Were they not expecting dinner guests within the hour? 'Clarice!'

The kitchen, stainless steel pans of water ready for the vegetables on the cooker and Spode coffee cups on a tray, was empty, as was the bedroom, where not only was the door to his cupboard open and his shirts had been disturbed but to his horror someone had defecated on the bedcover and urinated on the floor. With fear such as he had not known even during his war years now gripping his entrails, and in a state of panic and trepidation which froze his larynx and prevented him from calling his wife's name, he moved towards the drawing-room where the velvet and tapestry cushions had been plumped and arranged with military precision and the sherry decanter, eight glasses, and a small dish of salted almonds sparkled on a silver tray.

'Clarice?' His voice, tense now with fear, did not reach his lips. Crossing the Rubicon that was the two steps to the threshold of the dining-room, the disarray of broken glass, smoked salmon, halves of lemon, and thinly sliced brown bread and butter which littered the floor stopped him in his tracks.

Afterwards, when Milly had innocently returned in her white apron – later to be smeared with blood, when the ambulance crew had come with their stretcher and respectfully taken his wife's body to the mortuary, when the dinner guests he had forgotten to cancel had silently gone on their shocked way with their beribboned chocolates and their bottles of wine, when the police officer had finished questioning him as if he had soiled his own bed and murdered his own wife, when at last he was alone with the rest of his life, he had taken out his thoughts and examined them – to find that the mind which could plan and execute the most complicated of take-over bids was vacant, except for the image which he would be unable to expunge no matter how long he lived: the unequivocal imprint of the sole of a heavy boot on Clarice's dead face.

Having righted an upturned chair he was still sitting fully dressed in the dining-room when the newspapers arrived next morning. *Concierge in cupboard gagged. Kensington pensioner in savage murder. Drummond Street joy-riders in 150 mph crash apprehended, one dead, one in coma.*

ONE

As a Reader in Mathematics, accustomed to understanding averages and seeing through the political manipulation of statistics, Dermot Tanney thought he should have been able instantly to decipher the instructions on the sleeve of the box of steak and mushroom pie, which he had discovered wedged icily between the Chinese meal for two and the beef teryaki in the freezer. Wondering what madman had decreed that the instructions should be inscribed on the reverse of the package, so that it was necessary to turn the whole thing upside down to read, possibly damaging the piecrust, he put on the same recently acquired half-glasses through which he read the text of his lectures when he was lost for words (which having kissed the Blarney Stone was not very often). He sat down at the table, at which Sebastian, plugged into his Walkman, was ostensibly doing his homework, to give what passed for food these days his undivided attention.

'Your mother should be home soon.' Trying to hide the anxiety in his voice, he sent the first ball, a friendly lob, over the net that seemed relentlessly to divide the generations. The well-meaning remark with which Dermot had intended to open a hoped-for dialogue with his son fell upon deaf ears. He repeated it a semi-tone more loudly. 'Your mother should be home soon.'

Sebastian, in black regulation pullover (dotted with crumbs from his tea) and the regulation grey shirt from the open collar of which hung the loosened knot of limp string that was his school tie, did not look up from the exercise book where he was busy embellishing with extravagant doodles in the shape of space rockets the single line he had managed to write.

'Did you hear what I said?'

A grunt of assent emerged from between the earphones.

'Then why did you not reply?'

'It wasn't a question.'

Dermot could not dispute the veracity of the statement. Game to Sebastian. He felt the gall rise in his throat, the taste of which was familiar when he attempted any intercourse with the thirteen-year-old, and sent his next, avowedly sneaky, shot, on which there was a scarcely concealed back-spin, into the boy's court.

'Did you bring home your report?'

After a long moment's hesitation and without looking up, Sebastian reached into his bag on the back of the chair, removed a slim red booklet bearing the legend *Lion School* and flung it nonchalantly into the no man's land of marked and pitted oak which lay between his father and himself. Deciding to ignore the overt insolence of Sebastian's riposte, Dermot picked up the document and turned to the painstaking black copperplate of the first page:

'Dear Dr Tanney and Professor Sands, despite the difficulties at home, Sebastian has had a satisfactory year. Although the odd mild criticism emerges here and there in this report, his overall results may be regarded as satisfactory...'

Difficulties at home. To the outsider the problems could seem small and unimportant, facts interpreted according to the emotional assumptions of the listener, like the war that in the opinion of some was fought to protect a people and their culture from external threat, and in the opinion of others was waged with the aggressive intention of expropriating more land. Difficulties at home. Litotes. St Paul was a citizen of no mean city. The emotive power of language, in which the guerrilla was both freedom fighter and terrorist, the liberator an invader, the dissident a criminal, according to where one happened to be standing, according to one's point of view. Truth, with its potential for light and shade, its susceptibility to obfuscation, bothered Dermot, which was why he had embraced the science of mathematics with its proofs and certitudes, its concrete data, where your answer was either right or it was not. Forgetting the steak and mushroom pie as it slowly defrosted to leave a wet mark on the table (the domesticity in which he had to engage more and more lately did not come naturally), he returned to the report.

'...Sebastian is in the happy position of choosing his GCSE options from a position of strength. He is a delightful boy and, as his form master, I have no trouble with him. He clearly has much potential and I look forward to seeing this fulfilled in the future...'

Looking across the table at his son, who had added only one word to his *oeuvre* and was tapping his feet to the rhythm of whatever incomprehensible sounds were emerging from his headset, Dermot tried to see the boy through the eyes of Mr Blunt, a man whose surname was invariably replaced by the boys in his care with a more down-to-earth epithet. 'A delightful boy.' If Mr Blunt had seen his pupil, braces on his teeth, slumped with a bag of crisps in front of the television set each evening, glued to some sit-com with its maniacal and inappropriate post-production laughter when Dermot wanted to catch up with the news...or if he heard his every remark responded to, if indeed it was responded to, with the most cursory of grunts...if he were appraised of the boy's bedroom and bathroom habits which did not bear examination, if he had any intimation of Sebastian's determination to go through life with the minimum of effort and the least consideration for others, with an apathetic and often loutish demeanour which betrayed the lack of the most basic social skills, perhaps Blunt would not have regarded his pupil as being quite so delightful.

Dermot tried to remember his own childhood, but since his father, a pig exporter from County Cork, had left his home and his mother – a hard-working primary school teacher – for a nubile young vet when Dermot was three years old, there was no comparison to be made. He turned the page. 'English. Excellent year. In class Sebastian has continued to contribute helpfully although he still has a tendency to chatter...' A tendency to chatter. If he did converse in class, he left his vocal skills in school together with the rugby shirt that he invariably forgot to bring home to be washed until it was so permeated with mud that it could stand up by itself. 'Chemistry. With application and discipline Sebastian might improve his written work. Maths. B minus. Well below his excellent potential. Sebastian remains disorganised...' Looking at the confusion of sweet papers and exercise books, the Lion School scarf, the single plimsoll, the spilled pencil case, the well-thumbed comic, the calculator, the laser torch, the French verb book with its torn cover and the IT manual which lapped at Sebastian's feet, he thought that disorganised was hardly the word for it. B minus. B minus for maths! It was a bone of contention, but as his wife Sidney was fond of saying in defence of Sebastian (she spent her life defending him), not everyone can do fractals and Fibonacci numbers. Mathematics was not a question of fractal and Fibonacci numbers; not a question of how long it takes for a tap to fill a bath. It was a matter of being able check your change, to understand averages, to know that a fall in the annual percentage increase in the crime rate didn't mean that things were necessarily getting better. As he had tried to explain to Sidney on more than one occasion when the subject of Sebastian came up (which was too frequently for comfort), whenever one filled the freezer or attempted to fit luggage into the boot of the car, what one was doing was in fact quite complicated three-dimensional geometry…

'Why don't you put it in the oven?' The subject of his speculation did not raise his head from the table. He had problems with meeting his father's critical gaze.

'Put what in the oven?' Dermot remembered the supper he was preparing for Sidney's return. He opened the oven, slung the box, from which he had removed the sleeve and cardboard lid as directed, into its maw before turning his attention to the potatoes that he had bought from the Indian mini-market on his way home from the university, and which sat with accusing eyes on the draining-board.

Although the house was on five floors, the basement kitchen, French doors looking out on to the tangled garden which neither he nor Sidney had time to control, and front windows protected by an iron grille giving on to the Islington pavement with its miniature dust storms, was the hub. The house's warren of rooms was untouched by the prevailing designer ethos which made the surrounding homes of the professional middle classes with their Victorian baths and Conran sofas interchangeable. If the kitchen was the engine-room of the house, Sidney was its captain. Or had been. Organised and capable, she had taken up her position at the sink or the cooker after a full day's work almost without taking her coat off. No matter how late it was nor how traumatic her day, and apparently without effort, talking all the time, she would proceed to knock up an appetising meal for the three of them from ingredients she had bought on her way home from the hospital. Secure in the knowledge of her own proficiency, Sidney ran her home with the same lack of fuss and cheerful competence with which she ran her department, cutting through obstacles and tactfully solving problems. Both would have been hard put to manage without her. Dermot was not only a mathematician but also a popular science writer (he tried to show where mathematics fitted into human culture), a media guru beloved by female viewers who found his intellect sexy. He lived in his head, where the mental constructs of non-linear dynamics, algebra and topology – so vivid that he felt them to be real – took precedence over the problem of clean shirts (which he solved by wearing black polo-neck sweaters) and what they were to have for dinner. The one area where he took charge was the interiors of the cupboards. He lived his life by patterns, finding equations in fields of corn, in the movement of football crowds, and in share prices. Fascinated by the identical wave configurations to be found in sand dunes and liquid crystal displays, he would stand for hours mixing symbols and geometry, organizing tins of beans, packets of biscuits and canisters of rice into perfect symmetry in the larder. As far as visual splendour was concerned, computer graphics now allowed people to enjoy the glory of mathematics without having to do the hard work, but, as he told his students, the teaching of mathematics was like the teaching of music: anyone could be taught to listen, most people could achieve some degree of proficiency, but very few became virtuosi and fewer still composers. The job of musicians was not to sight read, and the job of mathematicians was not simply to understand what the symbols meant and to play around with them, but to use the symbolism as a tool for understanding the real nature of the problem: to emulate the creator rather than to read from the sheet music.

Just as at social gatherings the medical practitioner was often greeted with a catalogue of symptoms, the lawyer asked how he could tolerate the defence of one whom he knew to be guilty, the writer questioned about where he got his ideas, when the mathematician revealed his métier to strangers an embarrassed silence ensued, followed by, 'I was never very good at maths at school', as if the confession were something of which to be proud. Most people were better at maths than they thought. Mathematics was more than arithmetic, more than being adept at mental arithmetic, which, paradoxically, was often counterproductive: mathematics was embedded in the culture of everyday life. The surface of a mug of tea, no matter which way it was stirred, could be counted on to produce spirals rather than some other pattern, and the simple act of slicing a banana demonstrated the shape of energy at the surface of a pendulum.

Peeling the potatoes awkwardly with his left hand, using Sidney's right-handed potato peeler, Dermot cut them into satisfying shapes –

hexagons and rhomboids, triangles and rectangles – before fitting them neatly into the saucepan. This mundane task, during which he tried to come up with some revolutionary insight into the universe that could promote a new way of thinking about the natural world, of driving the planet forward, kept him from dwelling on what Mr Blunt had dismissed so casually as the 'difficulties' which had permeated the house and taken over their lives in the past six months.

At the age of forty-two, his darling Sidney was dying. Without medical intervention, in anything from a few weeks to a few months she would be dead. As a scientist who carried out no experiments, who solved problems with no direct practical application, he had tried to come to grips with the fact that he had to stand by, able to do nothing as she deteriorated before his eyes. He regarded it all as a river which had to be crossed and tried to invent a piece of mathematics which would take him to the other side. So far he had had no success and each time he thought about it or set eyes on Sidney he felt a sensation so devastating in the pit of his stomach that he was forced to hide behind a wall of flim-flam, which deceived nobody, least of all his wife.

Nine months ago he had accompanied Sidney to an endocrinology meeting in Paris where, suddenly overtaken by an episode of dizziness and exhaustion, she had spent much of the weekend in the hotel bedroom. Ignoring the fact that it was some time since she had felt really well and that she had progressive difficulty in climbing the stairs and walking, Sidney attributed her symptoms to a recurrence of the childhood asthma which had reappeared when Sebastian was born and had lately been troubling her again. She had refused to let Dermot call a doctor. She put her fatigue and breathlessness down to overwork, to too much travelling, to too many international conferences, to stress in the understaffed Department of Histochemistry, and to the fact that her routine asthma remedies no longer seemed effective. Apart from lamenting the lost weekend, neither of them had been too bothered. Back home again, Sidney took no notice of the fact that she was finding physical activity more and more difficult and she continued with her work at the postgraduate medical school, where for some time she had been collaborating with the head of cardiac surgery, Professor Eduardo Cortes, on research into terminal pulmonary disease.

A cursory examination by a colleague in the cardiology department to whom she finally confided her symptoms, which now included chest pain, endorsed her diagnosis of asthma. As the weeks went by, however, she became more and more incapacitated and could no longer make light of her condition. When she finally collapsed during a meeting in her office and announced that she would die if she were not looked at 'properly', she was admitted to a ward in the hospital to which the postgraduate medical school was attached. The consultant physician – to whom she confessed for the first time that her breathing had become so bad that she now had to sleep sitting up – had been horrified to find that the venous blood pressure in her neck was dangerously high and the veins above the collar-bone grossly engorged. When the diagnosis was made of 'right-sided heart failure secondary to pulmonary hypertension' – a condition in which the blood pressure in the arteries leading to the lungs is abnormally high – Dermot had at first felt a sense of relief. Primary pulmonary hypertension, or PPH, didn't sound all that serious, not like motor neurone disease or cancer, and when Sidney was discharged from hospital with her bottles of anti-coagulants and calcium blockers and instructions to go upstairs only once a day, her colour was good and she had looked rested rather than ill. Despite the massive side effects she experienced from her medication, which included weight gain and swollen legs, she refused to abandon her responsibilities. After a short period of bed rest and continuous oxygen, she carried on as best she could with the help of Dermot and Sebastian, who fed her peanut butter sandwiches and brought up slopping cups of tea.

When Dermot was summoned urgently by a neighbour who had found Sidney, rambling and confused, in the overgrown garden, he had called the ambulance and she was admitted to hospital, where tests revealed her heart and lungs to be so severely damaged that replacement organs were her only option. Without a transplant she would die.

At first Dermot had refused to believe it. He did not hold with illness, largely because he had never been ill. He realised that he had been deluding himself about the seriousness of Sidney's situation, which she had herself largely dismissed. Aware that even if organs were available they did not guarantee a cure, he took refuge in statistics. There were three hundred patients on the transplant list at the Fulham Hospital; one hundred and twenty transplants were carried out each year and half were successful; seventy per cent of these patients survived more than a few months. Repeating the facts like a mantra, but unable to assimilate them, he took Sidney home to face the psychological and physical burdens of confirmed heart failure. Each day that passed without a call from the hospital transplant co-ordinator brought Sidney closer to death, and Dermot, whose life had been spent unearthing answers, no nearer to finding a solution to the problem uppermost in his mind.

Despite Dermot's protests, and with the help of an oxygen inhaler, Sidney had managed to carry on working by sheer force of will. Today was the sixtieth anniversary of the Postgraduate Medical School, at which event she had promised to give the keynote lecture. With the permission and support of Professor Cortes, and despite Dermot's reservations, she had insisted on keeping her promise.

Putting the potatoes on a low heat, Dermot watched Sebastian remove the wrapper from a bar of Cadbury's Dairy Milk and absent-mindedly break it into mouth-sized portions.

'Do you know how many squares there are in that chocolate bar?'

Sebastian, who was more interested in eating the chocolate than in analysing it, shook his head.

'Suppose there are twenty pieces, what would be the minimum number of snaps required to break it into individual squares?' Sebastian brushed some escaped crumbs into his palm and putting his head back tossed them into his mouth. It was obvious. If there were twenty squares, twenty snaps must be needed.

'Twenty.'

'That's what I thought you'd say.' Sebastian fell into his father's traps every time.

'Nineteen. It's nineteen. Each time you break off a piece of chocolate the total number of pieces increases by one. Since you began with one square you will need to snap the chocolate nineteen times to create twenty individual squares!' Unimpressed, Sebastian offered his father a piece of chocolate.

Dermot sighed.

'I don't know why I bother. It wasn't some kind of test or examination, Sebastian. I wasn't trying to catch you out. I was trying to teach you something about mathematics. The fact that the slab was rectangular did not enter into the solution. It could just as well have been a single block of any shape. The argument is valid for any number of squares. If there are n squares then n-1 snaps are needed. This is what mathematics is about, finding general results and principals rather than solving problem for special values. Take a moment to reflect about it. What are you doing?' Sebastian was gathering up his books.

'I'm going to Rupert's. I'm sleeping over.' In one ear and out the other. Dermot didn't know why he bothered. No wonder Sebastian had a poor report from school. A walking sweetshop, Sebastian extracted a bag of licorice allsorts from his bag and put them on the table.

'These are for Mum.'

Looking through the grille of the basement window as the front door slammed (he didn't know how many times he had told Sebastian about slamming the door), Dermot noticed that it had started to rain. For the umpteenth time he dialled Sidney's mobile number. When there was no reply he glanced nervously at the clock on the wall and prayed, as he did every time she left the house, that nothing untoward had happened to her.

TWO

When Sidney finally put her name down on the transplant list, unlike many women who blithely signed hospital consent forms for cosmetic 'nips' and 'tucks' when what they were assenting to was major surgery with all its attendant risks, she knew exactly what she was doing.

Since the diagnosis had been made, she had thought long and hard about the possible cause of her illness. Very little was known about primary pulmonary hypertension, which ironically she was currently engaged in researching, other than that it was remorseless, progressive, and invariably proved fatal.

Throughout her childhood, encouraged by her mother who was an excellent cook and liked her food to be appreciated, Sidney had got into the habit of over-eating. A memory, as lasting as it had been mortifying, had been of trying on clothes in a communal changing-room where, struggling to get a size eight dress over her head, she had emerged hot and bothered to find her elegant mother, who never seemed to put on an ounce, gazing sadly at her daughter's plump reflection in the mirror. Tending to fat even as an adolescent, she had started to gain serious weight in her first year at medical school where she found herself responsible for the contents of her own fridge. Disgusted by her appearance, consequent upon an uncontrollable desire to binge on junk food resulting in a degree of guilt assuaged only by more junk food, she had successfully resorted to a then popular brand of slimming pills (which had done the trick but were later withdrawn by the drug company). She put her present dilemma down to their long-term effects. Whatever the cause, or causes, of her lung disease, she was now on the road that led to transplant or certain death. So far she had succeeded in coming to terms with neither.

Unable to get a clear directive from Dermot, who was too personally involved, as to whether or not she should opt for a heart-lung transplant (although there was in fact no choice) she had dumped her reservations on the Professor.

She had first met Eduardo Cortes at a pathology conference in Rio when she was making her way up the hospital career ladder. At the Farewell Dinner, by a trick of fate that was later to prove serendipitous, she found herself sitting next to a renowned Professor of Cardiac Surgery who, like many other physically unattractive men, made up with charisma for what he lacked in stature and conventional good looks. Born in Argentina, Eduardo Cortes had an incontrovertible way with women. He knew how to talk to them. Winning them over dissipated his deep and ineradicable strand of self-doubt, and he found their admiration reassuring. His accent, which he had never lost despite his many years in England, where he had qualified in medicine, added to the charm with which he had attempted to seduce his young dinner companion. Fifteen years later, as if it were a film seen yesterday, the scenario remained firmly in Sidney's head.

The conference hosts had been applauded and the speeches and votes of thanks to the organisers and participants were over when the Brazilian band in white satin shirts and red cummerbunds struck up an enthusiastic tango. Eduardo had dominated the conversation throughout dinner and entertained the table with his stories and amusing anecdotes. Putting down his napkin he had turned to Sidney, who was due to marry Dermot in three weeks' time.

'*Mi Buenos Aires Querido.*'

'Sorry?'

Languages were not her forte and her Spanish almost non-existent. She wondered if she had missed something. By way of reply the Professor had pulled her to her feet.

'My beloved Buenos Aires.'

Taking her arm, Eduardo had propelled her towards the mêlée of inebriated medical lotharios, dipping and preening inexpertly in a display of spurious sensuality. An enthusiastic dancer, she found herself clasped close to the Professor's solid body as his warm breath caressed her ear.

'Have you ever been to Argentina?' Before she had a chance to reply Professor Cortes continued: 'I was born in Argentina. Until I was eighteen years old I lived in Buenos Aires. Every day of my life I heard tango. Tango in bars, tango in restaurants, tango in shops… At home my mother danced tango...' He guided her firmly round the floor, flattening her breasts against his chest and thrusting his leg into her groin until her feet, in the three inch heels which made her more than a head taller than her partner, picked up the rhythm. He was a good teacher.

'...A sailor's song. An Italian dance. Played on a German accordion. Tango is the lingua franca of the brothel. It comes up from the streets. In Argentina we play it *a la parilla,* spontaneous, stir-fried, syncopated...'

Sidney was beginning to enjoy herself. 'Ninety per cent of the time it leads to sex...'

Sidney pretended that she hadn't heard. She noticed that the other couples on the floor had melted away and were watching their performance. 'Speed is what matters in tango...' Eduardo Cortes was surprisingly light on his feet. 'Speed...concentration...elegance... intuition... You have such beautiful green eyes.'

The band increased its efforts. Faces were turned speculatively towards them as they genuflected and bent.

'Have you ever been in love, Doctor Sands?' Sidney was about to tell the Professor about Dermot. He didn't wait for an answer. Years later she was to discover that Professor Cortes listened only to the sound of his own voice. That he never waited for answers. 'To understand tango you must have known love, you must have known suffering. Tango is about conquest. About desire...' Sidney felt herself held closer, the breath squeezed out of her. 'Through tango is expressed the personality. It becomes an obsession...' His voice became more intimate. 'I would like to make love to you.'

More than a little drunk from the wine with which Eduardo had assiduously plied her during dinner, and fired by the music and the exhilaration of the dance, Sidney considered the proposition. She remembered Dermot, who seemed very far away, at the same time as she noticed the gold band on the Professor's wedding finger.

'Are you married, Professor Cortes?'

The music rose to a sensuous crescendo. Cortes, his face damp from exertion, eased her backwards, pressing his body urgently against her own. 'Only a little bit!'

The encounter with Eduardo Cortes had proved to be the turning-point in her life. Years later, after sailing through her Membership and

Fellowship examinations, she had discovered that they had a mutual interest in diseases of the heart and lungs, and a productive collaboration had begun which resulted in a great many publications and a number of joint grants. Now Sidney's team and the Professor's team met on a regular basis and she always looked forward to pitting her wits against the Argentinian's scintillating mind.

When, soon after her diagnosis had been made, she knocked on the Professor's door, he knew that this time she hadn't come to discuss the markers for neuroendocrine differentiation or the importance of peptides in the respiratory tract. Sitting behind his desk, on which was a carefully placed silver-framed photograph of his family, Eduardo noticed that Sidney's erstwhile slight frame, the pale flesh dusted with freckles, had now thickened and that beneath the black leather canopy of her skirt the long legs on which she had once prided herself were swollen. He was not surprised when, before she had said a word, she was overtaken by a sudden and distressing attack of breathlessness. Puffing on her inhaler, she flopped in the armchair. Eduardo crouched silently before her, his probing thumb leaving deep indentations in her swollen ankles.

'I'm...dying...Eduardo.'

'My spies tell me that you are reluctant to put your name on the transplant list...'

'Reluctant? Reluctant! Wouldn't you be reluctant...?'

Releasing her ankles Eduardo stared out of the window on to the higgledy-piggledy complex of hospital buildings.

'Yesterday there was a cardiology meeting in Paris. I was due back here in theatre at six o'clock and had to take the Eurostar. I wouldn't tell this to anyone but you, Sidney, but I'm claustrophobic as hell. For the twenty minutes that the train was in the tunnel I was convinced that I would never see the light of day again. I was shit-scared.' There was one of the long silences with which Eduardo punctuated his conversations. Tapping his fingers on the desk he hummed a few bars of *Buenos Aires Querido*.

'Remember Rio?'

'You tried to get me into bed.' Laughing at the memory, Sidney stashed away her inhaler. 'I asked you if you were married.'

'What did I say?'

' "Only a little bit." '

13

'Such a long time ago.'

'They want me to give my informed consent…'

'What choice do you have?'

'…to the lethal risks of major surgery that offers only a notional hope of benefit…'

'One must think in terms of available alternatives.'

'When you and I are still struggling to understand the effects of transplantation, how can consent by a patient ever be informed?'

'How long have we been working together, Sidney? How many joint papers have we published? Transplant is not a difficult operation…'

Not a difficult operation. Although the spooky 'domino' procedure – in which she would hopefully receive a new thoracic set while her heart, thickened on one side only by her malfunctioning lungs, would be passed on to a patient with end-stage heart disease – sounded simple enough, it depended where you were coming from. Sidney had tried to discuss the issue with Dermot, but Dermot got too choked, too upset, and even though she had prided herself on her pragmatism, had always insisted upon calling a spade a spade, on knowing the truth about everything, she was finding the situation hard to handle. When they first told her she had completely flipped. She had felt like Sebastian's pet hamster, whose only option was to spin round and round on his wheel and for whom every exit was barred.

'I write about lungs every day,' she told Eduardo. 'I know everything there is to know about lungs. You would have thought…'

'Darling Sidney,' Eduardo came to sit beside her. 'You were expecting a clinical reaction and what you have is an emotional one. They are not the same.'

'Let me ask you something, Eduardo. Just suppose I do put my name on the transplant list. Suppose lungs do become available. I wouldn't want anyone else…'

'Of course I will operate on you, Sidney. Of course I will get you through the surgery. The plumbing is the easy part. Afterwards…'

'Afterwards?'

'Afterwards it will be up to you. I can't live for you. I can't breathe for you. I can't cough for you. You will have to do the fighting.'

'What are the chances…that I'll get that far?'

'You know as much about it as I do. Unfortunately we don't keep hearts and lungs on the shelf in theatre. There is an acute shortage of organs. For some reason people are unwilling to donate. Hearts and lungs have to be the right size and weight. You are nearly forty-three years old…'

'The young get Brownie points!'

'You want my advice…?'

'I've work to do, Eduardo. I've a department to run. I have a husband to consider. My son is thirteen years old…'

'Get your name on the list.'

She had already spoken to Debbie, the transplant co-ordinator, and tried to wheedle out of her what were her chances. Debbie had said: 'There's a great shortfall in organs, Professor Sands,' her Scots voice was sympathetic. 'We have some extremely sick people on the waiting-list. When lungs do become available, you know as well as I do that I have to evaluate them against the patients on the computer…'

Sidney looked at Eduardo. She noticed that his hair was going grey.

'I might just as well do the lottery.'

'If you don't play you don't win. Go and talk to Debbie. Get things up and running.'

'Is that what you would do if you were in my shoes? Would you put *your* name on a transplant list?' Eduardo looked at his watch and picked up some notes from his desk. Taking his white coat from behind the door and putting it on he resumed his professional demeanour.

'Medicine is a process of making choices, Sidney. Of learning how to agonize without destroying oneself.'

THREE

Sidney could smell burning the moment she entered the house. Parking her car in the disabled bay and struggling as usual to walk as normally as possible, she was aware that her progress was being monitored by a traffic warden, who found it hard to believe that the tall, Titian-haired woman wearing a black Armani jacket over a shocking pink skinny-rib top that matched her lipstick, and carrying a briefcase, was handicapped to the extent that she needed special parking facilities. Sidney was acutely aware that she didn't look disabled. She didn't look incapacitated. Even her mother had a problem believing how sick she was and had made her feel guilty, as if she were fabricating her illness. Sidney understood that Diana Sands was either unwilling, or unable, to accept the fact that her only daughter, her clever little star, was dying, and that it was only by denying the truth that she was able to cope with it. But the shock of discovering that she had PPH had been even more devastating for Sidney. Having not yet managed to come to terms with it, she still found it impossible to contemplate the proximity of her own death.

In terms of quality of life and life expectancy she had every right to a disabled bay, every right to a disabled sticker, yet the traffic warden with her accusing eyes made her feel a fraud, as if she were in fact malingering in order to obtain parking benefits. It was the same with her colleagues at the hospital, with Juliet her PA, with the departmental domestic assistant who looked after them all, and with friends and acquaintances whom she knew quite well. She caught them evaluating her when they thought she was not looking, seeking some reassuring sign of impairment, of wasting or terminal pallor. People liked to be able to believe their own eyes, to trust what they could verify. This accounted for the fact that appeals for heart–lung transplant funds went unanswered while the familiar white sticks and guide dogs of the visually-challenged inspired generosity, and no one had a problem with collecting-tins rattled for Save the Children or the Royal National Lifeboat Fund. Everyone had seen images of malnourished children and there were few who did not know what a lifeboat looked like. Although she hadn't realised it before, hadn't needed to think about it, it had been brought home to her in the past few months that death, or its imminence, changed relationships, marginalised one to the point of exclusion as if one were already defunct, and that it was the ultimate obscenity. People who knew about her illness and its prognosis, kept their distance. It was as though she were tainted, as if they feared she was contagious. Those who did not know but to whom she intimated that she had a life-threatening disease, because she wanted to share her predicament, changed the subject and withdrew. Only her friend Martha acknowledged her true feelings, only with Martha could she be herself. But Martha, a Professor in the Department of Radiology at the University of Pennsylvania, was in the United States. Lonely, isolated and rejected at a time when she most needed love and understanding, Sidney felt like a leper, even with Dermot, even in her own home.

Making her slow way into the house and down the basement stairs into the kitchen, she collapsed into a chair, her chest heaving.

'Some…thing's…burn…ing.' Dermot quick-stepped around her, removed her damp jacket, relieved her of her briefcase.

'I was getting worried. I tried to call you on the mobile…' He ignored her remark. Like many long-married couples their conversation consisted of a duet of apparent *non sequiturs*.

'…I could smell it in the street. Where's Sebastian?'

' "The vodaphone you are now calling, the vodaphone you are now calling…" '

'You'd…better…look.' Sidney fought for breath. Lifting her legs on to a footstool, Dermot handed her an inhaler.

'At Rupert's. He bought you some licorice allsorts. He'll call you later. You promised me…'

'I'm sorry. I switched it off for the lecture and forgot…'

'He's sleeping over.'

'I forgot… You want *me* to look?'

'How did it go? The lecture.'

'Dermot, darling, there is smoke coming out of the oven…'

'It can't be.' Dermot consulted his watch. 'Thirty minutes at 400 degrees…'

'Fahrenheit, Dermot. Four hundred Fahrenheit.'

'Dear God…!'

Opening the oven, Dermot who was knocked back by a cloud of smoke, removed a burnt offering.

'I was worried about you,' he said in mitigation, slinging what remained of the steak and mushroom pie into the bin. 'I don't know what I'm doing. The lecture finished hours ago…'

'I went to the department. To pick up some papers.' Sidney took the reprints and her laptop out of her briefcase and put them on the table together with her bleeper, which made her feel as if she were on the end of a piece of elastic and by means of which Debbie could get in touch with her quickly should suitable organs be found.

Having passed the assessment – both physical and psychological – to see if she could cope with the stringent demands of a transplant, Debbie had finally taken the draconian step of adding the name of Sidney Sands to the list in the computer. Amendments (when patients' medical conditions changed), deletions (when patients died before receiving their transplants), or additions (when new names were added) were made to the register by the medical staff, who updated the list continually and circulated it to relevant departments of the hospital. Sidney had had a long talk with Debbie, who liked to get to know the patients personally. As a member of the hospital staff she had been introduced to the nursing and medical personnel and had even visited the transplant ward to talk to the pre- and post-operative patients whose condition she had difficulty in equating with her own.

In Top Floor Surgical, Nicholas Lilleywhite, the consultant physician who was showing her round, had stopped at the bed of a seventeen-year-old whose translucent skin appeared to be stretched over her cheekbones and whose hair fanned out in dark corkscrews across the pillow. 'This is Anna.'

The girl, who appeared to be sleeping, had given up on a jigsaw (the fairy-tale engagement of Prince Charles and Princess Diana). It lay abandoned on her table. Nicholas touched her arm.

'Anna!' Bloodshot eyes met Sidney's and, forgetting for a moment her own problems, her heart went out to the fragile girl, young enough to be the daughter she had never had. 'Professor Sands would like to say hello.' The clubbed nails on the extended hand were, as were Anna's lips, an unhealthy shade of blue.

'Hi, Professor.' She followed Sidney's gaze to the unfinished puzzle. 'Just killing time. Until they let me out to the disco.'

'Professor Sands is waiting for a heart-lung bloc...'

'Join the club.' Anna reached for a badge from her locker and handed it to Sidney. Beneath the logo of the Fulham Hospital was the legend *Why Are We Waiting?*

Sidney guessed that Eisenmenger's Syndrome had affected Anna's circulation. Until the advent of transplant therapy, all that the medical profession had been able to offer for the condition were palliative treatment and bed-rest, and early death had been inevitable. Although neither of them had much to smile about, she smiled, in a way she hoped was reassuring, at Anna.

'Anna was born with holes in her heart.' The muffled voice came from a skinny youth with spiky black hair who sat by the adjacent bed in his bathrobe, pretending to read a comic. He removed his oxygen mask to join in the conversation.

'Thank you, Colin.' Nicholas replaced the mask.

'How long has Anna been on the transplant list?' Sidney addressed Nicholas.

'I speak English...' Anna said.

'Point taken.'

'Two years.'

It was like a slap in the face. If the length of time spent on the waiting-list was a criterion for transplantation, Sidney thought that she didn't stand much of a chance of getting a new heart and lungs.

'Colin's been on five years.' Anna rubbed salt into the wound. 'We've opened a book, which of us will snuff it first.' Since they had been on the ward together the two had forged a close friendship, keeping each other's spirits up, minimising the fact that every day that passed brought a deterioration in their condition. They ganged up like a pair of naughty children against the nursing and medical staff. It was their defence against what lay ahead.

In the kitchen Dermot fussed round Sidney as she opened her laptop and became immersed in her work.

'Sorry about the dinner.'

19

'Forget it.'

'I don't know what I'm doing these days. I can't concentrate.' He looked at the computer, at the recent copies of *Science* and *Nature*, the pages marked with Post-it notes, that were Sidney's reading for the night, spread over the table.

'I don't know how you can concentrate.'

'Nothing focuses the mind more than confronting one's own mortality. I couldn't have eaten steak and kidney pie anyway.'

'I'll make you some toast, then. Brown or white?'

'I'm not hungry.'

Almost worse than having to face her own mortality was having to cope with Dermot's anxiety, which manifested itself in his solicitude. Early on in her illness she had recognised that she would have to put up with increasing dependency and had made up her mind to accept help cheerfully no matter how she felt inside. Fiercely independent by nature and used to being in control of her own life this was not always easy. Sometimes she had to bite her tongue – loving Dermot and resenting him at one and the same time – when he insisted on treating her like a child. Acutely aware that something precious could be snatched from her at any moment, she had arrived at a point in her illness where it became clear that she desperately needed the support of family and friends if she were not to be overwhelmed. While she railed against her physical losses and the fact that her body had let her down, she cherished the functions that she had left and was determined not to let anyone undermine them. Disdainful of self-pity, she tried to avoid the 'why me?' syndrome which pre-supposed a Deity she did not believe in, and had moved beyond recrimination to acknowledging her not inappropriate sadness. She was sad most of all at having to leave Sebastian, who at the age of thirteen desperately needed his mother. Nobody really knew why she had got this illness, where it came from, or if 'God' had anything to do with it. Accepting that as a reality and recognising the important things that she was losing enabled her both to grieve and to accept the fact that in the absence of medical intervention she was pretty far down the road towards death.

Peering over her shoulder, Dermot read from her computer screen: '...the innate and unrelenting intolerance of individuals to grafts of other people's tissues and organs... Do you have to do that tonight, love?'

'They still expect me to complete the paper, even though I'm dying.' It wasn't only the paper. She was faced in addition with a deadline for a chapter she was contributing to a textbook of medicine, and was in the final stages of editing a book on lung transplantation. 'I spoke to Debbie again today...'

'And?'

Sidney shrugged eloquently. 'The usual. Could be tomorrow, could be eighteen months...' Sensing Dermot's distress, Sidney took his hand and laid it against her cheek. 'What do you want me to do, Dermot, run down a pedestrian on the way to work? Go round with a placard saying "No to road safety, no to speed limits, no to seat belts, no to crash helmets...?" Did Sebastian remember his PE gear?'

'I've no idea. He's thirteen years old. He's not a baby. You worry about him too much.'

'I'm a mother. It goes with the job.' Sidney yawned, fighting off the familiar fatigue that threatened to engulf her.

'Why don't you leave that? I don't understand you.'

'Because I am sick and you are well.'

'You have to think about yourself.'

'That's something I try to avoid.'

'Think about me then.'

'You know I couldn't hack this without you.' Despite his fussing, his over-protectiveness towards her, it was true. Embarrassed by her confession, Dermot wheeled out the ironing-board, one chore amongst the many he had taken upon himself. From the pile of clothes he had taken out of the washing machine he pulled a black cotton shirt.

'You can see your face in this.'

'It'll do.'

'Isn't it time you had a new one?'

'There's not much point...' She met Dermot's eyes. 'Sorry! Do you think they do drugs at these sleepovers? Do you think Sebastian takes Ecstasy?'

'Take it? I doubt if he can spell it. Have a look at his report.'

'What do you think he'll do? When he leaves school?'

'He'll not be a mathematician. That's for sure.'

'Sebastian needs a lot of love...'

'Do you think I'm not capable...?'

'You do go on at him sometimes.'

21

'For his own good. Only for the boy's own good. How does it look?'

Sidney glanced at the shirt. 'Perfect. It's perfect. I don't want to die...'

'Wouldn't we all like to live forever?' Dermot's voice was light.

'I'm afraid of death. The *total emptiness...*'

'That's a bleak vision...'

As she was driving home she had stopped at a zebra crossing to let an old lady, bent almost double and ninety if she was a day, make her painful progress across the road.

'I used to regard death as something which happened to other people, old people...'

'It's just another phase of life.' Dermot looked at the sole-plate of the steam iron as if he had never seen it before.

'It's all right for you.'

'I could walk out of here tomorrow and get run over by a bus.'

'Do you realise it's one of the few things no one has ever researched... *The British Journal of Mortality.* I'll write the first paper. "Sex-related differences in short and long term prognosis after death. A ten-year follow-up of three thousand and seventy-three patients in the database... Professor Sidney Sands, Dr Nicholas Lilleywhite..." '

In an attempt to distract her, Dermot held up a flesh-coloured bra. 'Do you want this ironing?'

' "...Introduction. The prevailing view regarding prognosis after acute death is that women fare worse than men... Patients and Methods. From the first of June 1979 to the 15th of August 1981, six thousand six hundred and thirty-one patients were buried... Results. No significant difference was found in decomposition before day 15 between the sexes... Discussion. The study indicates that short and long term prognoses after death does not differ between the sexes. Conclusion. Death by itself is not a risk factor..." '

'Not a word about the next world!' Dermot joined in the game.

'There is no next world. No pie in the sky when you die, though I'm not against it. It would be nice to think that one was going off to some celestial mortality conference. That one would run into people one knew in the bar. I don't believe it. The idea that we end up in some place in which there is perfect justice, perfect love, perfect truth, perfect happiness, is bullshit. There's not one shred of evidence...'

'You and your evidence.'

'…It's just a comforting idea for people who can't face the possibility of extinction. I can't face the possibility of extinction. If you want to know I'm shit-scared.'

'*Why are you afraid of death? Where you are, death is not. Where death is, you are not.*'

'It's all very well for you, you have your church…'

'That's not the church. That's Epicurus.'

'…you don't believe we are chunks of matter randomly generated by impersonal physical laws…'

'I have my faith…'

'Which is essentially and crucially nonsensical.'

'Substantiated by personal experience…'

'By self-delusion…'

'Confirmed by art and nature…'

'Created to pretend we never die.'

'And by some central kernel of meaning which we know as human love…'

'You can't argue people into faith, Dermot…'

'Without it you may as well put a gun to your head… Sorry!' They seemed always to be apologising to each other these days.

'Nobody knows what's really "out there",' Sidney said. 'Not Stephen Hawking. Not Richard Dawkins. Not even the Reverend Billy Graham himself. All the ways we have of approaching our existence, from science to religion, are ultimately no more than ideas, models, paradigms. You pays your money and you takes your choice. We choose our own paradigms. Sorry. I didn't mean to dump on you tonight. I know you don't like it. I get these sudden panics. I get frightened. Of being out of control…of letting go…I'm ashamed…'

'It's nothing to be ashamed of.'

'I don't mean for my lack of faith.'

'What then?'

'I'm ashamed because I listen all day for the sound of an ambulance, hoping that at any moment, somewhere in the Fulham Hospital donor zone, there'll be a road traffic accident or a mega rail crash and that someone of my weight, of my blood and tissue type… What if my donor's "intellectually challenged"…?'

'It's heart and lungs you're down for. Not a head transplant.'

'What if he's…?'

'Could be a 'she'.'

'She, then…'

'You won't know who the donor is.'

'What if I do know? Will you still love me if…?'

Choked by the conversation, Dermot truncated it abruptly.

'I'm going to make you that toast.'

FOUR

Martin Bond was accustomed to getting his own way. A New York attorney who now looked after the UK end of a multibillion dollar international company, he used his power and dynamism to further his ends be they commercial or personal. What he was unable to achieve with his highly developed business acumen and deceptively quiet powers of persuasion, he knew that money could generally buy. He was unused to being thwarted. He had been married three times. His first marriage was to a fellow law student whom he had mysteriously ceased to find desirable the moment the relationship had been ratified, and the second (on the rebound) was to a fashion model ten years his junior who anyone could have told him, but had carelessly neglected to do so, was intimate (in the most euphemistic sense of the word) with half the New York social register. Both of these unfortunate liaisons had ended in hotly contested divorces for which he was still paying through the nose. His third marriage, for which he made sure he had a watertight pre-nuptial contract, was to Mitzi, a warm and demonstrative Hungarian artist with whom he had found a happiness, contentment, and sexual fulfilment he had not dreamed existed. Three years after giving birth to their daughter, Anna, who had been born with holes in her heart and needed constant attention, Mitzi had died a lingering and reluctant death from the breast cancer which had been diagnosed too late to save her. Watching, impotent for once to influence the course of events, as his short-lived happiness slipped through his fingers, Martin had succumbed to a profound depression such as he had previously associated with the weak-willed, and from which he was saved in part by medication, in part by his determination to preserve at all costs his wife's imprint upon the sands of time. Anna became his be-all and his end-all. He devoted his life to caring for her, and his mind and his not inconsiderable resources, to so far vain attempts to restore his beloved daughter to health.

With the help of the latest textbooks of cardiology, and having read every paper on the subject published on the Internet and by dint of diligent study, he was now an expert on Eisenmenger's Syndrome. Anna joked that her father could qualify in medicine. When he was told by the doctors in New York that no operation on Anna's damaged heart was possible, not without severe risk of heart failure, not without risk of death, he took his daughter to Boston, where the surgeons shook their heads, and to San Francisco, where the sympathetic answers from the cardiologists were equally unhelpful. In a last-ditch attempt, when even he had to acknowledge that he was banging his head against a brick wall, he had had himself transferred to the UK end of his company, and brought his daughter to the Fulham Hospital, which was an international centre of excellence. Here two years ago, at the age of fifteen, Anna had been considered a suitable candidate for a new heart and lungs and had been put on the transplant list – on which she still languished and which was her only chance of survival.

Martin had made a friend of Debbie, the transplant co-ordinator, taking her out to dinner and buying her expensive presents, and had found an ally in the transplant physician Nicholas Lilleywhite. Nicholas had taken a personal interest in Anna (who was the same age as his sister Kate). She had inherited her father's brains and her mother's striking good looks (Martin was fond of saying that it was lucky it wasn't the other way round). As the longest surviving in-patient on the ward, Anna had become the pet of Top Floor Surgical. Sitting by her bed in his Jermyn Street shirt and his Savile Row suit, with its red silk pocket handkerchief echoing the spots on his immaculately knotted tie, Martin held his daughter's hand and stroked her clubbed fingers with his thumb while she slept, which lately she had been doing for more than eighteen hours a day. He watched her laboured breathing, which hurt him as much as it hurt her. In the next bed Colin Rafferty, plugged into his Walkman, listened to a football match between Liverpool and Manchester United. When a beatific smile illuminated his freckled face and he raised his fists in the air, Martin, who had befriended the lonely boy, knew that Liverpool had scored a goal. Colin's parents lived on Merseyside, the home of his favourite team, and his father was out of work. When Nicholas, who was doing his ward round, stopped by Anna's bed, Martin drew him aside.

'I hear Anna's been coughing up blood. Is that bad?' Martin's voice was anxious.

'It's not good. We have to face the fact that she's deteriorating...'

It was a verdict that Martin was both unwilling and unable to accept, as he had been unwilling and unable to accept the fact that Anna would never grow old, was unlikely to become a mother because carrying a child would kill her, that a transplant was her only hope. Since Mitzi's death he had devoted himself to saving the one person in the world who was precious to him, the one human being able to make sense of his life. He was not going to let her go now.

'I need to talk to Professor Cortes.'

'I've told you before Martin, the Prof doesn't talk to relatives...'

'What's with this guy? Who does he think he is?'

'It wouldn't help Anna.'

'It would help me.'

'That's the transplant counsellor's job.'

'I don't mess with counsellors. Did you give Professor Cortes my message?'

Warming the end of the stethoscope in his palms, Nicholas approached Anna's bed. 'I promise you I did my best.'

When Nicholas had gone, Martin, dehydrated from the overheated ward and with his back stiff from sitting, indicated to Colin to keep a watchful eye on Anna. Receiving the thumbs up from the boy, he took the elevator down to the basement canteen where he sat by himself, as was his wont, at the only available table, absent-mindedly stirring what passed for coffee.

'Anyone sitting here?' Dermot Tanney, wearing a Fair Isle waistcoat beneath his comfortable tweed jacket, stood by the plastic covered table with its plastic flowers, holding a mug of tea and a pack of digestive biscuits.

In answer to his question, Martin shook his head grudgingly. He had no inclination to hear the tedious details of someone's surgery, someone's broken leg.

'Tanney,' Dermot introduced himself. 'Dermot Tanney. I've seen you around.'

Martin concentrated on his coffee. He was in no mood for chit-chat.

'My wife's in for a check-up. She has PPH – primary pulmonary hypertension...'

'I know what PPH is.'

Dermot looked surprised. 'You a doctor?'

Martin shook his head. 'Not exactly.' The fellow was trying to be friendly. He decided to make an effort. Perhaps it would take his mind off Anna.

'My daughter's in Top Floor Surgical,' he volunteered. 'She's waiting for a heart-lung transplant.'

'So is my wife.' Dermot ripped open the biscuits with his teeth. 'How do you feel about it?' He said cautiously.

'Feel about it?'

'About organ transplantation.'

'Anna is seventeen. Her lungs are packing up. Her heart is under great strain. It's admitting defeat, in fact. How do you expect me to feel about it?'

Dermot held out the biscuits. 'Digestive?' The coffee was bad enough, Martin was damned if he was going to eat dog biscuits. Dermot removed his sweeteners from his pocket and dropped two into his tea.

'Mind if I talk?'

Martin was unwilling to take anyone else's problems on board. He had enough of his own. Dermot didn't wait for an answer.

'I've never really said this to anybody, certainly not to anyone in this hospital, but I have serious doubts about the whole business of transplantation.'

'What's bugging you?'

'Modern medicine has led to inflated expectations which are eagerly swallowed by the public. In many cases they are unfulfillable. It will need to redefine its limits even as it extends its capacities. To tell you the truth I'm seriously worried about the whole macabre business...'

'Go on.'

'Let me put it this way. Say you remove a human heart while it is still beating; say you transfer the parts of one human being to another human being. Surely you're transcending the laws of nature...?'

Recognising a mind as enquiring as his own, Martin began to take an interest in the Irishman.

'...Sometimes I wonder – I haven't discussed this with anyone, certainly not with my wife – if transplanting organs is anything other than cannibalism, the dark side of our quest for immortality, a secret desire to delay the day of reckoning...'

'What are you scared of, Tanney? Spawning a race of human monsters? Retribution from the grave?'

'We seem to have become so divorced from the natural process of life and death, so wrapped up in our western materialist dreams... What I worry about Mr...I'm sorry I don't know your name.'

'Martin Bond.'

'What I worry about, Martin, is the medical profession's commitment to ghoulish tinkering, to repairing and rebuilding people and keeping them alive by machinery, to the endless perpetuation of human life.'

'Your wife is dying!'

'That's the problem. It keeps me awake at night. Is it right to do what it is possible to do for her, or is it right to do what is right?'

'Do you know how many transplants are carried out in the US in a single year, Dermot? Eight thousand, eight hundred and eighty-six kidneys, two thousand, one hundred and sixty livers, four hundred and twelve pancreases, eighty-nine lungs and seventy hearts in combination with lungs...'

'I am a mathematician. Numbers do not move me.'

'Let me finish. The excavation of the body has a long history. Go visit any museum. You'll see lungs in alabaster pots, organs which have been dried, bottled, salted and pickled and used for anatomical teaching...'

'But *transplantation* is a modern invention.'

'All we've done is take it one step further. By applying current knowledge we've managed to defeat death...'

'Is death always an enemy to be defeated?'

'...and prolong life. To create one new automobile, if you like, from the spare parts of two.'

'The human body contains the human spirit, Martin. We are not Volvos. Not...Chevrolets. If it were that simple there would be no need for the metaphors of transplant surgery...'

'Metaphors?'

'Organs, so they tell us, are being "harvested" – suggesting fertility, natural ripeness – when actually corpses are being mutilated, ribcages sawn in two…'

'With the donors' permission.'

'…Vital parts surgically extracted…'

'Are you trying to tell me that Professor Cortes is some sort of demon or criminal, that he should be condemned to the electric chair?'

'…in a manner which ignores the sanctity and integrity of the human body…'

'How can you talk about the sanctity and integrity of the human body when your wife…?'

'…a manner which ignores the meaning of human relationships, a manner which disregards the significance of human death.'

'Be thankful that some people care enough about human relationships to carry donor cards.'

'Do you think I'm not thankful? Do you think I don't want, more than anything in this world, my wife to have a future, to be given the chance of having a heart and lungs that will function, air that she can breathe? It doesn't stop me being torn apart. It doesn't stop me having doubts.'

'Look, someone gets a heart and lives, someone else loses a heart and dies. It's the law of the jungle.'

'We don't live in the jungle. Unconsciously…deep down…I've never said this to anyone…I find the whole idea deeply distasteful.'

'Conscious acceptance and unconscious repulsion. The ambiguity and mystery of the human condition.'

'There's another thing. I'm a Catholic. The Church is not opposed to the use of organs from any human person. On the contrary it regards the signing of a donor card as an act of laudable generosity. Proper consent must have been given however and the person must not only be dying, or in a vegetative state, but actually *dead*…'

'Go on.'

'Until pretty recently, until the new technology arrived, someone was considered dead when there was no sign of life. A single heartbeat was the frontier between life and death.'

'Isn't that what they call "the boy-scouts' definition"?'.

'Suddenly the search for a pulse has been replaced by the search for activity in the brain.'

'All they've done is move the goalposts. Irreversible loss of all brain function, brain death, signifies the death of the patient...'

'...Who is then attached to a breathing machine and "kept alive" in intensive care where he is "treated" – often quite aggressively – in order to maintain his body for transplantation.'

'I agree it is confusing.'

'Everybody knows the patient is dead, but he is given fluid and drugs, even blood transfusions in some cases, as though he were still alive. Using the term "brain death" instead of simply "death" encourages us to believe that someone is not really "dead" but constitutes – I don't know – some other category of being.'

'It's a question of semantics. Why do we describe a sunset when we know full well – on an intellectual level, that is – that it is the earth that moves round the sun? How long did you say your wife has been on the transplant list?'

'Six months.'

'Anna has been waiting over two years! She's been in and out of hospitals since she was a kid. Antibiotics. X-rays. EKGs. Nobody really understands. They used to say I was obsessed with Anna. Told me I babied her. Why didn't I take her on vacation – travelling exhausted her – or for a brisk walk...?"

'People can't cope with the situation. My mother-in-law's the same. She makes my wife feel guilty.'

'It's pretty tough being positive all the time. Being optimistic. This thing takes over your whole life. You sense people avoiding you.'

'It's the aura of death they sense. They don't want to be touched by it. One becomes a pariah.'

'There's a kid in the next bed to Anna, Colin. By amazing coincidence they share the same birthday...'

'Mathematically that is not amazing. It is to be expected every once in a while.'

Martin ignored the interruption.

'Colin's a great kid. He keeps the whole ward entertained. Never complains, not even when he's feeling ghastly. He's been waiting *five years* for a transplant.' Five years. Dermot felt his heart sink. 'He's in pretty bad shape. I've been trying to talk to the Prof about Anna. Sometimes I get the feeling I'm up against the Law of the Washington Lobbyists...'

31

'Sorry?'

'It's not what you know but who you know. Rumour has it that if, and when, organs are harvested, Professor Sands – she's in charge of the Histochemistry Department – will get priority...'

'It doesn't work like that.'

'That's what they say. Everyone knows how the system operates. Professor Sands' team is researching PPH. She works with the Prof.' Dermot finished the biscuits and washed away the crumbs with the last of the tea.

'Sidney Sands is my wife.'

'I thought...'

'Tanney is my name.'

'Shit, Dermot...' There was a long silence while Martin fingered the plastic flowers with embarrassment. He shrugged his shoulders. 'What do you want me to say?'

FIVE

'Psst!' Colin aimed a crumpled tissue at Anna's bed. The youngest of five children, Colin had been born with cystic fibrosis, a hereditary and progressive disease in which, due to a genetic defect, his body's glandular functions were affected. Failing to thrive as an infant because of the 'malabsorption' and pancreatic insufficiency resulting from his illness, Colin had largely missed out on his schooling. Before he was eight, however, he could spell the mellifluous names of the complications that arose from his rare disease. Cirrhosis, diabetes mellitus, bronchiectasis: these came from repeated chest infections and frequent attacks of abdominal pain which had so far entailed surgical intervention for gallstones and 'acute obstruction'. Much of his young life had been spent in hospital wards where, fascinated by every aspect of the world within a world, he had made up his mind to be a doctor. He spent every available moment, when he wasn't too sick or following his beloved football, making good his lack of formal education.

Both of his parents – one of whom had worked diligently in a carpet factory while hauling up her family with what remained of her energy and the other who was a brickie – had been made redundant from their jobs with no chance of finding another. Watching his mother succumb to the unrealistic hope of winning the National Lottery, and his father to the destructive forces of drink and embittered disillusionment at the system that had deprived him of his livelihood, Colin was determined not to be dragged down into a similar abyss. With three siblings on the dole, one in custody for nicking handbags from pubs, and two nephews in care, he had vowed to break the pattern of resentment and deprivation and to get himself out of the poverty trap by his own efforts. It was in hospital, where for the first time in his life he had been well fed and cared for, that he observed that family life was not necessarily synonymous with altercation, blasphemy and physical abuse. That it had to do with offerings of Lucozade produced lovingly from supermarket bags, bunches of 'all-the-year-round' flowers (destined for a short life in overheated wards) and clean pyjamas, was an ongoing source of amazement to him. By the time he had made the long journey by ambulance from the Royal Liverpool Children's Hospital in Alder Hey, which he had mentally if not physically outgrown, and had been admitted to the Top Floor Surgical ward of the Fulham Hospital, the pancreatic disease which was associated with his cystic fibrosis (and which gave him a great deal of pain), was well advanced. Despite the relentless treatment (pancreatic enzyme replacements, vitamin supplements, a low-fat, high protein diet, physiotherapy, antibiotics and 'bronchodilators'), collapse and pneumonia were inexorably destroying what little remained of his lungs. Colin was able to see for himself the characteristic snowstorm changes on the X-ray pictures. A heart-lung transplant was his sole chance of survival into adulthood, of living an active and fulfilling life.

Unable to attract Anna's attention, Colin followed the crumpled tissue with another, which landed on his neighbour's nose. She opened her eyes.

'You awake?' Anna turned her head towards Colin.

'I am now.'

'There's...something's going on...' The effort of speaking coupled with excitement at what he was attempting to convey depleted the breath from Colin's puny chest.

Years of life in wards that had become home from home had trained his powers of observation, which he knew would stand him in good stead in medicine and earned him the reputation of the most reliable ear on the hospital grapevine. Unable to sleep, while the patients in Top Floor Surgical breathed stertorously, or made public proclamations from the clandestine depths of their tormented nightmares, or twisted and turned in drugged attempts to free themselves from the bonds of their pain, he had watched Debbie, roused hastily from her bed, in whispered consultation at the nursing station with an equally dishevelled Nicholas and the ward sister. The unmistakeable sound of the helicopter taking off from the roof of the building, as the morning lights were turned on and the ward maid clattered in with the tea trolley with its outsize aluminium teapot, confirmed that something was indeed afoot.

'Something's going on,' Colin hissed conspiratorially across the divide between his bed and Anna's, when he had regained his shallow breath.

'How do you know?' Interpreting the esoteric communication correctly, Anna raised her head. Colin tapped the side of his nose.

'I heard the 'copter.'

Dropping back on to her pillows as a thick cup of anaemic-looking tea was put on to her locker, Anna allowed her hopes, which were on a perpetual see-saw of anticipation and despair, to rise like a hot-air balloon in an opportune sky. *If* a heart-lung bloc was being harvested, *if* it was compatible and of the right size and weight, *if* she were selected for a transplant, much as she loved her father she might yet get the opportunity to enjoy what other girls of her age took for granted: the chance to walk down the street on her own, to look into shop windows instead of just using them as an excuse to get her breath back; the chance to go to college; the chance to 'do' Europe on a rail-card; the chance to pursue a career; the chance to go to parties; the chance to find a partner; the chance to look after her own home, not to mention to put on her own socks. This mundane task, like many others, had gradually become too much of an effort for her to manage. Aware that heart and lung transplants were still experimental and full of risks, she prayed nightly to a God (whom as a last resort she had recently acknowledged) not to let her die but to give her a final chance. She tried to think of valid reasons why she, of all the hundreds of patients on the transplant list, should be the one to be selected. She was not particularly good, she was not particularly clever (having missed out on so much of her schooling), she was not particularly accomplished and had nothing especially to recommend her. The only sphere in which she shone was in the eyes of her father. Unable to find even the humblest rationale to support her application, she consoled herself with the fact that even the most stupid donkey, the smallest flea, had *some* right to existence.

By the time Martin Bond arrived to visit his daughter, as he did every night after leaving his office in Berkeley Square, the rumour put into orbit that morning was common knowledge, even though nobody was supposed to know.

'Where's Colin?' Drawing up a chair next to Anna, who was fighting to keep awake, Martin looked fearfully at the eloquently empty bed with its curling pictures of footballers stuck on the side of the locker.

It was midday when they had come for Colin, moving him, with his oxygen cylinder, to a side ward with nothing to eat or drink. The moment he heard the story from Anna, flushed and excited as if it were she who had been sent for, Martin had stormed off to waylay Nicholas Lilleywhite. He found him at his computer in his office, which he had entered without knocking.

'Organs are being harvested, Nicholas...' The transplant physician, who looked exhausted, indicated the chaos on his desk without looking up.

'I'm extremely busy, Martin.'

'It's all round Top Floor Surgical.'

Nicholas tapped in some figures that appeared on his screen.

'I want to speak to Professor Cortes now!'

'Out of the question.'

'Don't bullshit me, Nicholas. It's not Joe Shmo you're dealing with. I don't know who you have to fuck to get a transplant, but I sure as hell am not going to wait quietly in line while somebody round here plays God.'

'Divine status is hard to imagine when you have twenty-three pages of paperwork to deal with for every organ we harvest.'

'So it is true! I demand to see the Prof.'

'Professor Cortes is in Cornwall.'

'I don't give a shit if he is in Australia. I know my rights...'

'Do you want me to call security...?' Nicholas was on a short fuse. 'To have you escorted from the premises?'

'I advise you not to try...' Martin advanced towards the desk, banging his fist on it with frustration. 'The minute he steps out of that helicopter... The minute he arrives...' He was growing purple in the face. Nicholas had been up all night and had worked non-stop all day. All he needed was to have a relative with a coronary infarct on his hands.

'Look, Martin, why don't you sit down for a moment?'

'It's my daughter's life I'm pleading for...'

'This is a hospital, not a court of law. Saving lives is our business...'

'Strange way you have of going about it.' Suddenly deflated, Martin collapsed on to the chair. 'Did you ever play a game on the sidewalk when you were a kid? If you don't step on the lines you promise yourself such and such? I tell myself each day if I do this, if I don't do that, organs will become available, the call will come and...Anna will be well.'

Passing a hand across his forehead, Nicholas leaned back in his chair.

'I've said all this before, Martin. It's time I said it again. We've been carrying out heart-lung transplants at the Fulham for several years now. The problems associated with it, *serious* problems – which Professor Sands and her team are working on – have not been resolved...'

'I know all that stuff.'

'Despite all the work which has been done, we aren't sure how transplanted organs will function.'

'I'm prepared to take that chance.'

'The human immune system is programmed to distinguish between bona fide residents and illegal aliens. Although it's very good at its job, it still does not recognise the life-saving elements of transplanted organs. It perceives them as "foreign invaders" and attempts to destroy them...'

'Immunosuppression.'

'In order to overcome this natural response – in the event that Anna did get her transplant – she would need to take certain drugs for the rest of her life.'

'That's okay.'

'Some of the drugs, such as cyclosporin, which brought transplant surgery out of the cave and into the daylight, have unpleasant side-effects. Some of them will make her extremely sick...'

'We'll face that problem when we come to it.'

'Even the most comprehensive knowledge of transplant immunobiology does not confer clinical insight. We cannot predict exactly how each patient is going to react. We are still faced with rejection and infection, twin evils that remain multifaceted and unpredictable. It's like walking a tightrope... Sharks on one side and piranha fish on the other.'

37

'Anna has hopes, dreams, aspirations. She wants to be able to go to the movies, to go dancing, to join in, to have fun. My one wish is to see my daughter grow up.'

'I hear what you're saying, Martin. I've grown fond of Anna myself. You have to take on board that transplantation is still only an "investigative endeavour". It must not, it should not, be looked on as a cure. We transplant patients to optimise their chances of survival. To offer them as enduring, active, meaningful, and normal a life as possible, for as long as possible.'

'Anna has never led a normal life…'

'Excuse me, that's my bleep.' Nicholas picked up the phone. 'Dr Lilleywhite…'

'Anna hates being dependent, hates asking for favours…'

'I'm sorry, Martin. Some other time. I'm needed on the ward. You must excuse me. I have to go.'

The emergency turned out to be a young man in need of resuscitation, to which end Nicholas skilfully introduced a central line into the jugular vein, enabling life-saving fluids to be given to him. Just as the procedure was finished and he was leaving the ward for the night, just as he was going off duty, he received a message from Sidney Sands, who wanted to speak to him urgently. Tired as he was, he weaved his way past the scattered outbuildings of the hospital in the heavy rain and, getting thoroughly soaked, sloshed the quarter-mile through the puddles to the Postgraduate Medical School building where he took the lift to the Department of Histochemistry.

While he admired, and envied, Sidney's achievements, sometimes Professor Sands got up his nose. Until she had become a patient under his care, Nicholas had known the Head of Histochemistry only by sight and reputation, and from watching her annual appearance in the Fulham Hospital Christmas concert where her long legs and skimpy costumes had always created a sensation. In the last skit he had seen she was dressed up as a chef, in white miniskirt and toque, and had high-kicked her way into *Burke and Hare* (the butcher's) to buy hearts and lungs for a Histochemistry Department dinner. While the sketch had brought the house down, Nicholas (who took his work extremely seriously) was not amused, and when Sidney had first attended his clinic for her transplant assessment they had got off on the wrong foot. Breathingwise it had been one of her better days and having been kept in out-patients for almost half an hour she had marched into his office looking pointedly at her watch. Finding the physician, who from now on would be responsible for her care, on the telephone to a nervous post-transplant patient, Sidney had done nothing to conceal her impatience. She attempted to drown him out while he was still speaking. The information that she was due shortly in the meeting did nothing to foster the necessary rapport between them. To be fair, when he had finished on the telephone, Sidney apologised for her intolerance, but Nicholas had been unable to expunge his irritation at her high-handed behaviour from his mind, and any subsequent dealings with Sidney, while on the surface entirely amicable, had been coloured by their first interview. He was only human. He was a good and caring physician. In this overstretched health service he had too many patients to deal with. All of them wanted his undivided attention – which in their shoes he would himself have expected – but with his limited resources he could only do his best.

Notwithstanding the fact that his shift had been a long one and that he desperately wanted to get home, he hurried through the rain at Sidney's bidding because her health had now deteriorated so much that he felt extremely sorry for her. From an energetic head of department, holding her team together and her finger on every pulse, she was struggling manfully to come to the hospital each day and to carry on with her job. He admired her courage.

The Histochemistry Department was deserted. He glanced in the molecular biology lab and the tissue culture section, but there was no one about other than Juliet, Sidney's PA, a spiky-haired girl with a ring through her nose who had told him, offering no apology, that Professor Sands was in conference with a member of her research team and why didn't he take a seat? Fuming, he sat on a stool in the tea room, next to its named mugs and electric kettle. Juliet offered to make him some coffee, which only exasperated him further. Nicholas was doing Sidney a favour. It wasn't his job to go running round the hospital after patients, and it was only her decreasing lung function, which now sometimes confined her to a wheelchair, that brought him to the Histochemistry Department when by rights he should have been on his way home. When Sidney wheeled herself into the tea room, her briefcase on her lap, his practised eye remarked her rapidly rising chest and the puffy feet, which overlapped the trendy shoes that made no concession to her condition. Sidney came straight to the point.

'I hear Eduardo's gone to Cornwall...' Nicholas nodded wearily. Another one trying to nobble the jury. '...I can't get anything out of Debbie.'

'I'm afraid that in this instance, Sidney, you're only a patient.'

'A dying patient.' The brisk tone belied the words. She took a reprint from her briefcase. 'Have you read my last paper? Myocardial localization and isoforms of neural cell adhesion molecule in the developing and transplanted human heart.' She handed the reprint to Nicholas. 'My work on pulmonary hypertension is crucial.'

'It's time you stopped working.'

'I can't swan off to the Mediterranean like Chopin or faff around in Rome like Keats just because I happen to be ill. I've work to do. The research programme depends on me. Have you thought how many patients' lives would be affected if... Have you thought of the knock-on effect?'

Nicholas hadn't the heart to reveal that at that very moment Colin was being prepared for a transplant, that the caution 'Nil By Mouth' already hung unequivocally on the side-room door.

'I'm afraid it's out of my hands...' It was no use giving Sidney the spiel about the sharks and the piranha fish. She knew about infection, she knew about rejection, better than he did himself.

'Of course it is,' Sidney sighed, dropping her professional mask to reveal a sick and frightened woman. 'I know nobody's indispensable, Nick...' It was the first time she had called him Nick. 'I was trying to save my own skin.'

When he finally left the hospital, retrieving his car from the flooded car park and driving home through the downpour that dangerously reduced visibility, Nicholas thought charitably that in Sidney's situation he would have acted no differently. *If I am not for myself, who will be for me?* As transplant physician he was familiar with the desperation of those who were dying before they had lived for want of available organs, and with his own impotence in the face of their desperate battles. While heart transplants had been going on for over thirty years, and heart-lung transplants for seventeen, they were still in the Dark Ages. Judging by the alarming rate at which biotechnology was developing, and at which scientists were reorganising life at the genetic level, in a generation from now both the definition of life and the very meaning of existence were destined to be radically altered. Like the Renaissance spirit that had swept over medieval Europe 600 years ago, the consequences for society and for future generations of cloned sheep, genetically engineered pigs, human organs grown in jars and vat-produced skin were likely to be enormous.

By the time he got home to the terraced house in Barnes where his wife Mary, a solicitor on maternity leave, was feeding Max, their eight-week old baby, it was almost ten o'clock. Nicholas had been working for sixteen hours on the trot – a circumstance that, where organ transplantation was concerned, was by no means unusual. While biological manipulation was changing the entire concept of nature and man's relationship to it, and interest was now focused on the thousands of chemical strands of genetic information that compromised the blueprints for living things, the fragrant smell of the evening meal and the sight of his newborn son at his wife's breast in his lamplit living-room brought him sharply back to the tangible world. He shed the preoccupations and heavy responsibilities of his working day at the same time as his anorak, and transferred his bleeper on to the waistband of his trousers. He embraced his family and reinforced his grip on reality.

SIX

It was not only the transplant patients in Top Floor Surgical but the Fulham Hospital itself with its ancient roofs and crumbling fabric, which was fighting for its life. One of London's oldest designated hospitals – catering for the sick rather than merely being an almshouse like many establishments of the same period – it had originally contained a hundred beds, but now accommodated more than a thousand in-patients, and had a thriving out-patients department serving a wide catchment area.

Amongst its earliest alumni were both eminent physicians and distinguished surgeons of the day who read lectures in anatomy in the dissecting room of the medical school. Over the years, the progress of science and the extension of medical education led to the establishment of additional lectureships on related subjects, and of courses of instruction in special branches of medicine and surgery. As the hospital slowly expanded over land purchased for it by its supporters, new operating theatres, residents' quarters, casualty departments, public health departments, pathological and isolation blocks were added, as was a new block containing 250 medical beds. The hospital now occupied several acres of land and provided medical and surgical beds, ophthalmology, dermatology, gynaecology, orthopaedic, ear nose and throat and maternity wards as well as an overstretched casualty department, but was now threatened with closure.

In a move to rationalise the National Health Service, successive governments had decreed that, irrespective of community needs, hospital services must be inconveniently and short-sightedly amalgamated, new hospitals provided (in some unforeseeable future), and those establishments not designated for rescue by the current powers-that-be were to go arbitrarily to the wall. Despite the fact that its Accident and Emergency Department was relied upon by the local community, that its teaching facilities were nonpareil, and that its reputation was worldwide, without the unlikely help of some *deus ex machina* the writing for the Fulham Hospital was on the wall.

In the side-room to which he had been moved that morning, Colin listened to his pangs of hunger, signified by the gurgling in his bowels which he now knew was technically referred to as borborygmi. Pondering his own uncertain future, he wished that there were 'Friends of Colin Rafferty' to plead for his survival with the same dedication as the Friends of the Fulham Hospital, who with their placards and appeals protested against its closure. The long and short of it was that he was lonely. Now push had actually come to shove, kind as were the nurses, attentive as were the medical staff, close as was Anna, his friend in adversity, seasoned hospital patient and operating theatre recidivist as he was, he wanted his Mum and Dad.

He knew that with his failure to thrive as a baby, his face pale and pointed and his physique frail and unattractive, he had since his premature birth been a thorn in his parents' flesh. His constant illnesses had enraged his father and exasperated his mother. Neither of them had been able to cope with the drain on their financial, physical and emotional resources. With their other five children, his diabetic and partially sighted Nana, who lived with them, and their daily struggle to make ends meet, they were already fully stretched. His parents made him feel guilty. As if he had brought his feeble constitution upon himself. What they were in fact doing was repudiating their own feelings of responsibility for his condition, the genetic component of which he had inherited from them.

Unlike his Mum and Dad however, for whom his removal from their sight was a blessing in disguise, Colin had found a way to escape from the terrible feelings of oppression and unworthiness that he visited upon himself. He lost himself in football, a game that owing to his disability he had never played. Empathising with the players in a fantasy world of flying feet, free kicks, seized chances, timely tackles, finely taken goals and midfield runs, his photographic memory enabled him to come up when challenged with the key results of any match played in the past few years, as well as to recite by heart the Premiership league table. When his Liverpool heroes appropriated the ball and dribbled it the length of the field, leaping and pirouetting like twelve-stone ballerinas, seeing off their opponents on their way to the goalposts as if they were so many annoying flies, he grew hoarse with the excitement of urging them on, so short of breath that he had to resort to his oxygen mask before his equilibrium could be restored. When the match was over, win or lose, he was Colin Rafferty again, alone with his cystic fibrosis. The doors of the dressing-room, where his muscular heroes were larking about in the showers and calling to each other with coarse familiarity in an excess of post-match euphoria, were firmly closed.

Although nothing had been said when he had been moved to the side-room – apart from the usual nonsense about needing his bed – he had been on Top Floor Surgical long enough to know that the tell-tale admonition to have nothing to eat or drink, to leave his stomach empty, presaged a visit to the operating theatre, and that, all things being equal, he was at last going to get the treatment he so desperately needed. Paradoxically, although he knew that his life was not worth a candle without a transplant, he feared that his enfeebled body would not withstand the trauma, that he would die on the operating table and there would be no one to notice his passing let alone to mourn him. Apart from the usual considerations of size, weight, and compatibility of organs, it was his rare blood group that had kept him for so long on the transplant list. Although from observing others on the ward succumb before organs could be found (he was well aware that his time was rapidly running out), there was a part of him that wanted to delay a little longer the deletion of his name from Debbie's computer. In the penalty box of his side-room, deprived of nutrition, he felt as if he were being disciplined – for hauling down another player, executing a flying headlock – by some divine referee who had given him a yellow card. As if he were being punished by being summarily sent off. Starved not only of food (there was sausages and mash for lunch) but of information, the nursing staff seemed to be avoiding him. He plugged himself into his Walkman and tuned into a match replay, occupying himself by reciting the mnemonic for the branches of the facial nerve, which had been taught to him by the medical students who surrounded his bed daily and whose mascot he had become. 'Two zulus buggered my cat': temporal, zygomatic, bucchal, mandibular and cutaneous. Anna's father had promised to buy him a copy of *Gray's Anatomy* for his birthday. He would become a surgeon like Professsor Cortes – of whom he had only once caught sight as he strode swiftly through the ward with his retinue, and whose name was spoken with awe.

'Colin?' Having headed the ball over the line from two yards out, Colin must have fallen asleep. When he opened his eyes he was surprised to see Alison, the transplant counsellor, to whom he had never spoken but had seen talking to other patients in the ward, sitting by his side.

'Hello, Colin, I'm Alison, I don't think we've met. I've got some good news for you. I've come to tell you that there are lungs being harvested…'

'I heard the helicopter.'

'I don't want to raise your hopes too much but they could just be compatible. What I want to do is to run through the procedure with you in case Professor Cortes decides to go ahead with your operation, so that you'll know exactly what to expect.'

Alison was wearing a short black skirt, a black polo-neck jumper and sheer black tights. Her creamy skin was like nothing he had ever seen before: clear and clean, like her healthy teeth when she smiled. Everything about her was shining, her glossy lips, her eyes – like blue marbles, as if you could see right through them – her short black hair the same colour as her long black lashes, which threw shadows on her cheek when she looked down at her notes. Colin decided that he was in love with her.

'The Duty Registrar will be along to examine you shortly. He'll discuss your present symptoms, then he'll explain the consent forms which he'll ask you to sign. He'll want to take some blood from you and measure your height, weight and blood pressure. He'll also want a nose and throat swab and a urine sample…' Colin wondered if Alison was married or if she had a boyfriend. She wore a silver ring on every finger. '…He may require another chest X-ray and an ECG. Professor Cortes' anaesthetist will also be along. She'll check you over and give you some medication to make you sleepy. When the results of your blood tests come back to the ward, you will be given some anti-rejection drugs, which you will continue to take after your operation. I won't bother you now with their names…

'Cyclosporin and azathioprine.'

'Well now, you know more about it than I do.'

'How long will the operation take?'

'Patients are usually in theatre a minimum of four hours. There's no need to worry about it...'

'England is playing Chile.' Alison made a note on her clipboard.

'I'll ask Sister to record it. You'll have something to look forward to. After the surgery you will be transferred to ICU – the Intensive Care Unit – where you can expect to stay for roughly two to four days. During your stay on the ward special precautions will be taken to minimise the risk of infection. The staff will wear aprons and gloves and the number of visitors will be kept to a minimum...' Colin wondered who was going to visit him.

'Flowers and plants are not allowed.' He loved it when she uncrossed her legs and wriggled into a more comfortable position on the chair. 'On your immediate return from theatre you will be deeply asleep, ventilated on a breathing machine and attached to numerous drips, drains and monitors. You will also have a urinary catheter, which allows us to check output from your kidneys hour by hour. As you wake up and your condition stabilises, the ventilator tube, which prevents you from speaking, will be removed to allow you to breathe on your own. You'll be given medicines to keep you free from pain. Any questions so far?' He wanted to ask her if he could touch her. If he could just hold the alabaster hand. He put his own hands beneath the cotton blanket.

'OK then.' She crossed her legs again so that her skirt rode up. 'When the doctors are happy you are making progress, more of the monitoring equipment will be removed and you will come back to the ward. At this stage you will still have a drip going into a vein in your neck via an infusion pump, which contains one or more drugs to stimulate the contraction of the new heart and stabilise the rate and rhythm of the heartbeat. You'll also have three fine wires which emerge from the skin beneath your breastbone and these will be connected to a small pacemaker box attached to your bed...'

'Bionic man.'

'You've got the idea. The wires are in contact with the outer surface of the heart, and in the earliest stages after the new heart is inserted this temporary pacemaker also helps to keep the heartbeat strong and regular. If the wires are not needed they are wrapped around a pledget of cotton wool and taped to the abdominal wall. They are pulled out easily after ten days. Electrodes attached to the skin of your chest and abdomen are connected to a computer screen which gives a continuous display of your ECG...'

'To measure the electrical activity of the heart.'

'I'd heard you were going to be a doctor. You will still have a urinary catheter...'

Colin stopped listening about chest drains to prevent the lungs collapsing, about being encouraged to do as much as possible as soon as he felt fit, about daily visits by the physiotherapist who would teach him breathing and leg exercises, about the Fulham 'Blue Book' which was given to all transplant patients and in which he would be required to enter all his drugs with the correct dosage and the appropriate times they should be taken. He was having trouble with his breathing, which was due not so much to his physical condition, his decimated lungs, but to the fact that his fifteen-year-old body was responding to Alison's tantalizing perfume, to the upsurge of her breasts beneath the close-fitting sweater.

'...Postural drainage and coughing techniques...' Alison was saying, as he made love to her beneath the bedclothes. 'Your voice may also be affected but this usually resolves itself after a few months. It is vitally important for lung recipients to continue the physiotherapy regimen taught to them on the ward and it should become a daily habit for life... Are you all right, Colin? Do you want me to call someone?' Watching, as she uncrossed her legs again, not bothering to pull down her skirt so that he was mesmerized by the deep cavern leading goodness knows where between her thighs, Colin did not answer.

'I'll help you with your oxygen, you're looking a bit strange.' Picking up the plastic mask she placed it over Colin's mouth, standing close to the bed and holding his hand as he shuddered convulsively, then was still. 'Better now?'

'Yeah, thanks.'

'Good. I'll leave you to rest. I have a surprise for you later.'

He was busy with the tissue box, hoping that Lucy or Fatima, who were on duty, wouldn't notice the state of his sheets when Father Thomas, wearing grey flannel trousers and a baggy sweater, put his thinning blond head round the door. Colin wondered if he had come to administer the last rites.

'Awake are we...?' Wanker. 'I've just heard the splendid news. You may be getting your transplant. I thought a little talk might...in case you were worried. Not worried are you?'

Father Thomas did his head in. He and Anna gave a passable imitation of his over-the-top camaraderie (designed to demystify the Church), which ended up with both of them in hysterics and struggling for breath. Stupid git, with his stupid smile, his suede shoes, his bony wrists. Of course he wasn't worried. He was scared shitless. It wasn't that he wanted a new heart, new lungs, just that he wanted to live. He would do anything to live.

'Is there anything you'd like to talk about Colin?' Colin couldn't think of a single thing he would want to discuss with Father Thomas. All Father Thomas could talk about was cricket and Colin wasn't the slightest bit interested in cricket. He didn't even know where Trinidad was. 'You're a brave boy. You've suffered so much. Now your suffering will be over...' Too late, Father Thomas realised the ambiguity of his words. 'What I mean is, with a new heart, new lungs, you'll be a new Colin Rafferty. Would you like me to say a little prayer for you?'

Please yourself. Colin didn't believe in God. The first time Father Thomas had stopped by his bed he had been unfazed by Colin's lack of faith. 'Be that as it may,' he said, 'As long as God believes in you.' Colin thought it was a load of cobblers. He wished Father Thomas would get on with it and hoped he would manage not to laugh. 'Our Father who art in heaven...' Colin closed his eyes. He thought about the friendly between England and Chile and prayed that Sister would remember to video the match so that he could watch it later. 'Through Jesus Christ Our Lord,' Father Thomas was saying in that special voice they had, 'Amen.'

When Father Thomas had gone, having consigned Colin to the care of the Almighty rather than Professor Cortes (Colin knew which he'd rather trust), he drifted off again until a once-familiar smell of stale smoke assaulted his nostrils. He woke to see not only his mother in her best coat, which had cigarette ash on the lapels and from which there was a button missing so was fastened with a safety pin, but also his father, who looked distinctly uncomfortable in an anorak which crackled as he moved and who was holding a bunch of mauve spray carnations. He sat by Colin's bed.

'Son?'

'We caught the eight-thirty,' his mother said. 'Awayday. The Friends of the Fulham Hospital paid.'

'All right, are you?' It was the question of the year. His mother took a card out of her amorphous handbag. She gave it to Colin. 'From Nana...' It was a Christmas card with the Christmas greetings heavily scored out and 'For Colin, love Nana' written beneath the indecipherable text. He recognised his mother's childish handwriting. 'Nana doesn't see too well,' she said in mitigation.

'All right are you?' His father clung to the flowers, cradling them in the crook of his arm like a baby.

'They've all asked after you,' his mother looked round the room as if she was checking her escape route. 'Our Doreen and our Arthur and little Kelly and Cassandra – daft name, I still can't get used to it – and Tom and Cathy next door...'

'She nearly won this week,' his father said. 'Tell 'im, Beattie.'

'Different numbers,' his mother brightened up. 'I felt like a change. In place of birthdays, yours and Doreen's and Tracy's and Frank's and Myra's, I did random...'

'You give it to Mr Patel...' his father explained.

'Who's telling this?' His father withdrew into his anorak.

'You give it to Mr Patel and the machine does it for you. Two boxes. Eight and thirty-two and nineteen...'

'I thought it was seventeen?' His father said. Colin was surprised his mother's look didn't wither the flowers.

'Now I can't remember where I got up to. Eight and thirty-two and nineteen and forty-three and twelve and twenty in one box, and four and six and forty-nine – forty-nine's come up I don't know how many times – and seven and eleven and nineteen...' – a look of triumph at his father – '...in the other.'

'Saturday night...' his father began. Colin had rarely heard him complete a sentence, he wasn't allowed. 'Tom and Cathy came over and we was all sat sitting on the settee...'

Colin could picture the four of them in the front room, with their beer and crisps on the coffee table next to Tom's filthy trainers (he always had his feet up on the coffee table), oohing and aahing at *Noel's Houseparty* on the TV and at the moment when the balls started to roll ('Arthur' or 'Guinevere' or whatever set had been chosen by the man with the white gloves). His mother would get the familiar red-on-white slip ready, although she knew the numbers on it by heart. There'd be great to-do to find a pencil that worked although Tom, being a carpenter and in work fortunately (albeit cash-in-hand, no questions asked), usually had a short stub with a chiselled end. She'd sit on the very edge of the settee and as the results were called, too quick for them to register, they'd argue about what they had seen but were unable to remember until the balls were flipped over on the screen as if by magic, and his mother repeated the numbered sequence checking them against the figures on her form.

'One, nine, thirteen, seventeen, twenty-six, twenty-seven…you don't often get a run like that…'

Colin checked the numbers in his head.

'I thought you said you nearly won? You didn't get any.'

'Because I didn't do birthdays. I changed me system. Just the once. It was Mr Patel made me do random. I would have won a hundred quid if I'd stuck to birthdays. "Better luck next time Mrs Rafferty." He was serving a sherbet dab. Not doing very well, he's not, not with the new Tesco's. He's feeling it is Mr Patel. I could have strangled him.'

'See Hoddle's giving Michael a chance tonight,' his father said. Football was their only point of contact. 'He's nowt more than a boy…'

'Eighteen and fifty-nine days,' Colin said.

'If you're good enough, you're old enough! There's not many can run wi' ball that quick. He's only played thirty-three club games. Youngest England football international this century. Takes me back to Duncan Edwards…' He noticed Colin's blank face. 'Matt Busby's Babes. The Munich crash. Before you were born. Let you watch it on the telly do they?' Colin nodded. He was tired now. Too tired to explain that while England faced Chile at Wembley he would most likely be in the operating theatre.

'Gloomy sort of place this.' His mother had been studying the dull linoleum, the green tiled walls. 'Worse than *Casualty*.' She always watched *Casualty* with Cathy next door over a cup of tea and a packet of Hobnobs, after his father and Tom had gone to the pub. 'Time they pulled these old places down. Got a canteen have they? I made sandwiches at the crack of dawn but I left them on the Easiwork. Three pound fifty for a hot bacon sandwich they wanted on the train. I told them what they could do with it. We can have them for tea, if we get back in time. I'm starving. Had yours have you?' Colin reckoned that the 'Nil By Mouth' notice on the door had gone over his mother's head.

'I'm not allowed.'

'Never mind. I remember when I went in for my veins. They give you a cup of tea afterwards. When you come round...' It was the nearest she got to acknowledging his transplant. 'Nothing to worry about. You'll be able to come home.'

'Be able to play football.'

'Be as good as new.' His mother stood up. 'We missed breakfast. I wonder if they do all-day breakfasts? I fancy a fry-up. Be all right will you, Colin?' She couldn't reach the door fast enough. He couldn't remember the last time she had kissed him.

'Course he'll be all right. You'll be all right, won't you son?' His father was out in the corridor when he realised that he had taken the flowers with him. Coming back into the room he laid them on the bed.

'Thanks Dad.'

Despite the lure of a fry-up in the canteen, his father seemed reluctant to leave the side-room, seemed riveted to the shabby linoleum, mesmerised by the mauve flowers in their damp paper. Colin saw something suspiciously like tears in his red-rimmed eyes. His voice was hoarse, but then his voice was always hoarse from the all the brick dust he'd breathed in over the years.

'Be thinking of you tonight, son...' Colin knew that his father didn't mean because of the football match: it was the nearest he could get to communication.

SEVEN

When there were hearts and lungs to be harvested Eduardo Cortes went into overdrive. Even on a normal working day, when he passed smoothly and swiftly through the swing-doors into the operating suite – a legendary conductor who ran imperiously on to the podium and galvanised the orchestra – everybody in theatre changed automatically into top-gear. Rising at half past five every morning and never in bed before midnight, despite the awesome demands of his job which might have kept a more susceptible being awake, he had never taken a sleeping pill – nor for that matter any pill – in his life.

His day, winter and summer, began with a three mile run during which he burned off not only calories, so keeping himself in trim, but any other extraneous considerations that threatened to cloud his judgement or interfere with his work. So far it had been a normal week. On Monday and Tuesday, before an audience of visiting professionals, he had performed intricate and delicate surgery on a newborn with congenital heart disease. On Wednesday he and his team had successfully implanted an 'artificial heart' in the chest of a woman with heart failure. On Thursday and Friday he had moderated at a conference in Zurich (on less invasive techniques in coronary surgery), which had been attended by 450 delegates; and on Saturday, in a procedure lasting seven-and-a-half hours, he and his colleagues had removed from a patient a blood-pump implanted six months earlier – there was bleeding from around the device. Thirty-six hours later, while he was still congratulating himself on the fact that the patient's heart had returned to normal and might now well be expected to function unaided, there had been a dramatic change in rhythm, a sign of danger after any heart surgery. Eduardo had been unable to resuscitate the man. While the death was a personal tragedy for the patient's family, to whom the implant had given hope, and was a genuine disappointment to the hospital staff who had cared for him, it was a most bitter blow to Eduardo, who blamed himself although his skills had never been in question.

Unflappable in theatre, where he worked in total silence, he repressed his frustrations and took them out on his wife and children when he went home. Achievements, goals, conquests and victories, whether over women or in his work, were important to him. Whether in the hospital or on his own territory he not only occupied a great deal of physical space – being short and heavily built enabled him to withstand the long hours on his feet both in the operating theatre and at the Albert Hall where he was a regular and enthusiastic promenader – but demanded an equivalent amount of personal attention from those around him. The combination of his Argentinian appetites and his wife's Italian flammability produced an ambience in which voices were frequently raised and it was by no means unknown for objects to be thrown. Francesca Cortes, with her black eyes and sable hair, had been born amongst the lemons, bitter oranges, and date palms of Pantalica. She was eighteen years old when Eduardo, with a sensuality and passion which matched her own, had swept her off her feet in the Excelsior Hotel in Rome, where she had been staying with her parents. After a wedding which had lasted for three Sicilian days and nights, he had transported her to the grey skies and diesel fumes of London where despite the fact that her husband was a notorious pouncer and had a habit of falling passionately in love with one woman or another at almost monthly intervals, Francesca, indulging and forgiving her husband's vanities and insecurities, remained faithful to him. They made a handsome if bizarre couple. Francesca was fifteen years younger and six inches taller than Eduardo and far more beautiful, and Eduardo was infatuated with his young wife who was equally enamoured of her spouse. Preoccupied as he was with the human heart – an organ that skipped when you kissed, broke when you were sad and thumped when you were frightened – he had discovered at a precociously early age that he had no trouble in conquering them. Luz, their baby daughter, was born nine months after their marriage to be followed eighteen months later by a son, Enrico, and soon after that by another daughter, Gianna-Maria. Refusing either to employ a nanny or give house-room to a dishwasher (when Eduardo was at home she washed and he dried), Francesca turned a blind eye to Eduardo's indiscretions, dismissing them as peccadilloes when rumours of his exploits reached her ears. When the indiscretions became major faux pas which were picked up by the press and he was pictured, on a visit to the States, in a tuxedo with a starlet on his arm, she called into play the conspiracy of silence with which she had been brought up – while every woman in Sicily acknowledged the presence and influence of those hostile to the law and its administrators, the word Mafia never passed their lips – and settled for a quiet life shattered only by Eduardo's frequent irascible outbursts and the occasional broken plate. While passion gave way to fierce loyalty, undying friendship and mutual affection, and her four children – Francesca included Eduardo – occupied more and more of her time, Francesca busied herself with their large Victorian house and garden in Dulwich, ate large quantities of sweetmeats (sent by her family in Syracuse) in front of the television, and abandoning her once shapely figure, allowed herself to expand. The more she took on the contours of Eduardo's late mother, of whom she had seen a picture wielding a banner in the Plaza de Mayo, the more Eduardo worshipped her, although since her transformation into Madonna his love for his wife had taken on a different connotation. Francesca kept the peace at home by the simple means of boosting Eduardo's frail ego. She agreed with everything he said – which while not politically correct was politically expedient – and fixed him *bife de chorizo* (often having to give the steak to the Schnauzers when Eduardo didn't come home), while she fed the children and herself on mountains of home-made pasta with which Eduardo, a dedicated carnivore, would have no truck. This seemingly compliant behaviour (she refrained from arguing with Eduardo who liked to persuade everyone to do what *he* wanted to do) was entirely foreign to her Latin nature and it was only a matter of time before, like the volcanoes of Sicily, her suppressed feelings bubbled to the surface and she erupted. All hell – both in Spanish and the Saracen invective of Francesca's native dialect (incomprehensible even to Italians), augmented by the barking of the Schnauzers and the noisy exit of the children from the line of fire – was let loose as the shit (sometimes in the form of a basinfull of spaghetti) finally hit the fan. Sometimes, unable to get his own way, Eduardo walked out of the house leaving Francesca, still threatening to kill him, and the children in tears; at others, in a melodramatic gesture (like the old-time heroines in the afternoon movies she watched), Francesca hurled a motley assortment of clothes into a suitcase and threatened to go back to her family, never to return. It always did the trick. The renowned surgeon, the celebrity of the conference circuit, the idol of the Medical School, the rock-star of the operating theatre, the sex-symbol of the hospital – where it was not unknown for him to be stumbled upon in one of the cubicles with a female member of his firm who were chosen, amongst other things, for their looks – fell on his knees and with tears rolling down his face promised his wife anything, anything at all if only she would stay. Francesca, who had no intention of going anywhere, and who adored both her husband and her children, informed Eduardo that he was haughty and arrogant and she had no intention of submitting to Argentinian domination, before taking him to bed where their differences were generally settled.

Eduardo would have been the first to admit that, often irritable though never a bully, he was not an easy man to live with and that had it not been for Francesca, upon whom he was as dependent as a child both in practical and theoretical terms, he would have had difficulty in living with himself.

While he was one of the few surgeons whose merit awards (which represented ninety-five per cent of his salary) kept him in the NHS, his career, like many other pioneering careers, had suffered lows, during which Francesca had sustained him, as well as highs in which she had shared. Dismissed unfairly by his detractors as a 'surgical opportunist' more interested in fame and éclat than in the advancement of science, he had twice faced legal claims for damages from families who maintained they had not been told of the possibility that their children could suffer brain damage as a result of heart surgery. Once, he had connected a young girl with a failing heart to a baboon in the hope of saving her life. When both the girl and the baboon had died and the news seeped out, there had been a public outcry. Eduardo would have been the first to admit that cardiac surgery was addictive and that in the operating theatre, where he swapped the halo for the scythe, he completely lost track of the external world. There was so much that could go wrong. Often the operations did not go according to plan; what he did sometimes caused damage – of that there was no doubt. All he could do was his best and sometimes, even though he knew very well that it was futile, he found it harder to make the decision to stop than to carry on.

At the same time as Colin Rafferty lay fearfully in his side-room at the Fulham Hospital, clutching his teddy-bear and anticipating his long awaited heart-lung transplant, Rosie Logan, a sixteen-year-old schoolgirl who had been knocked down and fatally injured by a motorbike outside her school in Cornwall, was being dosed with steroids and antibiotics and injected with an anticoagulant, prior to the removal of her heart and lungs, which had been generously donated by her grieving family.

Reaching St Austell in record time after the call had gone out, Eduardo Cortes had been immediately escorted to the operating theatre of the hospital where, having ascertained that the correct intravenous fluids and medications had been given to the donor, he confirmed that, although technically Rosie was 'brain-dead', her heart was functioning normally. High on the adrenalin which never failed him at such critical moments, he banished all irrelevant matter from his mind and concentrated on the task in hand.

Skilfully splitting Rosie's chest down the centre of the breastbone, he opened the pericardium and cut away the ligaments and tissues which were attached to the heart, the venae cavae, the aorta and the pulmonary artery. Noting the precise time at which the clamps were put on the pulsating vessels, and working rapidly with long, swift cuts of his dissecting instruments, he freed the heart and lungs from the fibrous sacs in which they were enclosed. An unhurried search of the organs for abnormalities which would render them unsuitable for transplant, told him all he needed to know. Leaving his team to sew up the cadaver, with as much respect as they would a live patient, he left the operating theatre to telephone Debbie, who had been anxiously awaiting his call.

Fifty minutes later he was back at the Fulham Hospital. Having missed breakfast, he went straight to the canteen where he picked up a tray, helped himself to soup and a roll and sat down heavily at a formica-topped table. Although he was aware that a well-dressed man was hovering in front of him, he did not look up.

'Professor Cortes?'

Eduardo did not respond.

'Professor Cortes? Martin Bond. May I...?' Bond's hand was on the second chair.

'The canteen's for everyone,' Eduardo broke into his roll with his powerful fingers.

'It's about my daughter, Anna. She's in Top Floor Surgical...' Martin was interrupted by the ringing of Eduardo's mobile which lay on the table before him.

'Cortes...' Speaking into the phone, Eduardo flung down his soup spoon and signalled to one of the volunteer canteen ladies who rushed to do his bidding. 'The soup is stony cold!'

'There's a long queue, Sir.' The woman took his plate.

'Tell them it's for me,' Eduardo resumed his telephone conversation. 'How long has the artery been blocked? What's his pressure?' Glancing at his watch, he closed down the call and immediately dialled a number.

'I know you don't talk to relatives...' Martin said.

'Get me Dr Blackley.' Eduardo ignored the intruder as a steaming bowl of soup was set before him.

'Thank you, darling.'

The canteen lady melted visibly.

'About my daughter...' Bond said.

'That unstable we saw this morning,' Eduardo snapped into the phone. 'The LAD's gone down. Organise a theatre and get him on bypass. Give me half an hour.'

'Anna has been waiting for a heart-lung transplant since she was fifteen. She is seventeen years old...'

Eduardo clicked his fingers, indicating the cruet from the next table. Bond passed him the salt and pepper which he sprinkled liberally on to his soup.

'... Anna's been coughing up blood. She has a nasty chest infection, arrythmia, and severe chest pain...'

'You a doctor?'

'Attorney. I look after the UK end of a multinational. Anna says I could qualify in medicine. I read all the books. No operation was possible. Not without risk of severe heart failure. Not without risk of death. For the last two years, she's been going downhill. The simplest task exhausts her... She spends most of the day doing jigsaw puzzles. She's seventeen years old for Christ's sake! Two years ago she was put on the transplant list...'

'There are 300 patients on our transplant list, Mr Bond...'

'The other 299 are not my concern. Every day that passes is a day nearer the time when Anna will be too sick to benefit from the operation. A heart-lung transplant is her only hope.'

'...We are able to do no more than one hundred and twenty heart-lung transplants a year.'

'What I want to know is, will one of them be Anna?'

'We have to be extremely rigid about whom we select. We don't want to put anyone through a great deal of unpleasantness for a life that may last a few months at most...'

'Let's cut the bullshit Professor. I understand the 'Save the Fulham Hospital' fund is strapped for cash. I understand that you chair the Medical Council.' Bond took his chequebook out of his pocket as Eduardo put down his spoon.

'Don't waste your time, Mr Bond. And mine.'

Bond slowly put back the chequebook 'I had to try. Everything. Wouldn't you, Professor Cortes, if your daughter could be saved by an organ transplant? If you had to watch your daughter disappearing, slipping further and further away from you every day? If it was your daughter's life on the line?' He made one last, desperate attempt. 'I understand from Nicholas Lilleywhite that you've been in Cornwall today, that organs have been harvested...' He was interrupted by Eduardo's phone.

Eduardo picked up the mobile, wiped his mouth, and exited the canteen with the phone at his ear almost in one fluid movement. 'Tell them I'm on my way.'

*   *   *   *   *

The moment he entered Top Floor Surgical, which was unusually quiet, saw the silent comings and going of nurses, heard the unmistakeable sound of sobbing through the open door of the side-room, Martin knew that something was amiss. By the look of her face, Anna had been crying. It did not help her breathing. As he smoothed the hair from her damp forehead, Martin noticed that Colin's bed was still empty. He felt his heart turn over.

'What's going on?'

'Nothing. That's the trouble.'

'Nothing?'

'Bad call.'

'Bad call' was a calamity shared by both pre- and post-operative patients. 'Bad call' meant that someone who had perhaps been waiting several years for a transplant,who had had not only his own expectations, but those of his family, raised by the knowledge that lungs were being harvested, only to have his hopes dashed. 'Bad call' was when organs – previously proclaimed to be of the right size, weight and tissue type for a patient on the Fulham Hospital transplant list – instead of being rapidly consigned to the innermost of four concentric plastic containers filled with ice-cold salt solution, instead of being secured inside a picnic cooler before being rushed to the waiting helicopter, were declared unsuitable for transplantation.

'Poor Colin,' Anna said, exacerbating her own breathlessness. For it was Colin, like a mourner at his own funeral, who had, despite his apprehension at the thought of a transplant, been sobbing his heart out in the side-room ever since Alison, as gently as she could, had conveyed the disappointing news.

By the time Colin was brought back to the ward where he refused to speak to anyone and lay supine in his bed with his face to the wall, Martin had gone down to the canteen.

'Colin,' Anna whispered.

Colin sobbed quietly, his whole body shaking. He had been given a tranquilliser. The supper trolley had been round but he had refused to have anything to eat.

'Everything happens for the best.' Anna said, although she did not believe it.

Colin held his threadbare teddy tighter to his struggling chest. It was all very well for Anna, she hadn't had her hopes raised, hadn't waited all day for the return of the helicopter the noise of which landing on the roof of the hospital had made his damaged heart sing with exaltation at the thought of the normal life he had never lived and which he had seemed within hours of leading.

A care assistant in a green overall brought the flowers from the side-room and set them gently on his locker. The heat in the ward had proved too much for them. At least it was the flowers that had died. The sight of their wilted mauve heads reminded him of his conversation with his Dad. He grinned at the sudden thought that, because the lungs were faulty, he would now be able to watch England play Chile.

Looking at Colin's thin body in its oversized pyjamas, which barely made a bulge in the covers as he adjusted his oxygen mask, Anna wondered what on earth the sick and lonely youth, whose parents had not been able to get out of the hospital quickly enough, could, today of all days, possibly find to smile about.

EIGHT

Every time Sebastian opened the front door and entered the house, his heart skipped a beat as he wondered if his mother would still be there. It sunk to his boots if the entrance hall was silent, and all that could be heard was the measured ticking of the long-case clock which had belonged to his grandfather Tanney and which was now part of his father's collection. There were clocks, of one sort or another all over the house, most of them antiques. A Victorian bracket clock in the bedroom struck the hour and was flanked by a rare, Lalique square-face clock by his mother's bed (a present from his father), and a French mystery clock, topped by a modestly draped lady, by his father's. He wondered how his parents managed to sleep. The carriage clock in the little-used dining-room also housed a compass and thermometer. There was a heavy, brass-cased desk clock in his father's ordered study, an Art Deco mirror clock in the living-room, an Act of Parliament wall clock in the basement kitchen, and countless others in the attic. Like his father, none of them was ever wrong.

If his first thoughts were about his mother as he entered the house, it was nothing strange. Ever since the word 'transplant', had become part of the household vernacular, he had thought about little else. It was the reason – rather than the idleness his father attributed to him – that he was unable to concentrate on such piffling considerations as maths or English. The day his mother had told him that a heart-lung transplant was on the cards was never far from his mind. Like the routine of the school curriculum with its monotonously regular timetable of lessons, like the recitative from an opera, it was – with variations in tone and content according to his mood – played out over and over.

The first time he had heard the word transplant was six months ago. His mother had been rushed off to hospital where he had been allowed to visit her in ICU. She lay, pale as the sheets which covered her, a drip fixed to her hand, a transparent oxygen mask over her nose and mouth.

His first reaction had been bewilderment. He knew that his mother suffered from recurrent asthma, but so did a couple of boys at school which just meant that they were excused from games. This common condition hardly seemed to qualify for a bed in intensive care. His father, looked almost as whey-faced as his mother, whose eyes were closed, and had shepherded him out into the rubber-smelling corridor.

'You realise she's dying?' His father's anxiety made him abrupt.

Sebastian hadn't realised anything of the sort. He was thoroughly confused. He knew that his mother was on occasions unable to breathe properly, particularly after she climbed the stairs when she complained of tightness in her chest, that sometimes her legs swelled and that, for some reason or another, she had to sleep sitting up. None of this – unlike cancer or AIDS or Creutzfeldt-Jakob Disease – had he equated with dying. He tried to take it in.

'Her only hope is a heart-lung transplant.'

It was weird. Unbelievable. His mother was a pioneering researcher into lung conditions and the problems of transplant rejection and together with her team she had actually witnessed many transplant operations. There was no way, outside a horror comic, she could have contracted 'her own' disease. His father was talking rubbish. He wasn't making sense.

'Mum will die if she has a transplant,' Sebastian said with certainty.

'She'll die if she doesn't,' Dermot forgot that Sebastian, who was unusually tall for his age, was only thirteen. 'It's her only chance.'

When his mother had been discharged from hospital with a supply of oxygen and a wheelchair for the times when she felt unable to walk, he had watched her carefully for evidence of mortality, just as he watched for tell-tale signs in the eyes of boys in his class who boasted that they had 'gone all the way' with girls. In neither case did he notice any appreciable change. Although his mother joked about the fact that she was no longer able to sing (being tone-deaf she never could), and on bad days she couldn't walk more than a few steps without having to rest, she continued to go to work every day, and although he and his father had taken over some of the more arduous chores around the house, she seemed to manage everything else okay. It did not appear to Sebastian, no matter how hard he scrutinised her tapping away at her computer or engrossed in her journals, to be a dying scenario. Whatever that was. By repeating the words, decease, demise, dissolution, extinction, non-being, nothingness, he tried to imbue them with significance, but found himself unable to come to get his head round death, despite the fact that there seemed to be so much of it around. You had only to read the headlines in the newspapers. *Two hundred and five die in airbus crash; muggers kill Briton in Kenya Game Park; pile-up on M6, family wiped out; female war reporter dies at 89; tide sweeps surfer to his death.* And that was without the obituaries. Offerings on TV were little better – 'A woman suspects her brother-in-law of murdering her sister.' 'Nick investigates a series of assassinations of religious leaders.' 'An executed serial killer returns from the grave' – not to mention the news bulletins with their images of starvation, of famine and slaughter, their explicit reproductions of human beings who had been shot and garrotted, tortured and slashed, mutilated or hacked to death. None of this carnage had anything to do with his mother going about her normal business, getting through the packets of licorice allsorts to which she was addicted, or cleaning her teeth.

Unwilling to believe that the sequel to death was annihilation, Sebastian had tried to discuss the matter with his father. The discourse had turned more on states of Grace, the Ultimate Spiritual Reality behind the universe and purging oneself of one's sins, than the difficulties Sebastian was having because he was terrified of losing his mother. Television and cinema notwithstanding, he had never actually seen anyone dead.

The silence in the house alarmed him. He had come straight from Karate and his mother should have been home from the hospital by now. As he flung his school blazer on the first available chair, a collage of disasters flashed through his mind. It had to do with collapse and ambulances, lungs which had ceased to function and heart attacks and shortage of breath...

'Sebastian?'

Sick with relief, he ran up the stairs. His mother was in the bedroom. She appeared to be packing. She was sitting on the bed and putting 'toilet items, night clothes and light outdoor clothing' – as requested by the Fulham Hospital – into the red cabin bag he equated with conferences. He stood transfixed in the doorway.

'I'm just getting a few things together in case they want me to go in. Had a good day at school?' As if nothing had happened. As if she wasn't a marked man.

'Yeah.'

'Homework?'

'Yeah.'

'There's some malt-loaf for your tea.'

'Yeah.'

His responses were eloquent. Sometimes he just grunted. It drove his father to distraction. Sidney had no idea what was going on inside her son's head. There were things she wanted to say to him, things they had to talk about. When she tried to broach the subject of the tenuousness of her hold on life, of what might lay in store for him if she did not get better, he was overcome with embarrassment and the door remained firmly closed. She had been unable to find a way in.

She could not blame Sebastian. When she contemplated her future, became absorbed in her own internal dialogue, she found the topic as distressing as did her family. It lay like a pestilence over their lives. But while Sebastian's difficulty was coming to terms with his mother's mortality, and Dermot's (although nothing had been said) with his punishing Catholic conscience, her own problem was the knowledge that recent advances in medicine were at best an evolutionary process. While effective preventive measures and new remedies sometimes saved lives on a dramatic scale, there was no such thing as a free lunch, no medical breakthrough that did not have its downside. It was the very nub of her research into PPH and chronic rejection which was severely hampered by an acute lack of cash and inadequate staffing levels. On more than one occasion she had brought the matter up with Eduardo Cortes, telling him (in terms he well understood) that trying to advance her investigations into pulmonary hypertension without the necessary resources was like having her legs tied together and being expected to dance.

For her research to be effective the hospital urgently required more lecturers and nurses to build up links with the European Database and the International Pulmonary Hypertension Research Consortium. Genetic studies, to characterise a possible familial link, had to be carried out as did investigations at the tissue and cellular level which would, in addition, require several researchers and a number of technicians for the laboratory-based aspects of the project.

A second proposal – concerning post-transplant chronic rejection/ obliterative bronchiolitis – required one new Senior Lecturer, to supervise research assistants, and another to carry out molecular and cellular studies together with an appropriate support team.

'Have you any idea,' Eduardo said on the last occasion she had discussed the question of funding with him, 'How much all this would cost?'

Sidney was lucky in that Dermot had not only translated her ideas into a business plan, but costed the entire project. Producing the figures triumphantly, she had presented them to Eduardo who gave Dermot's breakdown – which included staff, running costs, equipment, and alterations to the buildings – his undivided attention until he reached the bottom line.

'Six million pounds!'

'At today's prices.'

'And how do you propose we raise six million pounds?'

'Dermot suggests an endowment fund.'

Before she had had time to take the matter further, she herself had become ill. Although as a scientist she believed neither in God nor the immortality of the human soul, and certainly did not share with Dermot his hope of heaven and fear of hell, to her own surprise she found herself making pacts with Him. If she were offered a transplant, if she survived the operation, if she did not succumb to chronic rejection and obliterative bronchiolitis – the dangers of which she knew only too well – she would devote herself to raising money for the Fulham Hospital to fund her research.

This, however, was in the future, a future in which, in the light of her special knowledge, she was now anything but confident. If she herself took such a dismal view of what lay ahead, how could she inspire hope in Sebastian? Although he rarely communicated other than in monosyllables, he made it clear how he felt by the way he stared at her when he thought she wasn't looking – as if he were afraid that she might vanish into thin air before his very eyes. It broke her heart.

When carrying Sebastian, Sidney had refused to take time off from the hospital, where she was working as a Senior Registrar in Pathology. Insisting airily that she could keep her finger on the work pulse and be a mother at the same time, and that she would need no more than two weeks' maternity leave, she had been carrying out an autopsy (which she was not strictly allowed to do when pregnant) when her waters broke. Her son's birth had been both surprisingly prolonged and surprisingly traumatic. Not for one moment had she believed all the exaggerated complaints concerning 'unbearable pain' and 'wanting to die' disseminated both by patients she had delivered when doing her obstetrics and by her mother. She dismissed them all as fusspots. Brought up by her soldier father, Sidney Sands had believed herself not only to be capable of anything, but made of sterner stuff. She refused an epidural (about which she knew too much), and declined both the analgesics and the anaesthetics she was offered which she feared might harm her child. When she heard screams on the labour ward and imprecations to do with being unable to tolerate the pain a moment longer and expressing a wish to die, she had been flabbergasted to find that the noises came from her own throat.

Watched by Sebastian, Sidney put a hairbrush into the cabin bag and closed the zip. Exhausted by the effort, she lay back on the bed and patted the quilt beside her in silent invitation. Sebastian did not move from the doorway where he stood. Mumbling something about a geography test, she heard him slink away down the stairs.

There were few people she could talk to. Sebastian and Dermot were too emotionally involved, and Diana Sands was psychologically unable to acknowledge her daughter's illness as anything other than a temporary disability which, given time, would get better of its own accord. Had Sidney not had Martha to confide in, she did not think she would have survived without professional counselling, which she considered no substitute for the understanding of a friend. Martha, who had dropped everything and flown from Pennsylvania to London for the weekend when Sidney's PPH had first been diagnosed, was neither into sound bites like Sebastian, moral dilemmas like Dermot, nor denial like her mother, who telephoned frequently to ask how Sidney was but never waited for an answer. The two girls had met at school where they had not only forged a deep emotional tie but had been front-runners in their class, competing for the highest grades. When Martha had won a scholarship to Cambridge and Sidney took up her hard-won place at the Fulham Hospital, their paths had diverged. While Sidney married Dermot and had a child, Martha, who changed her partners with monotonous regularity, had serial affairs. When both of them were in their early thirties, Sidney having just made consultant grade at the Fulham Hospital and Martha co-opted to the Radiology Department at the University of Pennsylvania, they had run into each other at a conference in Bordeaux. They had immediately picked up the threads of a friendship which was impervious to the threats of time and distance. Sidney became the sounding board for Martha's erratic love-life and Martha supported Sidney both in her efforts to juggle the demands of her career with motherhood, which she discovered the hard way was not as simple as she had imagined, and the frustrations of working within the National Health Service. Although they did not meet often, they communicated frequently.

When Sidney had e-mailed Martha, to tell her that she was on 'death row', Martha had booked her flight.

'I presume you are numero uno on the transplant list?' she said over lunch at the University Women's Club.

'Unfortunately it doesn't work like that...' Sidney wondered how many times she had repeated the phrase. 'It's the luck of the draw.'

'I find that hard to believe. Have you spoken to the Prof?'

' "We have some extremely sick people waiting." ' Sidney gave a passable imitation of Eduardo Cortes.

'Tell him you happen to be one of them. Tell him there'd be a whole bunch more sick people if it wasn't for you.'

'It's hard to be your own advocate.'

Sidney's last discussion concerning the transplant list had been with Nicholas Lilleywhite.

'Can I ask you something?'

'Go ahead.'

'Suppose there are two people with the same profile on Debbie's transplant list. Suppose two patients fit the same organs...?'

'We take the one who's likely to do best.'

'In who's opinion?'

'Several people's opinions are taken into account.'

'Including yours?'

'I am the transplant physician.'

'And if there's a disagreement?'

Nicholas looked uncomfortable.

67

'In the final analysis, Sidney, although there are pretty straight-forward criteria...'

'Go on.'

'A decision has to be made...'

'By whom?'

'By the surgeon responsible.'

'By Professor Cortes.'

'How long before compatible organs are likely to come up?' Martha's voice broke into her thoughts.

' "Could be tomorrow. Could be eighteen months." '

'Can you afford to wait that long?'

'It's not a question of affording. If I don't get a transplant PDQ I'm a dead man...'

Martha put an eloquent hand on Sidney's.

'...I know that in the grand order of things one person's death is insignificant but when they told me I had PPH I was gobsmacked at my own reaction. I thought I could handle it. I couldn't handle it, Martha. I can't handle it. I'm frightened.'

'Anything unknown is bound to be frightening. Let's face it, the prospect of one's own death is frightening.'

'Going somewhere and not being able to return? Being totally powerless to reverse the process?'

'It's pretty scary.'

'It's the personal annihilation bit that freaks me out. I can't get my head round the idea that that sooner or later, and probably sooner, Sidney Sands – the person eating this God-awful omelette – will cease to be.'

'In her present form.'

'Meaning?'

'Meaning, when a caterpillar changes into a butterfly it no longer exists as a caterpillar but that doesn't signify it ceases to exist. Look at it this way, someone who is born blind, no matter how hard he tries, cannot imagine what colour is: someone who is bound by matter is unable to contemplate a spiritual existence...'

'Come off it, Martha. You don't believe that afterlife crap any more than I do.'

'It was worth a try.'

'After they'd told me about the PPH, when Dermot had gone, when everyone had gone, I howled. And howled. All this 'why me'? stuff – as if there was any reason 'why not me?' It doesn't make a pennyworth of difference that I know everything there is to know about PPH. When push comes to shove I'm no different from anyone else. There's not one morning I don't wake up and hope it's been a bad dream, hope it's gone away. I *can't* leave Sebastian. He needs me. He needs his mother. He's thirteen years old, Martha. It's so damned unfair.'

'Who said life was fair?'

'I can't talk like this to Dermot. Dermot tries to cheer me up. He doesn't acknowledge my feelings.'

'I expect he has enough of his own to manage.'

'I daresay he has. What am I going to do?'

'Take one day at a time, Sidney. One step at a time. It's the only way. You have immense resources. What was it they called you at school?'

'Ms High Achiever.'

' "A" for everything.'

'I had to keep up with you.'

'Remember how your parents used to hand round your homework?'

'Everyone who called at the house – even the milkman – had to see my homework.'

'Ask Sidney' had been a Sands' catchphrase. As far as her mother was concerned, Sidney was infallible.

Tears were dropping into Sidney's abandoned omelette. 'They were so proud of me.'

'They gave you confidence. Confidence is the greatest gift a parent can bestow. If anyone can make it, Sidney, you can.'

'This isn't a case of dedication and hard work, Martha. Whether or not I'm going to be alive in six months is out of my hands. You're the only person I can let my hair down to. The only person I can dump on.'

'I only wish I lived nearer. I want you to promise to call me night or day…'

Sidney dried her eyes. 'If you knew how much better that makes me feel. Sorry about the self-indulgence…'

'That's what the girl's here for.'

'Take no notice…' Sidney blew her nose and put away her handkerchief. 'I'm fine now.'

Martha looked at her friend, her twin, across the table. 'I'm proud of you. I don't know where you get your courage.'

'Don't tell anyone, but courage doesn't come into it. Courage is when there's no choice. Courage is when you've nothing to lose, when you've reached the end of the road.'

NINE

A bad call affected everyone. Debbie, an ex-nurse from the Edinburgh Royal infirmary whom five years ago Eduardo Cortes had seconded to the transplant unit, took it personally, as if the inadequacy of the donor organs was down to her. Although there were confidential details of three hundred patients – with ailments ranging from pulmonary hypertension and cystic fibrosis to complex congenital heart defects and lung tumours – on her register, there was only sufficient money in the Fulham Hospital kitty for one hundred and twenty transplants a year. Last year sixty-four people on the waiting list had sadly died before their number came up.

As transplant co-ordinator, Debbie received the details of organs, usually from patients on life support machines, as soon as they became available. The confidential information was sent out by hospital duty officers in the donor zone which, in the case of the Fulham Hospital, covered Oxfordshire, Devon and Cornwall, and South Wales. Once the call came, it was Debbie's job to ascertain that the lungs were suitable, with regard to tissue matching and compatability, and that they were the correct size and weight. She had to satisfy herself that they were clear of AIDS or other viral infection, and make absolutely sure that permission had been given by the donor's family for the organs to be harvested. Only then, after taking account of how critically ill a potential recipient was, as well as his or her age, did she highlight a suitable patient. If – and it was always to her profound regret – she was unable to make use of the organs for anyone on the Fulham hospital database, the details had to be forwarded either to the UK Transplant Centre in Bristol or to Eurotransplant, who would hopefully find a match. Pairing donor (whose identity was never disclosed) with recipient was only the beginning of a responsible and frequently distressing job on which lives depended. Many patients had reason to be grateful to Debbie (although not all were), and as she became privy to their real, and often complex, problems, those who were awaiting transplants came to mean a great deal more to her than mere names on a computer. Family breadwinners had sometimes lingered so long on the waiting-list that they became too incapacitated to work and were forced to give up their jobs; the self-employed became desperate, and as their reserves of physical health dwindled so did their incomes; wage-earners often had to leave their nearest and dearest in other parts of the country and endure lonely and impoverished lives in London in order to be near the transplant unit should the call come. Sometimes – and this was the most heartbreaking of all – when the wait proved too long, Debbie had to delete names which over the months had become real flesh, real blood, and tactfully and sympathetically inform the next of kin. For all her cheerful exterior, sometimes her capacity to inspire hope and instil confidence deserted her, and by the time she got home at night she felt as if she had been eviscerated.

Nothing made her feel more impotent, more useless than a bad call, which was sometimes one of several for the same unlucky patient. She was well able to understand why, thus faced with impossible choices, many medical practitioners had now turned to animals in their search for an alternative source of organs, an avenue which was not as unexplored as it at first appeared. Those who maintained that exploiting animals in the interests of science was morally indefensible, and that xenotransplantation raised ethical and safety issues, rarely took into account the fact that for many years insulin from animal pancreases and heart valves from pigs had been responsible for saving lives. While *homo sapiens* could well survive without eating animals, animals had nonetheless been bred for food from time immemorial: it hardly seemed rational to baulk at raising them in order to save human life, and in Debbie's book only if the animals were made to suffer needlessly did problems arise. The hearts of specially-bred transgenic pigs, which had been given the outer appearance of the human heart so far as the immune system was concerned, were already being utilised experimentally in the laboratory. But the only real test of these animal hearts would be on selected patients who had everything to gain and little to lose. While the risks of infecting those selected with animal diseases were, according to the proponents of xenotransplantation, small enough to be justified, there were wider issues at stake. For some the hope of saving thousands of lives far outweighed the risk of infection, despite the fact that viruses carried benignly by pigs, could turn out to be extremely harmful to humans not previously exposed to them. Eduardo Cortes, Debbie's boss, was of the opinion that it was reckless to go ahead with xenotransplantations while the downside was the possibility of the spread of retroviruses or other hitherto unknown diseases. In the foreseeable future, animal transplants – and the construction of human beings by sewing parts together, already an anatomical possibility – would be as common as kidney transplants today. But a great deal more research was necessary and greater certainty needed, before this huge step was taken.

As far as Eduardo was concerned the work of transplanting human hearts violated no fundamental principle, and he experienced no basic contradiction between his religious and scientific beliefs. He was of the firm conviction that not only a person's memory but his identity and his character lay in the brain, rather than in the heart. Encouraged by the Holy Father, who accepted the concept of brain death that had created a new class of dead persons and who had never raised any theological or ethical objection to organ transplants, he had firmly retained his faith in God.

While Professor Cortes put his trust in the Deity, Debbie, like many others at the Fulham Hospital, both staff and patients, put her faith in Professor Cortes. When the call came to say that the lungs from St Austell had been pronounced unsuitable, she had run up the five flights of stairs to Top Floor Surgical to break the news to Colin.

'Look, Colin,' Debbie sat down on the bed and took the boy's hand. 'I've just had Professor Cortes on the telephone...'

Colin had been in Top Floor Surgical too long. He had started to get worried when nobody had come to administer the pre-med which would make him drowsy before he was taken to theatre. He guessed what Debbie was about to say.

'I'm afraid the news is not very good.'

Colin was breathing heavily.

'The lungs turned out to be faulty. I'm afraid it was a bad call.'

Bad call. How many times had he heard it, seen disappointed patients trundled ignominiously back to the ward? Bad call. He tried to make it mean something, to apply it to himself. A few minutes ago he had been anticipating the moment when the two gentle porters –

Jampel from Tibet, who was studying to become a software analyst, and Mohammed from Nigeria, who was into his final year of engineering – would come in their green hats to put him on the trolley and push him on rubber wheels to the operating theatre where he would be consigned to oblivion from which he might or might not return. A few minutes ago he had been scared stiff of the transplant and its chance of life. Now he was panic stricken by the absolute certainty of his own death. Debbie had let him down. She was going to let him die.

'It's a great disappointment for you. I know how you must feel.'

How could she know how he felt? She wasn't dying. She hadn't been making plans. For going back to school. For working hard. For taking exams. For qualifying in medicine. For breezing down Top Floor Surgical, his white coat flapping, his hair flopping over his forehead, like Nicholas Lilleywhite.

'There's bound to be another call shortly,' Debbie said gently, stemming the tears which were coursing down Colin's face. 'As soon as Sister returns from her tea-break we'll get you taken back to the ward.' Anna would comfort him. 'It's best they discovered it, Colin. You couldn't be doing with faulty lungs, now.'

Colin's body was juddering with quiet sobs. When the sobs grew louder, shaking the thin body in its striped pyjamas, Debbie cradled the boy in her arms, trying to make him see reason when she knew that there was none to see. She was unable to pacify him and the sounds of his distress could be heard by the other patients, so she rang the bell. Colin refused to speak to the nurse as he had refused to speak to Debbie. Even when Nicholas, his knight in shining armour, came to write him up for a tranquilliser, he plugged himself into his Walkman and turned his face to the wall. His hopes of becoming a doctor had all been a dream. He had been deluding himself. He was Colin Rafferty from Liverpool. He had cystic fibrosis. The game was up. He was going to die.

Back in the ward, he was still sobbing when Martin Bond returned from the canteen.

'He refuses to speak to Nicholas, he refuses to speak to the nurses, he refuses to speak to Alison, he won't even speak to me...' Anna whispered.

Martin sat down on Colin's bed. 'Colin.'

'…You're wasting your time, Dad.'

'I caught the tail-end of an interview with Glen Hoddle in the car,' Martin said. 'He didn't sound all that happy. What was the result of the match?'

After a long pause, there was a movement beneath the blanket and Colin turned round cautiously. 'Two-nil. We were never in it.'

'How come?'

'Batty and Butt are arseholes. Phil Neville's a nerd. Hoddle never took Chile seriously. They were a different class.'

'What about that Liverpool striker, what was his name again?'

'Owen. He was brill. It was the team let him down.'

'How about I try to get us some tickets for the World Cup?'

'You what!' Colin couldn't believe his ears.

'Get us some tickets for the World Cup.'

He would buy a hospitality package. It would cost him an arm and a leg, but it would be worth it.

'World Cup's in June!' Six months! When every day counted. Tears flowed again down Colin's face. Martin dried the boy's cheeks with his handkerchief.

'Not if you're going to cry.'

'Any road it's in France.'

'So?'

'I've never been to Paris. Has Anna been to Paris?'

'Anna doesn't like football. We'll leave Anna at home. There are strings attached.'

'Sorry?' Colin blew into Martin's handkerchief.

'Keep it. You have to shape up. One bad call doesn't mean…'

'What do you know about it?'

'Look Colin, life is a lottery. You have to keep playing the numbers…'

'That's what my Mum does.' Colin looked surprised.

'You never know when yours is going to come up.'

'Do you really mean it? About Paris?'

Martin took his out his pocket organiser and tapped away at the keys. He showed the LCD to Colin. *Two tickets for World Cup.*

'Blimey! Can we go to the top of the Eiffel Tower?'

Colin was not the only one marked by the traumatic events of the day. When Eduardo Cortes arrived home earlier than expected he found his family installed comfortably on the sofa in front of the TV enjoying a Chinese take-away. Ignoring the canned laughter which erupted in regular bursts from the set, he made straight for the fridge and removed a bottle of Corton-Charlemagne, a case of which had been a present from a grateful patient. Reading his face, Francesca put down her crispy noodles and followed him into the kitchen.

'Something happen, Eduardo?'

'Bad call.'

The dreaded words. The adrenalin had been flowing when he had arrived at St Austell. He had listened carefully to the catalogue of events which preceded the sad 'death' of the Rosie Logan, and ascertained that there were no circumstances – such as drug ingestion or chest trauma – which could adversely affect the performance of the heart and lungs. Had he had the slightest doubt at that stage that there was a problem he would have cancelled the procedure and not even the first of the many hurdles would have been cleared. It was only after the organs had been removed, cooled down, and treated with special solutions to minimise tissue damage in transit, that he had discovered anomalies which would make transplantation too risky and, to the disappointment of all concerned, had called the whole thing off.

The first heart transplant had been carried out in South Africa, more than thirty years ago. The patient, a brave man in his fifties, had lived for eighteen days. A year later, Geoffrey Gordon-Blake, Eduardo Cortes' mentor and immediate predecessor, had followed suit. While the Fulham hospital held its breath, Gordon-Blake's patient had survived for forty-six days only, which was both a public defeat and a personal disappointment. For the next ten years heart transplants – in the UK at any rate – were put on a back burner and it was not until the discovery of the powerful new immunosupressant drug cyclosporin, which revolutionised the procedure by reducing the chances of rejection, that the transplantation programme which had made not only Gordon-Blake's but Eduardo's reputation had swung into action. When he succeeded to the Chair of Surgery on Gordon-Blake's retirement, his reputation was on the ascendant and the survival rate of his transplant patients exceeded that of his closest rivals. More than seventy-five per cent of his heart-transplant patients now survived the critical five-year period and his success rate for heart and lung transplants was well above the world-wide average. Although there were several surgeons in Britain whose skills equalled his own, none could match the record which had won him both fame and fortune. Giving his all not only to the Fulham Hospital but to the advancement of science in many parts of the world, it was hardly surprising that there was sometimes very little left of him for Francesca and the children.

Francesca opened the cavernous fridge. 'I fix you steak, *caro*.'

'I'm fine. I had a sandwich in the canteen.' Taking a glass from the cupboard, Eduardo made for his study where, from past experience, Francesca knew he would spend the evening listening to his favourite music, reliving the frustrating events of the day, and castigating himself for his inability to live up to his own expectations.

TEN

Nicholas brought his tray over to the table in the canteen where Eduardo was simultaneously eating his lunch and reading the *Lancet*. If the previous day's bad call had been frustrating for Eduardo, it had proved equally disappointing for Nicholas. On the assumption that Eduardo would be bringing organs back from Cornwall, his job as transplant physician had been to check that the designated patient was sufficiently fit to receive them. The bird-like dimensions of Colin's thin chest with its transparent skin was just one of many reasons the boy had been so long on the waiting-list: Debbie had never been offered lungs small enough. Given a new heart and lungs, a balanced healthy diet and the bit of luck he deserved, there was every hope that if the transplant were successful Colin would not only continue to grow but would develop some much-needed strength in his frail body. While Eduardo was doing his job in Cornwall, hoping to bring the thoracic set he was removing from Rosie Logan, back to the Fulham, Nicholas had made his way to the side-room of Top Floor Surgical. As he examined Colin's chest, listened to his damaged heart, palpated his stomach, probed gently beneath his prominent ribs, Colin had watched his every move. When Nicholas reached for the chart at the end of the bed, the boy had pre-empted him: 'BP 120 over 80, temperature 37, pulse 80, respiration 15...'

Nicholas confirmed the observations for himself, then, as gently as he could, tapping them into prominence, he extracted some blood from Colin's collapsed veins.

'OK?' he asked, as the lad winced.

'Fine.' Colin hid his internal terror about what lay ahead from his hero.

Handing Colin his pyjama top Nicholas patted him on the shoulder.

'We'll have you running round the ward in no time.'

'How's the boy taking it?' Eduardo glanced up from his journal.

Colin, who appeared to have got over his disappointment at the bad call, was once more in good spirits. Nicholas was not so happy about Anna who had had another poor night and who had clung to his hand as he attempted to leave the ward.

'Tell me about baby Max. And about Mary...' He had to bend his ear to Anna's blue lips to hear what she was saying, for her voice registered little above a whisper. While she enjoyed listening to stories of his home life, and to hearing about the outside world which she hoped to be part of one day, the truth of the matter was that she was jealous of his wife, whom she had never met, and passionately in love with the good-looking young physician who lavished such attention on her and upon whose imagined powers of healing she relied.

Nicholas sat down on her bed. After the setback of the bad call, for which the entire unit had been psyched up, he had dismissed his worries from his mind. While Max was being put to bed, he had cooked dinner for the two of them and afterwards had spent an uneventful evening in front of the television with Mary. To Anna, the minutiae of his domestic life represented not only an ideal to be aimed at but were as desirable and as unattainable as the Nobel Prize.

'Nicky...'

Nicholas tried to release his hand but Anna clung to it.

'You won't let me die, will you?'

Answering Eduardo's question as to how Colin was faring after the previous day's ordeal, Nicholas said crisply, 'Colin's fine.' Eduardo looked at him sharply. Nicholas was not into feelings, least of all his own. The fact that Colin was eating again, talking again, reading the medical journal that Nicholas had brought him from cover to cover meant, as far as the transplant physician was concerned, that the boy had taken the bad call in his stride. Sometimes Nicholas, with his youthful arrogance – which reminded Eduardo uncomfortably of his own – irritated him beyond belief. Suppressing his emotions was the physician's way of coping with the more distressing aspects of his work.

Eduardo had his own stratagems to which he had resorted last night. The malfunctioning lungs had been a bitter blow. Like a dog to a juicy bone, he had been looking forward to his night in the operating theatre sewing the new organs into Colin Rafferty's chest. When the bone had been snatched away from him at the very last moment, the excess hormones coursing through his body that gave him the energy to spend all night if necessary on his feet working flat out with his concentration fully charged had no outlet. His adrenalin levels sank like a stone and he was engulfed by a great wave of dark depression that pulled him back into a familiar abyss from which there was only one way out.

Feeling the need for peaceful reconciliation with himself after a day of conflict, he was listening to the last movement of Beethoven's last sonata and making inroads into the Corton-Charlemagne when he heard Francesca put the lights out and the children creep up to bed. Leaving the house, he shut the front door quietly behind him and removed his Jaguar from the drive.

He parked outside a white stucco house in Pimlico and rang the bell. A well-endowed brunette – who bore an uncanny resemblance to Francesca in her young days – wearing beaded trousers, a diaphanous blouse and a nimbus of opulent scent, opened the door of the basement flat.

Greeting Eduardo she led the way into a tidy sitting-room adorned with polished reproduction furniture, freshly plumped cushions, pleated lampshades, ruched curtains, and a neatly ranked collection of china shoes. Taking her by the hand, Eduardo pulled her towards the bedroom. He had come to seek oblivion, not to look at china shoes.

In the morning, showered, shaved and happily whistling a tango, he had breakfasted with the children, and clasped them in turn in a bear-like hug before they went off to school. Before he left the house he embraced Francesca who had been sleeping when he finally came to bed.

'*Va bene?*' Francesca was still in her floral housecoat.

'*Muy bien.*'

Although they spoke different languages they understood each other. Eduardo's marriage fulfilled his basic human needs for attachment, bonding, intimacy and love, even if it did not always satisfy his insatiable appetite for sex.

Removing his lunch from the tray and setting it on the canteen table, Nicholas sat down and glanced across at the *Lancet*. Eduardo was reading the paper on "Myocardial localization and isoforms of neural cell adhesion molecule in the developing and transplanted human heart..."

'Sidney's?'

Eduardo nodded. 'What's the situation there?'

'She's not responding to the diltiazem. Her PA pressure is still running at ninety to a hundred...'

'What's the prognosis?'

'If she doesn't get a transplant soon... She's not going to make the Christmas party.'

Eduardo shook his head.

'Her work is crucial...'

'I've told her it's time she stopped working.'

'That's ridiculous. Our entire research programme depends on Sidney. We can't afford to lose her...'

Nicholas picked up his knife and fork.

'Anna Bond has a nasty chest infection, arrythmia, and severe chest pain. She's deteriorating pretty rapidly.'

Eduardo was not listening.

'...Have you considered how many patients' lives would be affected? Have you thought of the knock-on effect? How old is she?'

'Seventeen.'

'Sidney?'

'I thought we were talking about Anna. Sidney is forty-two...'

'A gentleman never discusses a lady's age...' Sidney appeared at the table in her wheelchair. They had not heard her approach.

'...I only use it to get attention.' She glanced at Nicholas' empty plate. 'What's on the menu today, Nicky, liver, kidneys, or a nice bit of heart?'

Nicholas stood up abruptly. 'I'll get you some fish pie...'

'I'm not hungry.'

'See you later then...' Nicholas picked up his tray.

Eduardo's eyes followed him as he left the canteen.

'You've upset Nicholas.'

'That's not difficult.'

'Should you be here?'

'I've a job to do, Eduardo. A son to bring up.'

'How is Sebastian?'

'He's in France. On a cultural visit with his class. He didn't want to go but it does him good to get away. Away from...' Her voice tailed off. 'Dermot gets impatient with him. Because he's no good at maths, because he's hopeless at chemistry. Debbie says there was a bad call yesterday. I don't think I could bear that.'

'Let's hope you don't have to.'

'I'm sick of waiting, Eduardo. Sick with waiting. Everything seems pointless. My work, my life. I'm tired of being tired. When I think about what's happening inside me, I feel...threatened.'

She didn't tell Eduardo about the isolation and the loneliness – which she couldn't confide to Dermot because he felt responsible – or that she had several times considered taking more than the prescribed dose of the pills by her bed, and that it was only the thought of Sebastian and how he was going to manage without her that had stayed her hand. She had felt herself spiralling downhill since her assessment, when the medical social worker had knocked on the door of the lab and put her through her paces to see whether she was a suitable candidate for transplantation.

'Professor Sands...?'

The girl, who was Australian, was young enough to be her daughter. She was brisk and professional. Sidney liked that. 'My name's Denise Butterworth, I'm the medical social worker. Can you spare a few moments?' She looked round the friendly room with its views over London, its cluttered desk, its microscopes under dust covers, its bookshelves and conference table. 'I'm really sorry, have I caught you at a bad time?'

'It's always a bad time,' Sidney pulled up a chair beside her own which had been a gift from the department and which had her name blazoned across the back. 'Let's get it over with.'

'All right. Firstly, Professor Sands, we do like the patients under assessment and their partners to feel that they are in this thing together. Transplantation is a very big step – I don't need to tell you – and we need to make absolutely sure that you both have a clear understanding of the implications. Have you discussed the procedure with your husband?'

Dermot speaks to me about Sebastian. He speaks to me about the ironing. He does not speak to me about the transplant. He is a soul in torment. They had never discussed it fully.

'We've talked about it...'

'What does he think about it?'

He doesn't want me to be disappointed. He's scared I'll be turned down. He is reluctant to raise my hopes.

'He wants me to have a transplant,' Sidney said brightly. She knew that the report of the medical social worker would be instrumental in getting her name on to Debbie's computer. She wanted to make a good impression, to give a good account of herself.

The social worker was making notes.

'That's fine, Professor Sands. Let's move on. Are both your parents still alive?'

'Only my mother. My father was in the army.'

Utterly reliable, intensely loyal, holding to the highest principles and values of Church and State, Major-General Roger Sands OBE, a very special person who was considerably older than her mother, wasted little time on those who did not come up to his own high standards. He had instilled in his daughter not only the concept of hard work and dedication but the importance of being kind and fair to others. All her life (when she was not away at boarding school) Sidney had heard tales of jungle warfare, in which her father was an expert, under daunting conditions, of rivers and rainforests, foot-rot and tree-top snipers, amphibious landings and bloody battles. After a final tour as major-general, her father had retired in triumph and accepted several civil posts including partnership secretary to a prestigious firm of accountants, chairman of the board of governors of various schools and prime-mover in a military museum which under his aegis raised millions of pounds to become one of the finest in the country. A man of stature both physically and mentally, Roger Sands had suffered a massive coronary infarct and keeled over on the golf course more than ten years ago.

'What does your mother do?'

'Do?'

Diana Sands didn't *do* anything although she had always been a talented homemaker, running up her own curtains and cushion-covers and turning her hand to anything that needed doing either inside or outside the house. Once a keen sportswoman, she now captained the local team at bowls. Fortunately for Sidney – who according to her mother had been able to read at the age of eighteen months – she had never been forced to do anything, such as sports or needlework, which she hated and had been left to her books. She remembered trying to make a pinafore at school. It had taken her a year and in the end her mother had done it for her. As an army widow, living on a pension, her mother's life now revolved around her spaniels and her garden (she was creating a wild-flower meadow) whilst in her spare time she campaigned against perceived injustices such as the closure of the village post-office (the longstanding postmistress had refused to log on to the information super highway) and the decimation of the swallow population.

'What does your mother think about the transplant?'

'Dermot says she's afraid. He says she doesn't want to think about it; to consider the alternative. He thinks she's too scared. She lost a baby, a boy – cot death – before I was born. I'm all she has.'

'Do you see much of her?'

Entrenched in the country, Diana Sands hated coming to London. She hated the traffic, she hated the overheated shops, she hated the crowds. On her last visit Sidney had taken her to lunch at the Royal Society of Medicine where she had told her over the poached salmon that she was waiting for a transplant. That without it she would die.

'They say these things, darling,' was her mother's response. 'Remember Marjorie Hutchins – Major-General Hutchins, Mountbatten, South-East Asia – they gave her five years after she discovered her breast lump. She lost all her hair and had to wear that frightful wig... That was ten years ago. They honestly don't know what they're talking about. I bought you a marble cake. I left it in the cloakroom.'

'She's firmly convinced,' Sidney told Dermot later, after her mother had gone back to Sussex, 'that marble cake is a panacea for pulmonary hypertension.'

'She would like to believe it. She lost one baby and she's lost her husband. She doesn't want to lose you.'

Looking at Sidney in her wheelchair, Eduardo noticed how short of breath she was and wondered if the emerald green suit which reflected the colour of her eyes was an act of defiance.

'I've been reading your last paper...'

'My *last* paper?'

'Your latest paper. What do you expect from a foreigner!'

'I hope you're right.'

Sidney sounded down.

'Is something the matter?'

'I had a row with Dermot. He falls over backwards to be nice to me and all I do is shout at him. I may be dependent on him but I'm not a child.'

'It is not an easy situation. I've spoken to Debbie. Thing's have gone a bit quiet. Let's hope she gets a call soon.'

'That's what the row was about. I want you to be honest with me, Eduardo.'

'I'll do my best.'

'Dermot is afraid. He worries that medicine's quest to further scientific knowledge may not always be in the best interests of the patient.'

'He doesn't want you to have a transplant?'

'He hasn't said so. Not in so many words.'

'Listen to me, Sidney. Since I was nine years old I have wanted to be a heart surgeon. All my professional life I have tried to be the kind of physician whose example led me to choose medicine as my life's work: the kind of physician who cared for my mother who died from her bullet wounds. But alongside that example has been another, more powerful image, the challenge that motivates most persuasively, the challenge that makes each of us try to improve our skills; the challenge that results in the pursuit of a diagnosis, the search for a cure...'

'I think that's what worries Dermot. That the motivation of the transplant surgeon may be to experiment on the patient, to solve the riddle of the disease. He thinks too many patients are mesmerised by their doctors. That they create a transference with them – in the psychoanalytic sense – and want to please them; that they talk themselves into believing that doctors know exactly what they're doing, and the more high-tech the doctor, the more they think he must have good scientific reasons for recommending a particular course of action.'

'Every medical specialist must admit that at times he has been driven by a desire not to give up, but when moralists and ethicists try to judge our clinical decisions they come unstuck. The professional code of the surgeon demands that no patient should be allowed to die if a – reasonably straightforward – operation could save him. Are you asking me to break that fundamental rule?'

'Not me. Dermot.'

'Tell Dermot that we live today in the art of saving life, and that there are a great many dilemmas in that art. Half a century ago, that other great art, the art of medicine, prided itself on its ability to manage the process of death, making it as tranquil as possible. That medical art has been replaced by the art of rescue...'

'And abandonment when rescue proves impossible?'

'If I had a major illness requiring highly specialized treatment, I would seek out a doctor highly skilled in its provision. I would not expect him to understand my values, my expectations for myself, my spiritual nature or my philosophy of life. That is not what he is trained for, not what he will be good at. Since the invention of the stethoscope, nearly two hundred years ago, physicians have learned to distance themselves from their patients. Tell Dermot my skills are super-specialised, that if he wants clinical objectivity he must talk to your GP. I do my very best to treat my patients with empathy; I try to help them make decisions that will lead to their recovery. That's not enough to improve my talents, not enough to maintain my enthusiasm, not enough to fuel my passion for my work. I am a technician, Sidney, a highly skilled technician; my not inconsiderable record in the operating theatre comes not from my heart, but from my head. I cannot be your conscience, darling. Don't ask me to be your guide.'

ELEVEN

Bernice Partridge was tired. Tired of living at the top of a tower block whose lift, daubed with graffiti and smelling like a public urinal, was usually broken. She was tired of the new baby who never stopped screaming; tired of the two-year-old twins who were still in nappies and into everything; tired of never having enough money for smokes or food despite the fact that she was working and signing on and turning the odd trick; tired of the dailiness of her days and the brokenness of her nights; tired of travelling on the tube from Hackney to Knightsbridge which was where the work was; sick to death of cleaning other people's houses.

On Mondays, Wednesdays and Fridays – leaving the children with her friend Alice, an outworker who lived downstairs and whom she had to pay handsomely – she cleaned for Fiona Frost, a minor actress with a bijou mews house. On Tuesdays and Thursdays she cleaned for Ralph (pronounced *Rafe* for some reason) Hawkes, a bachelor tycoon with a shady reputation who lived in Norfolk and had a pied-à-terre in Rutland Gate.

This was Monday and Fiona had gone for an audition – she spent most of her time going for auditions – leaving a note for Bernice to take down the nets in the bedroom and hoover the mattress. Fiona was allergic to house-mites amongst other more bizarre things.

Knowing that an audition meant that Fiona would be gone all morning, Bernice scrumpled up the note with its childish handwriting and made herself a Royal Albert cup of Earl Grey tea. Fiona was okay. The same age as Bernice, although she let it be known in *Spotlight* that she was several years younger, she treated her cleaning lady like a friend and, with her ravishing good looks, her exotic wardrobe, and her frequent appearances in *Hello!* magazine on the arm of the latest hunk, brought some glamour into Bernice's drab life.

Taking her time over the tea, and searching in vain for a biscuit (there was nothing but a jar of stuffed olives and a tin of macadamia nuts in the cupboard, and a tub of cottage cheese and a bottle of champagne in the fridge), she opened the security grilles and shutting the French windows behind her – Fiona went ballistic about smoking and it was as much as her job was worth to get herself caught – she stepped out on to the patio for a drag. When she had finished, she buried the cigarette butt in the potted geraniums and made her way up the cream-carpeted stairs to the bedroom where the chaos that greeted her came as no surprise.

She didn't mind picking up after the actress because it gave her a chance to go into the mirrored wardrobes, to indulge the fantasies that sustained her inner life. She was not exactly organised herself. In her three-roomed, unheated council flat, she and the children lived and slept on mattresses on the floor in the smallest bedroom. The other two rooms were let to lodgers which was strictly against regulations. There were no cupboards to speak of, let alone mirrored ones, and any floor space there was, was usually littered with clothes, discarded nappies she hadn't got round to disposing of, and second-hand toys she picked up in the Oxfam shop. Untidy as she was, and it was usually *force majeure*, her debris was as nothing compared with that in what Fiona referred to as her 'boudoir'.

As soon as she opened the bedroom door Bernice knew that there had been a man in there. The unmistakeable odour of recent sex rose from the king-sized bed, with its satin sheets and pink quilted headboard, almost filling the room, and hanging heavily on the air. Letting her imagination run riot, Bernice opened the windows on to the mews house opposite, into which you could almost stretch your arm, and set to work on the filmy nightdress and peignoir, the wired bras, G-strings, suspender belts, stay-up stockings with lacy tops and sundry outfits which lay in heaps on the shag-pile carpet and which Fiona had obviously tried on and discarded before going to her audition.

Having made the bed – not bothering to hoover the mattress as requested – with its satin-bound blankets, embroidered cover and scatter cushions which had to be arranged in just such an obsessional way, (Fiona would have nothing to do with duvets which she considered vulgar). She sorted the undergarments according to whether or not they needed washing (by hand and in Woolite).

Bernice opened the mirrored wardrobes with their internal lights which illuminated the sharp jackets and the skirts, the ponchos and pedal-pushers, the dresses and the velvet coats, the tee-shirts and boob-tubes which topped the umpteen pairs of stiletto-heeled shoes and with which the wardrobe was crammed.

Looking at her watch, she riffled through the garments prior to trying them on. Luckily for her, she and Fiona were not only the same age but the same size. Zipping herself into the close-fitting dresses and minuscule skirts, Bernice became, until the clock struck twelve, the actress' alter ego.

Struggling into a pair of narrow black leather trousers, a recent addition to the wardrobe, and selecting a scarlet camisole to wear beneath the matching bomber jacket, Bernice inserted her bare and calloused feet into a pair of strappy sandals and struck a macho pose before the mirrored doors.

While accepting that life was unfair, it never occurred to Bernice to be jealous of her employer or to resent either her wardrobe or her lovers. On the contrary, she considered herself lucky to have access to the actress' glamorous world and to enjoy vicariously the fruits of her minor success and her minimal fame.

Not completely satisfied with the scarlet camisole – too flimsy a garment in her opinion to wear beneath the black leather jacket – she took down an armful of tops from the shelf and sorted through them. Sometimes her forays into the wardrobe involved more than simply trying-on. If there was a sweater or a skirt which really took her fancy and which she was unable to live without, she nicked it. Whether or not Fiona was aware of Bernice's predilection for her clothes, she was uncertain. When her scatty employer noticed that something was missing the conversation went something like this:

'You haven't by any chance seen my black skinny-rib, Bernice?'
'No.'
'I thought you might have put it away in a different place.'
'No.'
'It's not in the wash?'
'No. Only the white one.'
'You didn't take it to the cleaners?'

It was Bernice's job to drop off the dry-cleaning on her way home.

'No. Maybe you left it somewhere,' Bernice would say helpfully. Fiona was always going away, to Germany for voice-overs or to Cannes for the film festival. 'Maybe you left it in Cannes.'

'I didn't take it to Cannes. Be an angel and look for it for me, would you? I'm due at San Lorenzo at twelve.'

And Bernice would tidy up the sweaters, replacing them in neat piles and colour coding them if she felt so disposed. Because Fiona's black sweater was stashed away beneath her bed at home, and she had already worn it on a couple of occasions to the pub, she would declare that hard as she had looked she had been unable to find it.

'I expect it will turn up,' she'd tell Fiona sympathetically. Sometimes, when she was fed up with the garments she had taken, she'd fetch them back again and put them away reeking of smoke.

'I expect so.' At this point Fiona would look her cleaning lady in the eye, but Bernice didn't flinch. She was an old hand at prevaricating. It was her stock-in-trade.

Having extracted herself, with difficulty – she had to lie down on the bed – from the black leather trousers, Bernice decided on a Ghost skirt and a diminutive cherry cardigan which revealed her belly button for her second change of outfit. She had just managed to do up the satin buttons and find some suitable shoes, when she heard Fiona's key in the door. Bloody hell! Switching on the hoover, she ignored Fiona when she called, pretending she hadn't heard, and wriggling out of Fiona's clothes, grabbed her sweater and pulled on her jeans, guessing that Fiona would check her messages, which would take her a vital moment or two, before coming upstairs.

By the time her employer came into the bedroom, Bernice was hoovering assiduously.

Fiona hurled a well-thumbed script disdainfully on to the bed. 'Another one to bite the dust. It was an absolute nightmare, darling. A mega-shambles. A part to die for and that silly bitch from EastEnders – she can't remember a line for more than a nanosecond – is shagging the director. I don't know why they bother. Getting up at six and schlepping all the way to Kennington for fuck all! I'm absolutely knackered. You wouldn't be an angel, Bernice, and fix me a teensy weensy G & T while I give my agent a piece of my mind?'

She was far too preoccupied to notice that her Ghost skirt, which Bernice had had no time to hang up, was incriminatingly over the chair, or that her Manolo Blahnik sandals lay higgledy-piggledy on the floor. Switching off the hoover, Bernice put the outfit away in the cupboard, and went down to the sitting-room to look for the gin.

She sat at the kitchen table with her mug of Typhoo (she didn't let on she had already had a slug of Fiona's Earl Grey) while Fiona, holding her portable phone in one hand and her G & T in the other, walked round the kitchen slagging off her agent for sending her on a wild goose chase. Bernice admired the porcelain finish of Fiona's blemish-free skin, her expensively streaked blonde hair, her lustrous black lashes beneath the silver-shadowed lids, the full red lips with their well-defined outline, the subtly rouged cheeks achieved with a battery of skilfully applied make-up without which Fiona never faced the light of day, and the apparently effortless way in which the reed-like, almost anorexic actress, always managed to put herself together.

When she had downloaded her exasperation, she collapsed on to a chair opposite Bernice and put her telephone on the table close beside her just in case Steven Spielberg, or even Mike Leigh, should take it into their heads to call and offer her a part.

'What an absolute prat I am,' she said when she'd drained her gin and tonic, 'banging on about a part I didn't even want, with a director who's an out-and-out shit, when you've got your own troubles, Bernice. Tell me,' she leaned across the table and assumed her Lady Macbeth voice, 'How is your son?'

Feeling the tears prick her eyes, Bernice would have killed for a cigarette. Getting up from the table and fussing with the tea bags and the kettle, she got her emotions under control.

'They want to turn off the ventilator.'

'I'm so sorry.'

The tears which Bernice was unable to hold back made their slow way down her cheeks.

'That's not the worst of it. They want me to donate Wayne's heart and lungs.'

Wayne, who had been born when she was sixteen, was the oldest of her four children. They had been fathered by three different men, all of whom had in their various ways, managed to evade paying child support. Thrilled with her achievement, and secretly envied by her peer group, she had left the baby with her mother while she went to work in the Co-op, where she sat for eight hours a day behind the till. Wayne, a model baby, grew up to be a model child. He gave her no trouble. Until he was twelve years old, when her white-haired angel turned like a poisoned chrysalis into an adolescent lout.

First she blamed his behaviour on his father who had done time for fraud. When Wayne came before the magistrates for thieving, first comics and fags, then CDs, which he sold down the market, and bicycles, she blamed it on herself. When he started doing drugs and she suspected he was dealing, she blamed it on the appearance of the twins and finally the new baby, by which time Wayne had left school and stayed in bed all day – either sleeping or reading his comics – and out all night. When he refused to get a job, or even to sign on so that he could help her with the rent, and began to be violent and abusive, she became worried about the other children and threw him out, slinging his collection of some 300 comics after him. It was the last she had seen of him until the fuzz was on the doorstep telling her there had been a road traffic accident and that Wayne, who had been taken to the Smithfield Hospital, was in intensive care.

She had not at first been able to take it in. Erasing the past five years, during which Wayne had been known to attack her physically, from her mind, she still thought of him as her platinum-haired angel, docile and adoring, and kept a special and unusurpable place in her heart for her firstborn, flesh of her flesh and blood of her blood. Asking the police inspector to come in, she had enquired politely how the accident had happened, and if Wayne was badly hurt. Since the baby had colic and was screaming, making it necessary to jiggle it up and down, she had been unable to make sense of the evasive words which had to do with the serious crime of which it seemed Wayne was suspected. Something to do with appropriating motor vehicles, with the instant death of the driver of said vehicle, with Wayne's critical state. A scan showed that he had suffered a catastrophic brain haemorrhage – and his internal injuries (which she attributed to his failure to put on his seat belt), from which he was not expected to recover. By the time she had taken the children down to Alice, and accepted a ride in the police car to the hospital, Wayne had been officially declared dead. Paradoxically however, and for reasons she was at a loss to understand, he had not only been put on a ventilator, but according to the monitor suspended from the wall, his heart was still beating.

Sitting by his bedside, where she was given cups of tea and treated like royalty – nothing seemed to be too much trouble – she recognised the old Wayne. The Wayne who had fetched and carried and helped her round the house; the Wayne who had rushed to do her bidding and who, while he had not found 'book learning' easy had been no trouble at school. Looking at his angelic face, stroking his silver hair, urging him to look at her or to say something, she refused to believe that he was dead.

Yesterday afternoon the surgeon had invited her into his consulting room. He was a Mr Ahmed, which put him at an immediate disadvantage as far as Bernice was concerned (she had enough trouble with the Paki kids setting fire to mattresses outside her flat). He gave her a long spiel about body parts and that it was an honour and a privilege to be a donor family and how he was sure she would want to be responsible for saving another human being by donating organs from her dead son, for giving someone else the gift of life. The flaw in his argument was that she was not at all sure Wayne was dead, when with her own eyes she could see that his body was pink and warm and that his heart was still beating. Once she had even imagined that he had squeezed her hand, although the nurse had assured her that this was a common occurrence and was down to a lingering spinal reflex. She was not at all sure that he was not going to wake up.

Mr Ahmed was patient. Many times he explained to her that someone who had suffered massive internal injuries, as Wayne had, could be resuscitated and kept 'alive' on a mechanical ventilator for weeks and even months and how physicians and nurses in the intensive care unit could now perform many of the integrative functions previously automatically carried out by the brain, such as regulating body temperature and blood pressure. He explained how, while Wayne's heart was still pumping warm, richly oxygenated blood round his body, two series of stringent tests had been carried out and death had been legally certified. He told her how organs would only be removed after two independent doctors, who were not concerned with organ donation and were not part of the transplant team, had confirmed brainstem death; and only then would she be required to give her informed consent after which they would take Wayne to the operating theatre and turn the ventilator off. He said how two minutes after the life support had been removed and Wayne's heart had stopped beating, they would remove his heart and lungs as quickly as possible and put them on ice. It was the 'putting them on ice' that had done for her, as she thought of the duck breasts and the chicken legs in the freezing cabinets of Iceland, where she shopped for the kids' fish fingers and peas, and forced her sobbing from the room. Mr Ahmed's nurse put a comforting arm round her and gave her a cup of tea.

'It's all right for them,' she told Fiona. 'It's no skin off their nose.' Ignoring the fact that Wayne had grown up to be a vicious and dangerous psychopath, she added, 'He's my little boy.'

Fiona, who had no children, tried to empathise with Bernice.

'If they say Wayne's dead...'

'Brain-dead.'

'Think of it this way, Bernice, he's never going to wake up. Never. He's never going to be alive.'

'So they say.'

'Suppose Wayne's only chance of surviving was to receive organs from someone else? Wouldn't you want that person's family to give their consent?'

'I never thought of it like that. They had this programme on the telly. Foreigners kidnapping children – they said they were going to find work for them – smuggling them into...India I think it was, and selling their organs to the hospitals. So many dollars for kidneys, so many for eyes, so many for hair, so many for blood...'

'They can only get hearts and lungs,' Fiona explained gently, 'from a person who's already dead.'

'I can't do it,' Bernice shook her head. 'It's out of the question. They can talk till they're blue in the face. I'd never forgive myself.'

TWELVE

Each time the telephone rang or her bleep went, Sidney panicked, and the more it happened the more catatonic she became at the sound of the bell. Since Colin Rafferty's bad call, the Fulham Hospital had been the recipient of three hearts, several pairs of kidneys and some corneas for transplant. As far as thoracic sets were concerned, Debbie's computer had been strangely quiet.

As Sidney felt her lungs become less and less competent and her life ebb inexorably away, her colleagues in the increasingly pessimistic Department of Histochemistry, who had always relied on her to inject unity into the team and help avoid internecine strife, fought hard to keep her spirits up.

At home, Sebastian and Dermot were at a loss to know how to deal with a situation which as the days went by, with no call from the hospital, became increasingly grave. Whatever conversation there was between Sidney and Dermot, went round and round in circles. Dermot tried to generate an optimism he did not feel, to counterbalance Sidney's increasing certainty that the call from the hospital on which she had pinned her hopes, would now come, if indeed it came at all, too late. There were days when she felt so ill, so short of breath, so weak and so dizzy that death seemed not such an unacceptable option. Her recurring dream, from which she woke sweating and distressed, betrayed her conscious mind. She was alone in a room. Looking down on herself, like a camera on an open set, she was small and frightened. Hearing footsteps, she knew that 'they', 'it', 'death', had come for her. There was nothing to conceal her. No place to hide. The room was devoid of furniture. Making herself as small as she could she slunk into a far corner. They were disguised as nurses, three or four of them. They took her by the hand, pulling her towards the door. She knew what lay beyond it. She fought them with all her strength, resisting annihilation.

There was no one to help her. She was on her own against the forces of destiny. She always woke before they dragged her away, sobbing in Dermot's arms.

On her better days her inner fury was turned outwards. It fuelled her temper which she directed at whoever happened to be nearest. It was not an easy time.

While others who awaited the grim reaper cultivated their gardens in the futile hope that by some miracle they would live to see the trees blossom, the plants grow, Sidney, typically, planned a two day symposium: Lung Transplant – Impact on Lung Disease, which was to be held at the Fulham Hospital in eighteen months' time. She wrote letters to eminent speakers from centres of excellence in Cambridge, Boston, San Francisco, Pittsburgh, Chicago and Colorado, inviting them to attend. With dogged optimism she named Professor Sidney Sands the speaker on The Pathology of Pulmonary Hypertension.

The determination with which Sidney threw herself into organising the conference seemed to Dermot not only an act of bravado, but an imprudent bid to tempt providence. A recent visit to Top Floor Surgical with Martin Bond, where he made the acquaintance of Colin and had helped Anna with her jigsaw (Princess Diana was still only partly dressed), had brought home the fact that it was not only Sidney's life which was at stake, but that there was a whole doomed community whose survival was dictated by the availability of suitable organs. In worrying about Sidney, he tried to concern himself neither with the sufferings of the wider population nor with Anna and Colin who were not his responsibility.

Still agonising about the morality of transplantation, and torn apart by the leviathan struggle between his punishing conscience and genuine concern for his wife, he had more than enough to think about. He knew that there were sufficient injustices in the world without tormenting oneself about the ethics of a comparatively simple surgical procedure, for which the donor or his family gave permission and to which the recipient agreed. The deeper he delved, however, into the murky waters of organ grafting, the more anomalies he found. In China – according to human rights campaigners – a country in which three times as many prisoners were executed than in the rest of the world put together, there existed a chilling trade in organs towards which the government turned a blind eye. Drugs were administered to criminals on death row to facilitate organ removal before their owners were shot and their body parts sold to unscrupulous dealers. On what was a gruesome stocklist, the going rate for lungs (non-smoking) was currently $20,000, livers fetched $25,000, kidneys $20,000, and corneas, at $5,000 the pair, came with the assurance that the offender had been despatched by means of a bullet through the heart, rather than the head, and that the eyes were undamaged. If particular organs were not available, additional inmates were shot by willing executioners with little regard for human life. Some detainees had their kidneys removed and were then left to die (which saved the authorities the trouble of shooting them); death sentences were passed on others simply to serve the demands of the organ trade, and executions were carried out for such trivial misdemeanours as breaking into cars or stealing VAT receipts, which would barely qualify for custodial sentences elsewhere. Chinese doctors who had fled to the west told blood-curdling stories of how corrupt officials had summoned them in the dead of night to select body-parts, which were then shipped to the United States where terminally ill patients gladly paid through the nose for a chance to live.

When Dermot had brought this aberration to the attention of Martin, during one of their regular sessions in the hospital canteen, the lawyer had dismissed the obnoxious trade as no big deal.

'If you had to take a second mortgage on your home to pay for a heart-lung bloc for Sidney, you'd do it, Dermot.'

'I wouldn't be happy about it.'

'It's not your happiness – or your life – that's at stake.'

While the Holy Father himself had voiced no objection, even to attaching one person's head to the body of another (the head of a monkey had been transplanted more than twenty years ago), Dermot considered the procedure hardly Christian. There were no reasons other than emotional ones against head transplants which seemed not to violate any fundamental theological principal. He couldn't help wondering however how the donor's relatives would feel about the head of their loved one being attached to the body of a stranger and whether any person in his right mind would consider it. Would the new, composite person be their relative with a new body, or a different person altogether with their relative's head? While it was widely accepted that the personality lay in the three-and-a-half-pound lump of white jelly that was the brain, Dermot was of the firm belief that it was a person's soul which defined his identity. As he struggled to get to grips with the dilemma, he tried to imagine himself paralysed from the neck down as the result of an accident. His body was as inert as a sack of potatoes and he was able to move only his head although his brain was functioning normally. What would he say then to a body transplant, presuming the complex problem of attaching the spinal cord to the new head had been solved, presuming it could be done? As a scientist, he did not much care for hypotheses and dismissed the question from his mind. Unwilling to burden Sidney with his uncertainties, he kept his reservations to himself and their conversation revolved around practical rather than ethical problems. Usually it involved Sebastian who seemed more withdrawn than ever.

Sometimes when Sidney was working, often into the small hours, catching the moments as if each was her last, she'd raise her eyes from the computer screen and fighting her fatigue and breathing with difficulty, lean back in her chair. Thinking that she had a question for him about the symposium, or the new paper she was struggling to complete, Dermot would put down his book.

'Will you see that Sebastian has a bath every day..?'

Although he knew very well what lay behind the question, Dermot was unable to acknowledge its significance and did not reply.

'...You know what boys are like.'

'You're not going anywhere, Sidney. A heart bloc will be available shortly. I know it will. You'll be able to tell Sebastian to take a bath yourself.'

'Dermot, we have things to discuss.'

She not only felt like a leper at work because her colleagues, uncertain how to make contact with the 'dead among the living', treated her with kid gloves, but also at home where she felt she had to sound a warning bell before bringing up the vexed subject of the future and where Dermot seemed unwittingly to have made her the target of some terrible rite of exclusion.

'We have to talk.'

'I'll see that Sebastian takes a bath.'

'I wasn't thinking about Sebastian. I was thinking about you.'

'Isn't it time you went to bed?'

'There you go again. We need to talk. While there's time.'

'What is it you want to talk about?'

'You're an attractive man…'

'Why, thank you!'

'I want you to get married…'

'I'm already married.'

'If I die. If there's no transplant available. I wouldn't want you to feel guilty about it. If somebody came along. I just wanted you to know.'

'Had you anyone in mind?'

'You're being facetious. I'm being serious. There is so little time. And Sebastian…'

Sebastian. Thirteen years ago, with the birth of her child while she was still trying to make a career in medicine, no one had warned her about the transformation that was a *sine qua non* of childbirth which would tie her in perpetuity to another human being. No one had prepared her for the emotional consequences of motherhood or told her that for the first few months at least she would be on a roller-coaster of worry, guilt and exhaustion and that henceforth her view of the world would change. Accustomed to being in control of her own life, it had come as a shock to discover that she was the willing slave of a nine pound bundle whose physical presence made sense of human existence and whose innocent dependence upon her provoked feelings she had never experienced before. Her two weeks' maternity leave had turned into two months, and the two months into four. Reluctant to abandon her child to the care of strangers, she had returned to work with a heavy heart. Dermot, who was as delighted with the baby as she, played his part in looking after Sebastian but he too had a demanding job and she was always fearful about leaving him in the care of strangers. Like many women trying to juggle a career and motherhood, she worked out a *modus vivendi* in which she found herself pulled in two directions, able to give neither her work nor her child the one hundred per cent which, in an ideal world, they merited. Never having experienced an excess of hands-on love in her own childhood – the combined result of army life and being sent away to boarding-school – she rushed home each day to lavish her love and attention on Sebastian.

When Sidney had discovered that, despite the pill, she was pregnant, she and Dermot had had their first major disagreement. In the midst of applying for consultant jobs in pathology, the pregnancy could not have come at a more inconvenient moment. Resolutely refusing to let the career upon which she had expended so much time and energy take a nose-dive, she was prepared to take whatever steps were necessary to stop it crashing altogether. Although it was by no means an easy decision to make, after much soul-searching she decided that she would rid herself of the foetus. Dermot was horrified. He categorically forbade what he regarded as a mortal sin. Sidney told him that she was going ahead with an abortion. Dermot forbade it. Who would give her a consultant job when she would need almost immediate maternity leave? Dermot was adamant. She was not to murder his child. Strong-minded as she was, as she had always been, when the chips were down, Sidney discovered that she loved and respected Dermot too much to implement her plan. Despite fierce opposition and without concealing her condition from the selection committee, on the strength of her references and qualifications she was given the fiercely contended job of consultant at her own teaching hospital and Dermot's decision was vindicated.

Having worked until she was nine months' pregnant, she had airly declared that there was no way she was going to breast-feed her baby. She would hire a responsible nanny, express her milk, and return to the hospital two weeks after her confinement. The moment she set eyes on Sebastian, who had very nearly made his debut in the post-mortem room, she realised that she was irrevocably in love with him and, in view of what was a totally unexpected occupational hazard, her views on childrearing underwent a dramatic change. Privately she thought Dermot was jealous, although he never said so. An impractical man as far as domesticity was concerned – his mind was always on more abstract problems – he undertook what he considered his fair share of the chores. However, he had never so much as sewn a name-tape on to Sebastian's school uniform nor had *his* working-day dogged by worry about the reliability of the current carer or remembering whether Wednesday was rugby or recorder. Sebastian adored his father and later even seemed to revel in the mathematical patterns (with their subliminal lessons) in which from the moment he could handle them, Dermot helped him to arrange his coloured bricks. While the birth of Sebastian set the seal on their marriage, brought unanticipated joy into their lives and was a source of great happiness to them individually, the appearance of a third extremely vocal person in the household gave rise to confrontations and difficulties sometimes hard for two equally purposeful people to resolve. While Dermot thought Sidney too soft with the boy, making excuses for his peccadilloes and a rod for her own back, Sidney accused Dermot of expecting too much of their son – just as her own father had imposed impossible targets on her – and of becoming angry when Sebastian did not fulfill his expectations. The older the boy grew, the more his father demanded of him and the more Sidney felt constrained to protect him.

In view of her impending death, Sidney wanted to be certain that Sebastian, now thirteen, would be in as safe hands with his father as he had been with his mother. In reply to her intimation that she wanted to discuss Sebastian's future before events over which she had no control overtook her, Dermot said:

'What about Sebastian?'

'He loves you.'

'You got him to say three words!'

'There you go again. You're so hard on him.'

'I don't mean to be, Sidney. This is a difficult time.'

'It's difficult for all of us. You remember when my 'asthma' reappeared? When Sebastian was born. I think that somewhere you blame him. You think he's responsible for my illness...'

'That's an outrageous suggestion!'

'Is it so outrageous? Sebastian needs a lot of love.'

'You think I'm not capable of giving it to him?'

'You're the most loving man I know.'

It was true. Shy and undemonstrative in public, Dermot went out of his way to care for and protect her. It was his unspoken concern, the depth of his regard for her, as if she were the only woman in the world, which had attracted her to him in the first place.

Neither of them had intended to get married. Dermot had been an impecunious young mathematics lecturer at Goldsmith's College and she a Senior Registrar at the Fulham when Martha, then married to Don, her first husband, had set them up with each other. Sidney told her she shouldn't have bothered. Working a ninety-hour week and studying for her Membership, she not only enjoyed her state, single apart from a couple of short-lived relationships, but was too tired at the end of the day for social life and found most of the men with whom she came into contact, especially those with whom she worked, both immature and intellectually challenged. Although they didn't exchange more than half a dozen words – which included Dermot's delight at her name which she had inherited from an Irish great-grandmother, during the course of the evening which had begun in a riverside pub and ended in a Greek restaurant where they had sat at opposite ends of the table, each had been acutely aware of the other's presence and although she thought herself the last person to whom it would happen, love, unbidden, had knocked upon her heart. Two weeks later Dermot had invited her to a lecture at the Royal Society after which, as if it were the most natural thing in the world, she had gone back to his flat.

On the day that Sidney received her Membership they decided to get married. Having given up her daughter as lost to medicine, Diana Sands was delighted. She thoroughly approved of Dermot with his tall good looks, his Celtic charm and his obvious regard for her headstrong daughter, and lost no time in contacting the local vicar, fixing up the parish church, investigating the cost of marquees, and arranging for Sidney and Dermot to be photographed for *Country Life*. She was deeply disappointed when, at the couple's insistence – they had made up their minds – the marriage took place at St Joseph's, Bunhill Row, followed by lunch at a nearby Chinese restaurant which reverberated to medical student humour and went on late into the inebriated afternoon. Their honeymoon was spent in Mexico, where Sidney suffered acute food-poisoning, and they returned to the large but shabby house in Notting Hill which they had bought jointly with the help of their respective bank managers and modernised as and when they could afford it.

Acceding to Dermot's suggestion that it was time she went to bed, Sidney switched off her computer screen before persisting with the dialogue that made him so deeply uncomfortable.

'Why are you so afraid of showing Sebastian how you feel about him?'

'You tell me.'

'I'm a histologist, not a psychiatrist. Look Dermot, I'm fed up with this pussyfooting around. If no transplant is available, sooner or later, and probably sooner, rather than later, you and Sebastian will be left on your own. I have to satisfy myself that the two of you will cope.'

'What choice will we have? I know you like to control things, Sidney, to enter everything on a spreadsheet. Even you can't control things from the grave.'

'At least I've got you to consider the possibility...'

'Do you think that I've not considered it?'

'Then why can't we discuss it?'

'Because you are going to get your transplant.'

'How can you be so certain?'

Lifting her laptop into her briefase, Dermot put his arms tightly around her and his face against hers.

'Because I pray for you every night.'

THIRTEEN

Despite her meticulous contingency plans, when the call finally came Sidney was unprepared. While she had been unable to get through to Dermot, who apparently preferred to skim over the thin ice of her days on the twin blades of his faith and his confidence, Sebastian's refusal to face up to his mother's imminent death was based on the fact that not only was the contemplation of it too painful (he found any overt discussion excruciatingly embarrassing) but that he was angry with her. His anger was the apotheosis of the anger he had felt, but which he was unable to name, since he was a baby when notwithstanding her undisputed love for him – she smothered him with it when she was around – Sidney had not only breast-fed her son with a text book or journal in her hands, unwittingly sustaining her intellectual requirements at the expense of his emotional needs, but whenever there was a conference or seminar to attend she had disappeared abruptly from his horizon, sometimes for days at a time. While he was growing up he saw his mother only intermittently – he was often asleep when she got home. A constantly changing carer, or occasionally his father, had presided over bath and bed times and later attended such seminal events as school plays and sports days, and his holidays were often spent with his grandmother (who not only knew the names of all the trees but made her own pastry). This had given rise to the dual sensations of overwhelming love and fierce resentment towards his mother which struggled within him, like Jacob with the Angel. Now, or so it seemed to the thirteen-year-old, she was abandoning him for good. She was finally going to leave him on his own.

When he found himself alone with her and sensed that she was going to open up a dialogue his fists clenched involuntarily, his stomach went into spasm and his face flushed with the strength of the ambivalence he felt towards her. Unacquainted with death, which was too painful to contemplate, he preferred, like his father, not to think about it.

Once Sidney said, by way of bringing up the subject which vis-à-vis Sebastian, was never far from her mind.

'It's not unreasonable, Sebastian, given the way things are, for me to be concerned about your future. I know you don't like me to talk about it, but a death in the family is always harder on those who are left behind…'

Sebastian, who was doing his homework, gave no indication that he had heard. Aware that he was listening, Sidney knew that it was the most she could hope for.

'What I'm trying to say, Sebby, is that there's much less heartache for the person who dies than it is for those who survive.'

'Dad says you're going to be OK…' He addressed his exercise book.

'It's wishful thinking, Sebastian. You and I have to be realistic.'

'He says you're going to get a transplant.'

'Suppose I do? Transplants are not always successful. Have you thought about that?'

Sebastian gathered up his books and stood up.

'Where are you going?'

'I'll finish this upstairs…'

'I'd really like us to talk.'

'I have to give it in tomorrow morning.'

Sebastian's room, with its dormer window, was on the top floor of the house. Since Sidney had been ill she rarely disturbed him. Hearing, as she went to bed, the raucous and incomprehensible cacophony that came from his stereo, loud enough to waken the entire street, she climbed the steep stairs to the third floor, taking one slow step at a time and stopping to regain her breath. Pausing outside his bedroom, she heard another, unmistakeable, sound above what passed for music. Waiting until her heart had stopped thumping, she knocked softly and opened the door. Sebastian was lying on the bed, his face wet with tears, his fists clenched, sobbing as if his heart would break.

'Go away!'

Sidney stood in the doorway. She took in the mêlée of clothes and school books on the floor, the sports gear and guitars, one with its strings broken, which covered every available surface, at the abandoned computer game transfixed on the screen.

105

'Go away!' Turning on to his stomach, Sebastian buried his face in the pillow.

Sidney approached the bed.

'Sebastian…'

'This is my room. I don't want you in here.'

'Please don't cry. Why are you crying?'

'I'm not crying.'

Sitting down on the bed, she reached out to touch him.

'Leave me alone!'

Her hand on his shoulder was shaken off.

'Get out of my room!'

'What am I going to do?' She asked Dermot when he came home from his meeting. 'He's breaking my heart.'

'Leave the boy alone.'

'I need to know he's going to be all right.'

'You cannot order the universe.'

'Why is he like this?'

'Only he knows, and he's not going to tell you.'

'I'm his mother.'

'He's not a baby any more.'

'He's my baby.'

'Sebastian's fighting to become a man.'

'He's no right to play his music so loud.'

'The music can be fixed…' Dermot made for the door.

'Dermot please…'

'Don't worry, darling. I'm only going to ask him to turn it down.'

Leaning against her Everest of pillows – which was the only way she could get any rest at all – while Dermot slept, Sidney thought that she should not have found it strange that Sebastian was part of the conspiracy; that like his father he had cast her out from all normal social contact. We are born alone and we die alone. Everyone, even her own beloved son, was withdrawing from her. It was as if she were already dead. Half dreaming, half musing, as the shadows cast by the street lamps made surreal patterns on the wall, she suffered the stigma of the isolation to which she should by now have become accustomed.

* * * * *

On Sunday mornings Debbie, whose job as transplant co-ordinator was a sedentary one, worked out at her local leisure centre. Her pulse rate was up to 135 beats a minute and she was into her third mile on the tread-mill when the bleep she carried with her at all times and which was hooked into her track-suit pants, disrupted her early morning reverie. Half an hour later she was in her office liaising with UK Transplant in Bristol who thought that a thoracic set *might* shortly be available.

Downloading the particulars on her computer, she felt her pulse-rate quicken as if she were still on the treadmill. Over the months and years she had been doing a job that demanded that she treated human body parts as a commodity, she had got to know and empathise with the patients on the transplant list; those who fell by the wayside, those whose number came up, and those who 'competed' for the same organs.

Often when she searched for patients to marry with available organs offering them the chance of life, images of the Third World, where children were dying daily for lack of food and water and medical care, flashed into her mind. While she was powerless to help these innocent victims of world politics, she wished that at least there were enough money in the Health Service, where each procedure was looked at in financial terms, to keep pace with medical science: one transplant equalled a hundred appendectomies, ten hip replacements, or the possibility of yet another anti-smoking campaign. The figures seemed so insensitive, the cost of operations being calculated not in human, but in monetary terms with heart lung transplants being the most costly and the most risky procedure of all.

The more sensational newspapers sent reporters to the transplant unit and had a penchant for showing patients previously at death's door walking away from the hospital, apparently bursting with health, to live happily ever after. It was a long way from the truth. Far from walking off into the proverbial sunset, far from bursting with health, those patients who managed to come through the trauma of a transplant operation had to cope with the horrific drug therapy, with the heartache, with the emotional and physical pain which formed the intricate pattern of their daily lives.

Medicine had always been involved in matters of life and death but the recent proliferation of new artefacts – dead bodies with living parts, living bodies with parts from the dead – was a comparatively new departure impinging upon the fundamentals of human life. Debbie had been long enough in her job to know that at the heart of resistance to organ donation lay fear, much of which derived from entrenched attitudes both towards the body and towards the dead; fear of mutilation, fear of inflicting pain upon the dead, belief in the sentient corpse, fear of retribution from beyond the grave. Likely donors often expressed the fear that in an emergency – if they were to carry a donor card – their lives might be considered of less consequence than someone else's, that medicine might be more interested in their death than in their survival, that their body parts might be perceived as valuable and that they were worth more dead than alive. It was not difficult to dismiss such fears as irrational, but irrationality had a long history of being applied to unpalatable truths. Like public opposition to body-snatching in the nineteenth century, resistance to donating organs not only existed but was measurable. In a survey carried out some time ago, of those who were asked to donate organs of brain-dead relatives for transplantation, thirty per cent had refused. Although this result was disappointing, set against the hundred per cent resistance rate for the dissection of cadavers less than a century previously, it compared extremely well: it was hard to know whether it was better to focus on the seventy per cent who generously agreed to donate their organs rather than on the thirty per cent who declined.

Debbie had been born in the Outer Hebrides and had spent her early years amongst three generations of her extended family. Sometimes, trawling through her list of names, comparing tissue types and blood groups, matching donors to recipients, the thought occurred to her that despite all the so-called technological advances, the world was not only spiritually impoverished but a great deal harder to live in than that lost world of several centuries ago in which admittedly short-lived lives were spent in close-knit communities in a limited geographical context. Reducing human beings to a data bank of medical statistics, despite the possibility of prolonging their lifespan, and even the removal of death itself from the warmth of the family to the chill impersonality of the hospital ward where it somehow became disassociated with life, led to the increased levels of anxiety with which modern man was beset.

Engrossed in spiritual consideration, Debbie was shocked to see not one name but two displayed as suitable on her screen. It was a nightmare situation and meant that it fell to somebody, most probably Nicholas or Eduardo – or if there was disagreement to Eduardo alone – to make an unenviable decision. Dismissing all metaphysical thoughts, all consideration of the ultimate beginning and the ultimate end in which she had been raised to believe, she printed out the names of the two patients and snatching up the paper ran quickly downstairs, unaware that Martin Bond, who had come up in the lift, was on his way to her office.

*   *   *   *   *

When Nicholas Lilleywhite was bleeped by Top Floor Surgical he was taking advantage of baby Max's peaceful and angelic sleep to make love to his wife. 'Shit!' he said. 'Shit, shit! Shit, shit, shit!'

Summoned by the news of a possible transplant, he dressed quickly. Medicine was like that, everything came at the worst possible time. At the hospital, outside his office, he found Martin Bond in a high state of agitation.

'Can I have a word?'

'Not now.' Nicholas opened the door.

'Have you had news of a transplant?'

Nicholas picked up the phone and dialled Debbie's extension.

'It's too early to say.'

'Debbie was called in this morning…'

Debbie's extension was engaged. She was most likely talking to the Professor. 'You appear to be well informed.'

'This is Anna's last chance…'

Nicholas tapped his fingers impatiently on his blotter. 'I understand your concern Martin. Firstly, as far as I am aware, there's no definite news of any organs. Secondly, if there were they might not be the slightest use to Anna. Thirdly, I must ask you to excuse me now, I have work to do…'

'Not so fast. I'm a desperate man. I'm not leaving this office Nicholas, until I'm satisfied…'

Debbie's line was still engaged. Nicholas replaced the receiver. It would probably be quicker to run upstairs to her office. He had a soft spot for Anna but Martin Bond was beginning to be a pain in the ass.

'I'll talk to you later.'

Martin Bond barred the doorway. 'You'll talk to me now. I happened to be taking the elevator to talk to Debbie as she was going downstairs to brief the Professor. I knocked on the door of her office and when there was no reply I thought that she might be on the telephone and opened the door. The room was empty. The monitor was switched on…'

Nicholas was getting angry, his short temper had not been improved by having his coitus interrupted.

'Please get out of my way.'

Martin Bond stood his ground.

'There were two names on Debbie's computer, Nicholas. One of them was Professor Sands…' he looked up at the transplant physician, 'The other was Anna Bond!'

*   *   *   *   *

As soon as Eduardo came back into the house for breakfast Francesca knew that something was wrong. Giving him the space she knew he needed, she poured him coffee and made some fresh toast. The Sunday newspapers were by his side but he did not read them. Even when he had finished eating he sat on at the kitchen table. Anyone who did not know him might have thought that he was staring vacantly into space. Francesca came up behind him and laid her cheek against his.

'Bad call?'

Taking the hand which was on his shoulder, Eduardo shook his head. A bad call was easier. It presented no dilemma. Did not require him to play God.

He had already spoken to Debbie by the time Nicholas had knocked at his door.

'Sunday, bloody Sunday.'

The reference to the movie was lost on Eduardo. Work was not only work but, apart from his seasonal attendance at the proms, his main leisure pursuit, and it was only through Francesca and the children that he kept up with the distractions of the outside world. Despite the fact that the telephone had rung while he was still dreaming, he had showered, shaved and, impeccably dressed in a cashmere sports jacket, had reached the hospital with fifteen minutes of Debbie's call. Looking at his transplant physician in an ancient sweater hastily pulled on and in which Nicholas had seen fit to come to the hospital, noting the fact

110

that he hadn't bothered to shave, irritated him before Nicholas had said a word.

He explained that the tentative offer of a donor heart and lungs had come from Bristol where a prospective donor had sustained a fractured skull after falling from a sixth floor window and was not expected to regain consciousness.

'There appear to be two suitable recipients...' Eduardo said.

'Anna Bond and Sidney Sands.'

'You've spoken to Debbie?' Eduardo was surprised.

'Martin Bond was in Debbie's office. The two names were on the screen.'

'Debbie is supposed to lock her door. I hope you fobbed him off with something.'

'Bond is hardly a man to be fobbed off.'

'What did you tell him?'

'I haven't told him anything. He thinks Anna's number has come up.'

Anna's notes were on Eduardo's desk. He fingered the thick file which he had been reading whilst waiting for Nicholas.

'Anna has low bone density. Her mean kyphosis angle is forty-four per cent. She's lost 5.85 centimetres of height and has vertical compression fractures.'

'We've transplanted plenty of patients with osteoporosis, Eduardo. It's not exactly a big deal.'

'Anna's been with us a long time. She's formed a transference with you. Bond has been getting at you. You mustn't let their feelings sway your professional judgement.'

Nicholas ignored the implication which impugned his clinical judgement and made him see red.

'Anna is going downhill fast. I give her three weeks on the ward at most.'

Eduardo picked up a thinner file.

'Tell me about Sidney.'

'Sidney has been on the transplant list for six months against Anna's two years. She has no osteoporosis, no complications of her pulmonary hypertension... She can afford to wait a bit.'

'I don't think you appreciate the fact that without Sidney we might as well scrub our entire research programme. Without Sidney it will be put back several years. Until she gets her project on the road she is a one-man band. We have the future to think about.'

'Whose future did you have in mind?'

Eduardo closed the two files and stacked them neatly on the desk. First Anna's on top of Sidney's then Sidney's on top of Anna's.

'I don't know, Nicholas. I have breakfast with Francesca on Sundays. If Debbie has no more news for us at the moment, I think I'll go home.'

Confiding his problem to Francesca as they sat at the kitchen table, helped him to think it through. His wife was his sounding board, the Father Confessor he had given up long ago. The fact that he spoke to her neither about his visits to the mews house in Pimlico, nor about what he got up to at the conferences he attended without her, did not mean that she did not know.

With the help of Francesca, he was trying to get to grips with his dilemma when they were interrupted by Gianna-Maria who, at the age of fourteen, was preparing for her first date with a sixth former who had invited her to go skating. She came into the kitchen in the oversize tee-shirt which passed for a nightdress, clutching two outfits for her mother's approval.

'I've tried them on a hundred times,' she held them in turn close to her body. 'Which one do you think I should wear?'

Looking at the red and the black skating skirts, at his daughter's striking, Italian good looks and troubled brow, Eduardo wished his own dilemma could be solved so easily, that he were not a self-appointed gatekeeper, that his was not a choice between two human beings both of whom had a right to life, but a question of the red skirt or the black.

That he was not alone in his predicament he knew. Since ethicists had first tackled the problem, the transplant issue had been hotly debated but still remained unresolved. Did organs go to the patient who was sickest or to the one with the most promise of recovery? On a first-come, first-served basis – like the queue in the hospital canteen – or to the patient who was most 'valuable' in terms of wealth, education, position, contribution to society? To women and children first; to those who had adequate family support for post-transplant care; to those who could pay? Or should lots be drawn, impersonally and uncritically and leave it to the luck of the draw?

By the time he left the house half an hour later in response to Debbie's second call, bringing all his medical acumen, his long experience and his judgement to bear, he and Gianna-Maria had made their respective decisions. He hoped that his own had been made on a clinical basis and with his head rather than his heart.

FOURTEEN

As usual the news had reached the ward. No one ever knew exactly how it got there. Even the tea-lady was in on what was supposed to be highly confidential information.

'Somebody for the high jump this mornin'', she said as she pushed her trolley, lifting the heavy metal teapot and handing out the thick chipped cups. 'Everybody jumpin' like a cat on a hot tin roof.'

Colin, who had been on oxygen now for several days, was plugged into a rapturous account of how the new kid on the block, Michael Owen, who had made such a scintillating debut against Chile, had scored his first hat trick in the League and salvaged a draw for Liverpool at Sheffield Wednesday. At the age of eighteen (plus sixty-two days), this made the player the youngest to score a treble in the Premier League, and the third youngest to achieve the feat in a top division of English football behind Alan Shearer and Jimmy Greaves.

Although Michael Owen was his hero, Colin was not really paying attention to the football commentary. He was praying to a God with whom, *pace* the chaplain, he was unfamiliar but whom he imagined looked like the Father Christmas he had once been taken to see in Alder's, the Liverpool department store. Sitting on Santa's knee, in the lighted grotto decorated with cotton wool snow scenes, he had thought he had reached heaven. All he asked was that the heart and lungs which were being bandied about the hospital from the operating theatres on the sixth floor to the ultrasound and MRI departments in the basement, be for him. After the last bad call it was only fair. By the sombre manner in which Nicholas looked at him when he did his ward rounds, by the fact that the nurses and care assistants, who were kindness itself, avoided his gaze, by the hours he spent on oxygen and the increased difficulty he had in breathing (sometimes he could hardly talk), he knew that he was getting weaker and was scared that he would shortly die.

Although the frequent deaths on the ward took place behind the poppy-flecked curtains, and the porters in their silent shoes appeared in the small hours to take the bodies to the mortuary, he had seen his Grandad succumb to a heart attack. He knew what death was like.

Grandad had been sitting in his mother's kitchen holding forth about the council which, despite his severe angina, was dragging its feet about installing central heating in his flat, when he had crashed from his chair on to the speckled linoleum, sending his Coronation mug of tea flying over the floor. By the time the ambulance arrived, Grandad's eyes, which had at first looked glassily up at the ceiling, had lost their lustre, the pupils were dilated, and their watchful light had gone out. Even before the paramedics had confirmed the old man's absence of pulse (Grandad had seemed old then although he was not yet sixty), the ten-year-old Colin knew that his mother's father, who now had a grey-white pallor and appeared to have shrunk to half his normal size, was dead. He did not want to end up in the mortuary, a flaccid lump of meat on a butcher's slab, like Grandad.

Torn between his morbid deliberations, thoughts of a possible transplant – about which he tried not to get too excited as it interfered with his breathing – and the football, Colin did not notice Nicholas' approach until he came to stand contemplatively by his bed.

'How was the game?' Nicholas took his stethoscope from his pocket.

Colin removed his earphones.

'Brill. Liverpool was three-one down. Owen had a strike in the first half. Seventeen minutes to go in the second half, he went like the clappers and kicked two goals in five minutes...'

'A draw.'

'Yeah. But we gained a point and now we're in second place. Am I getting my transplant today?' He felt Nicholas' stethoscope cold on his chest and knew his heart was thumping.

'Take a deep breath. Now breathe out for me. Good lad. Now cough...' Nicholas played for time. 'Who said anything about a transplant?'

'Come off it. Everybody knows.'

'It's the first I've heard about it,' Nicholas lied.

'The last one was a bad call. It's only fair.'

115

Nicholas wondered what fairness had to do with it. Eduardo's face when he returned to the hospital, the fact that he had difficulty in meeting Nicholas' eyes, had told him that if the heart and lungs from UK transplant were available they were not going to Anna Bond whose words, pleading with him not to let her die, still rang in his ears. Sometimes he wondered what had made him take up medicine and in particular his specialty with its unacceptably low rate of cure.

While he usually knew long before his patients that their illnesses were likely to prove fatal, once the sufferers themselves realised that they were dying it had a profound affect upon the doctor–patient relationship. No matter how much they looked to him for treatment, he was no longer possessed of the power to cure; no matter how much effort he put into saving lives, he was impotent to prevent their deaths. Patient and doctor were left facing not only each other but the predicament confronting two people both of whom knew that one of them was doomed. Like other terminally ill people, those under Nicholas' care in Top Floor Surgical varied in their response to what lay ahead of them, from having no awareness of it – or being reluctant to talk about it – to acknowledging the possibility, or certainty, that their lives were shortly to end. Although there was usually sufficient evidence for them to suspect that their diseases were incurable, they might well elect either to ignore that evidence or to regard the clues in an optimistic light. Transplant patients were often alerted to what was going on by a breathlessness so severe that it took them to the very threshold of mortality, or by a steady deterioration accompanied by a catalogue of new symptoms which augmented those which previous treatment had failed to relieve. Sometimes it was the attitude of relatives and friends which rang the warning bells, or a chance remark from the nursing staff, not intended for their ears, which confirmed the fatal nature of their diseases. Consciously or unconsciously, patients sometimes chose to deceive themselves. They joined in a tacit conspiracy colluding with doctors sensitive to their needs. Nicholas' approach was to be frank with those in his care – he had no deep-seated need to encourage their pretence – but sometimes, as in the case of Colin Rafferty, alone in London with no loving family to support him, he found himself manoeuvred into expressing dishonestly optimistic opinions.

Keeping the boy supplied with back numbers of his medical journals, encouraging him to think that he was going to be a doctor, promising him that one day he would be playing football, reassuring Colin that new treatments were on hand and that his recovery was only a matter of time, forced him to assume a role which did not fit with the direct approach which led patients such as Anna, who welcomed his forthright manner, to trust him. In Colin's case Nicholas felt that the masquerade was justified. He sensed that while the fifteen-year-old could take a certain amount of disappointment, he preferred to hear good news.

Replacing Colin's oxygen mask, he handed the boy his earphones.

'See you tomorrow.' Even this little flag of survival sometimes rang hollow.

All the while he had been examining Colin, he had been aware that three feet away, holding Anna's hand – although his daughter appeared to be asleep – Martin Bond waited to talk to him. Acutely aware of the bad tidings he had sooner or later to impart, Nicholas had been hoping to avoid him. Drawing back Colin's curtains with exaggerated slowness, he met Bond's eye. There was no escape.

'Any news?'

The strain of Anna's steady deterioration was beginning to tell on Bond. The dark shadows beneath his eyes revealed his lack of sleep and there was a gap between his neck and the collar of his Jermyn Street shirt. While Nicholas was prepared to prevaricate with Colin, it was futile to lie to Martin Bond.

'I'm afraid not.'

'Anna is not going to get the organs?'

Nicholas looked at the bed, unsure if Anna was listening.

'The situation is unchanged.'

'Listen Nicholas, Anna cannot afford to wait...'

'I understand your feelings.'

'...*If* the thoracic set is harvested and brought to this hospital, if it is not given to Anna, whose name was on Debbie's screen, there will be serious repercussions. I shall take this to the highest authority.'

'You should be speaking to Professor Cortes.'

' "Professor Cortes doesn't speak to relatives." You are the transplant physician. You are in charge of the patients in Top Floor Surgical. I am speaking to you.'

'I hear what you say and I take the matter extremely seriously...'

While Bond was talking, Nicholas had been observing Anna's breathing. He did not like what he saw.

'If Anna dies I shall hold you personally responsible. The solution is in your hands.'

Nicholas knew better than to reassure Bond, as he had reassured Colin, that Anna would be all right, to give him false hope of salvation. It was not Bond's menaces, but his own failure to give comfort which had made him want to avoid the confrontation in the first place, that made him feel threatened. He was aware that a barrier of distrust was quickly arising between them.

'I'll speak to the Professor.' he said lamely.

As he left the ward, Anna opened her eyes and looked at him accusingly, as if he had already broken his promise to her, as if she knew very well that she was not going to survive. Although he was less perturbed than he might have been earlier on in his career, he was only human and was forced to acknowledge the hurt he still experienced when he knew for certain that one of his patients was going to die.

*   *   *   *   *

Although Dermot was in effect helping Sebastian with his homework, he found it hard to concentrate on statistical graphs. His thoughts kept sliding from bar charts and pie charts, from line graphics and tables, to the semantics of transplantation which were never far from his mind.

Dishonest language bespoke dishonest intentions. It served only to deny the reality of the activities it contemplated, cast problematic matters in a favourable light and dehumanized the patients whose bodies were the real purpose of debate. Referring to human body parts as HBP neatly divested them of their emotive meaning, ignored the physical and emotional connotation of the heart and denied the cultural dimension involved in its removal. While the acronym purported to convey scientific objectivity, the reality was physical and of passionate importance. Referring to HBP made human organs sound as if they were industrial components, just as the euphemistic 'explantation', for their extraction or removal, conjured up the less brutal and more organic image of vegetation. 'Procurement', when used of organs, had an unsavoury association with commodities and commerce or even prostitution, while the term 'donor', so glibly used, denied, or lost sight of, the enormous value implicit in the gift in which no actual 'gift' was envisaged nor any reciprocation recognised.

Those who employed this nomenclature revealed unspoken attitudes. By romanticizing transplantation and casting it in a more positive light, they devalued, or even denied, the humanness of the donor and concealed the 'healing–harming' paradox of the venture, with its unpalatable truths, both from the patients and from themselves. While new treatments, experimental work, specialist training and professional zeal required human organs and tissues for their continued sustenance, frequent publicity promoted public hope of benefit from transplantation and increased patients' expectations. Medicine, like history, was not necessarily progressive. Human beings could choose paths which led to catastrophe. Would organ transplants, like the ancient slingshot, end up as the megaton bomb?

As usual, Dermot's rationalisations were at variance with his feelings. He wished that his mind were not so analytical and that he could simply accept the situation, that he could try to make the best of it, like Martin Bond.

Unaware of the battle taking place in Dermot's mind, Sidney had conflicts of her own. Watching him from the sofa, as he explained to Sebastian that the trouble with statistics was that there was scope for deception, two heads bent over the open book like a tableau in a Dutch interior, provoked sensations both of overwhelming happiness and overwhelming grief. When she realised that the print on the pages of the journal she was reading was damp, she was not sure whether her tears sprung from joy or from sadness.

Sunday lunch, cooked today by Dermot, was the only meal the three of them could be sure of eating together. It was a ritual they had maintained since Sebastian had been old enough to sit at the table. Last Sunday her mother, on one of her rare visits to London for a wedding, had joined them. She arrived by taxi and had been amazed at the extortionate fare from Knightsbridge, where she had been staying with friends. She had treated them to a blow-by-blow account of the wedding complete with a resumé of the speeches, followed by a castigation of the local log merchant (who had tried to fob her off with birch and sycamore, which lacked the body of oak or ash), and a critique of the new production of *An Ideal Husband* at Chichester before, terrified of the answer, she could bring herself to enquire about her daughter's health.

When Dermot, advisedly, managed to steer the conversation to Sidney's deteriorating condition, Diana Sands produced her diary.

'I wrote something down for you Sidney...' She flicked over the pages. 'Here it is. Eighty-six B Wimpole Street. A healer. He does it with his bare hands. They say you can actually feel the heat emanating from them. People swear by him...' She glanced at Sidney's impassive face before putting away the diary. 'Surely anything's worth a try.'

Sidney's mother was not the only one ready with useless suggestions. Everyone she met, outside the hospital, had a personal panacea. She had been advised to seek the help of alternative practitioners of every hue, from reflexologists to craniologists – as if her illness could be cured by changing her miasma or paying attention to her chakra – by well-wishers who felt compelled to come up with something in the face of mortal disease. She would have liked to have been able to talk to her mother. In the sitting-room, after lunch, whilst Dermot and Sebastian did the dishes and her mother put on her reading glasses and opened the plastic bag of old photographs she had brought up from the country, of Sidney as a little girl – some of them taken abroad where her father had been posted – she had tried.

'This was in Aden when you won the Beautiful Baby competition. I think you must have been about two. That wonderful red hair. Roger and I were so proud...'

'Mother, things have been going from bad to worse lately, I think we need to talk.'

'...You in your first school uniform. That was when you were five. You used to run all the way home. It was only round the corner and you could in those days. You were always smiling. We used to call you our little ray of sunshine. Even when you went away to school everyone wanted to be your friend. You were such a popular child.'

'If I don't get a call from the hospital soon...'

'This was taken in the garden. Unfortunately, the sun was in your eyes. For some reason I had a passion for pansies. Did I tell you I was opening the garden to the public next summer?'

Sidney gave up, exhausted. She needed to rest. Slowly, her mother replaced the photographs. She looked at each one as if it had suddenly become precious, so revealing her true feelings, as if Sidney were already dead. When Dermot put his head round the door to enquire if anyone wanted coffee, she was sitting on the sofa beside Sidney, stroking her hand.

Dermot and Sebastian always took Grandma to the station. When it was time for her to leave she had embraced Sidney warmly, holding her for a long moment in her arms.

'See you soon. Such a dreadful expression. Look after yourself, darling.'

Sidney only wished she could.

Glad that this Sunday there was just the three of them, Sidney watched her two men clear away their books preparatory to setting the table for lunch.

'Any afters, Dad?' Sebastian hesitated with the spoons.

Dermot had bought a *tarte tatin* from Marks and Spencer because he knew that Sidney liked it although these days she was sometimes too exhausted to eat. He did everything he could to please her, which paradoxically only made her feel worse. Although she had never been an emotional person, as the days went by without word from the hospital, a sign from Debbie, little things – the *tarte tatin*, the sight of Dermot and Sebastian disputing the degree of readiness of the lamb, the exchanges concerning the vegetables and whether or not the mint sauce was past its sell-by date – wrung her heart.

They had just sat down at the table, Dermot helping her across the room, when the telephone rang. Dermot went to get it.

'That'll be Grandma,' Sidney said, as the lamb, surrounded by crisply roasted potatoes, grew cold. Sidney glanced at Dermot who was still on the telephone and listening intently. When he finally put down the receiver he seemed to have difficulty in moving. Sidney and Sebastian stared at him, waited for him to speak.

'It wasn't your mother. It was the hospital…'

'It's Sunday. The lab's closed. I suppose it's those Animal Rights nuisances again…'

'It wasn't the lab. It wasn't the Animal Rights Campaigners. It was Debbie…'

'Debbie?'

'They've got some organs for you. They want you to go in straight away.'

Unable to take in the news she had been waiting for, Sidney felt herself freeze like a threatened animal.

'Tell them I can't.' She stared at the roast potatoes as if she had never seen a potato before. 'Tell them anything. Tell them I haven't had my lunch.'

FIFTEEN

Sidney lay in the narrow bed in a side-room in Top Floor Surgical knowing, although she was not supposed to know, that not ten yards away, on the other side of a flimsy partition, lay Gavin Wyatt, a 35-year-old TV soap star who was dying of end-stage heart disease and whose ghoulish future depended upon receiving her discarded heart. Now that the crunch had finally come, now that the moment which had been uppermost in their thoughts and almost the sole topic of conversation in the Sands–Tanney household for the past six months, had arrived, all Sidney could think about was how hungry she was, and that Debbie's call had deprived her of even a taste of the tantalising leg of lamb. Although she was no psychotherapist and was proud of her scientific pragmatism, she admitted to herself, for there was no one else in the side-room (Dermot had gone to find the coffee machine) that the leg of lamb was a defence against the terror which gripped her, causing her to hyperventilate and giving her pins and needles in her hands, as she waited for the pre-med which would hopefully allay her fears.

When Dermot had finally convinced her that she must go into the hospital immediately, not to deal with a break-in by Animal Rights Campaigners but because Debbie *thought* (she always erred on the side of caution) there might be a donor, she had been paralysed with fright.

'Nothing to eat or drink,' Dermot had said, more calmly than he felt, staying her hand as she reached for a roast potato to allay her fears. 'Wait there while I get your things.'

Alone with Sebastian, faced with the leg of lamb rapidly congealing on its dish, Sidney could not have moved had she wanted to. Like one who was drowning, the panorama of her life fast-forwarded before her eyes. Now that the call had come she knew, with an absolute certainty, that once she left the safety of the house she would not come back.

123

Sitting opposite her at the table, Sebastian stared at his empty plate. Their poignant silence was broken only by the suddenly audible tick-tock, tick-tock, of the long-case clock.

Sidney was the first to speak.

'Let's be practical for a moment, Sebby. I know you don't like talking about what may happen, but I think we'd both regret it if...'

Tears sprung to Sebastian's eyes, which were grey like Dermot's. 'If...if anything were to happen to me and the worst absolutely came to the worst.'

A single tear overflowed. It rolled down Sebastian's cheek. He made no attempt to wipe it away.

'Look please don't cry,' Sidney's own tears were not far away. 'I can't talk to you if you cry. It's a very straightforward operation. I've explained the whole thing to you. And I'm not going to die. But just in case something goes wrong, I want you to know that I love you. I love you very much. And no matter what happens I'll always be there for you. And I know you love me. And it wasn't such a bad report. And your father loves you very much. And you can come and see me afterwards. I won't be able to speak to you, but I'll know you're there. And...please don't cry, there's nothing to cry about. I'll only be gone for a little while. You won't know me when I come home. And everything will be back to normal again. I might even come swimming with you. They say exercise is very important. And there's really nothing to worry about. Why don't you let me give you some lamb? And a couple of potatoes. You can eat it cold tomorrow. Remember to put it in the fridge. In tinfoil. But not until it's quite cold. Perhaps you should tell Daddy it's in the wardrobe. My case. I expect he's looking everywhere. He can never find anything. Did I put a hairbrush in? Look, there's no need for you to starve...'

'I'm not hungry.'

Getting up with difficulty, Sidney went to sit on the chair beside him. She sensed him withdraw.

'Don't make this difficult.'

As if he could make it easy. Picking up Sebastian's napkin, Sidney dried his face.

'I'm all right.' He snatched the napkin from her.

'Of course you are.' Putting some lamb on his plate, she raised it to his mouth.

He turned his head away.

'I'm not a baby!'

'I know you're not. And I'm relying on you to look after…things…' She meant Dermot. 'While I'm away.'

Daring to put an arm round him, expecting a rebuff, Sidney was surprised when Sebastian put his head on her shoulder. She felt his hot tears through the thin cotton of her blouse. Holding him to her, his body giving way to his distress, they rocked silently to and fro, neither of them aware that for the past few moments Dermot had been standing in the doorway.

'I can't find any case,' he said eventually. 'I've looked everywhere.'

'In the bottom of the wardrobe.'

Dermot looked questioningly from herself to Sebastian, cradled in her arms.

'I was just telling Sebastian to remember to have a bath.'

Finding a million things to do, Sidney was disinclined to leave the house. She could not. She checked her case, tipping the contents out on to the floor. Wrote a note for the cleaner. Picked up her laptop which Dermot removed from her hand, telling her she would not need it. Watered the plants. Emptied her bladder, three times. Tidied the papers she had been working on. Stacked her journals in neat piles and then in neat piles again. Finally, when she had exhausted herself and had to resort to the oxygen, Dermot had had to be firm with her, and propelled her down the steps, from which she said a silent farewell to the lamposts, and practically carried her into the car.

Like son, like father. Dermot talked about everything except the transplant. He cursed the slow-moving traffic, the Sunday drivers, the shoppers who filled the streets and overflowed into the road impeding their progress. Faced with the crowds of shoppers in the King's Road, he castigated the godlessness of a society that had lost its way, sold its soul to the devil of materialism, of consumerism, that sought happiness in pursuing what it thought it wanted rather than enjoying what it had, then attempted to heal its festering wounds with drink and drugs. He might have been taking her to the dentist.

'Did you speak to your mother?' He asked, by way of conversation, when they stopped at the traffic lights.

Sidney nodded. She had made the call while Dermot was fetching the car.

'She wanted to catch the next train.'

'Will I meet her at the station?'

'I managed to dissuade her. I said you would keep in close touch. I think she was quite relieved.'

Arriving at the hospital Sidney was glad of a wheelchair. She had been expecting a red carpet. This was a momentous moment in her life. A few visitors passed through the desultory foyer with children by their sides and flowers in their hands.

'Professor Sands,' she announced herself at the admissions desk anticipating immediate recognition. The Sunday porter looked at her blankly.

'They're expecting me in Top Floor Surgical.'

Laying aside the racing results the man returned his reading glasses to their worn case and ran his finger down the ledger in search of her name.

'Won't keep you a moment.'

He had difficulty in getting through to the ward where nobody seemed to know anything about her. Sister was not on duty and Staff Nurse was at lunch.

'Let me have a word with the transplant co-ordinator,' Sidney held out her hand for the phone.

'I can't let you, Madam. Not on this one. There's a pay phone down the corridor.'

'I work here. Don't be ridiculous!' Sidney was angry and depressed at her reception. No one seemed interested in her. She wanted to go home.

When Dermot had parked the car, he accompanied her up to Top Floor Surgical. From Anna's bedside, Martin Bond followed their progress along the ward to the nursing station. Sidney was directed to the Day Room where on the TV screen a Jamaican choir was giving an enthusiastic rendering of *Amazing Grace*. After half an hour she was sent down to the medical ward on the fourth floor because Top Floor Surgical didn't have a bed. Finally, when Sister came back from lunch, when they had managed to find Debbie, and Nicholas had been bleeped, they took her back up to the ward and showed her to a side-room where no one seemed bothered that she had come to have her life saved and she was left on her own, feeling dismal, to get between the uninviting sheets.

Dozing off, she opened her eyes to find Nicholas looking down on her. He seemed distracted, as if this moment were not the be-all and end-all for him as it was for her, as if there were more important matters on his mind than Sidney's transplant. Handed the consent form, which Nicholas explained in detail just as he was required to do, she attached her signature to it as if it were her own death warrant, almost forgetting how to spell her name. Before he left the room Nicholas took her hand and squeezed it reassuringly: 'All the best then…' Coming from Nicholas it was volumes. 'See you later.'

Eduardo's anaesthetist was a woman with short grey hair and dangly ox-blood earrings and a key member of the operating team. She bustled in to satisfy herself that Sidney was fit enough to undergo the operation, and confirmed that everyone was now on full alert. In view of the fact that the expected organs were due to arrive at the hospital at any moment, she authorised Sidney's pre-med, and suddenly it was all systems go.

When Dermot returned with his coffee in a polystyrene cup, he pulled up a chair close to Sidney's bed and took her hand. 'You're cold as ice. Will I get another blanket?'

'I'm fine. Don't go away.'

'You're shaking. There's nothing to worry about. Just a small scratch in your hand. You'll go to sleep. When you wake up it will all be over…'

It would all be over.

'…You'll be a new woman.'

'Maybe you won't like her.'

Dermot managed a smile.

'Maybe I won't. What did Sebastian have to say?'

'This and that. I tried to reassure him. You won't be hard on him if…?'

'What do you think?'

Dermot and Sebastian would be all right. They would have to be. She could do no more.

'When this is over,' Dermot said. 'The three of us will go away. Florence, Venice…'

'Sebastian's growing up. He was talking about going to summer school with his friends…'

'Then we'll go on our own. A second honeymoon.'

'I hope it will be better than the first.'

'You spent most of the time in the bathroom.'

'Mexico was your idea.'

'How was I to know Montezuma would take his revenge?' Releasing her hand, Dermot threw the remains of the coffee into the wash-basin and the empty cup into the bin. Whistling softly, he stared out of the window at the car park far below.

'Look, Sidney,' slowly he turned to face her. He was silhouetted against the light. 'I don't have the right script for this. There are things I ought to say. Things I want to say.'

'You don't have to say them, Dermot.'

He sat beside her on the bed.

'There's times I may have been less than…'

'There's no need.'

'When I may have seemed unsympathetic.'

'You are a kind and caring man.'

'Times when I've been angry with you. When I feel I have taken second place to the research. I didn't mean it.'

'You were entitled to be angry. I would have been angry.'

'I do love you.'

'I know you do.'

His hands embraced hers, warm and reassuring.

'With all my heart and soul.'

Sidney tried to say something, to tell Dermot that she loved him and would never have got through the past six months, through the waiting, without him, but her words were drowned by the sound of the helicopter as it hovered menacingly overhead.

'You're going to be all right,' Dermot said when it had landed, wishing he felt as convinced as he sounded. 'I know it. You'll be climbing mountains again.'

'I've never climbed a mountain in my life.'

'I was speaking metaphorically. I'd better leave you to rest now. I was told not to stay.'

'What will you do, while I'm…?'

'Don't worry about me. I'll find something. I'll be fine. You look tired. You look exhausted,' he put his face to hers. 'Sidney…' his voice was breaking.

'It's all right, Dermot.' She was reassuring him.

'I do love you, darling. I do.'

'I love you too, Dermot.'

Perhaps they should have said it more often, perhaps they should not have waited for this. She saw Dermot leave the room, following him with her eyes as he reached in his pocket for his handkerchief and she heard him blow his nose. The next thing she remembered was that nurses had come in to prepare her for the operation and had efficiently remade the bed so that she could be transferred to the trolley when the time came. The nurses had laughed and joked – one of them was getting married – and she had laughed and joked with them to join in the fun, and they had given her the pre-med and she was on the conveyor belt and there was no getting off now. Not that she wanted to. She was looking forward to her new heart and her new lungs and being able to breathe again and run up the stairs and do her own shopping. Dermot did his best, but he always bought too much of one thing and not enough of another or forgot something altogether and had to improvise or go back to the supermarket. Not that he minded, but she couldn't help being annoyed. Little irritations. She hated being dependent. She had always been independent which often set them at each other's throats. Normal service would soon be resumed and they could settle down again at home and in the department where she had fallen behind in her work and where the atmosphere was awkward as they watched her health deteriorate. All that would be a thing of the past...

'Sidney?'

She hadn't heard Eduardo come in. His face appeared to be swimming. She couldn't focus very well.

'Are you sure the organs are for me?' she asked stupidly.

Eduardo nodded.

'All ready for the big fight?'

'What are the odds? Heads I live, tails I don't.'

Eduardo looked at his watch.

'What's the matter? Don't you trust me? You don't mind taking your car to the garage for someone else to sort out.'

'I was wondering, Eduardo, what sort of a man is willing to carve up a woman, take a saw to her ribcage when there is only a fifty-fifty chance of saving her life?'

Eduardo sat down on the bed.

'A man who grew up during the Dirty War, during the 'purification' of Argentina, during the mass abduction and murder. A man who, when he was nine years old, heard a knock on the door in the middle of the night. A man who watched thugs in dark glasses drag his father from his bed, with the sleep still in his eyes, and take him away in his undershirt. A man who saw his mother gunned down in the Plaza de Mayo as she protested against the 'disappeared'…I'm sorry, Sidney. I didn't mean…'

'Of course you didn't.'

Patting her shoulder reassuringly, Eduardo pulled himself together. 'I'm just going to have a bite to eat and take a look at the cricket…'

'The cricket!'

'It's pouring with rain in the West Indies. They hadn't taken the covers off. England were 200 for six. When you wake up…'

'If I wake up…'

'You'll have tubes everywhere,' his voice has resumed its normal briskness. 'Not worried are you?'

'Why should I worry, Eduardo, about going towards what might very well be the last hours of my life?'

'I promise you it's a straightforward procedure. We've discussed it all before.'

There appeared to be two Eduardos in the doorway. Sidney felt herself drifting. She decided to go with it. There was nothing more she could do.

'I have faith in you Eduardo. I am in your hands.' She wasn't sure if the Professor of Cardiac Surgery had heard or even if he was still in the room.

SIXTEEN

Despite the fact that he lived his life by numbers, Dermot had not realised that there were so many long hours, so many interminable minutes in the day. Once the helicopter landed and the donated organs had been rushed to the operating theatre, the grisly scenario that had been set in motion gathered momentum, and he took the first steps into a phantasmagoria which someone other than himself seemed to be living and which he prayed would turn out to be nothing but a bad dream.

When the diminutive Jampel and the handsome Mohammed finally arrived in their crumpled greens to transfer Sidney expertly on to a trolley she awoke from the never-never land into which the pre-med had precipitated her. Calling Dermot's name, she clung to his hand and refused to let it go. He accompanied the rubber-wheeled trolley on its sepulchral journey to the operating theatre. In the dilapidated lift, the two porters joshed each other, keeping up a crossfire of banter to allay her fears as the cage halted slowly, taking its time to come to rest at every floor, to admit patients consigned apathetically to wheelchairs and long-suffering ward maids who gazed over the tops of their wheelie bins full of linen into Sidney's drugged eyes. Convinced that there was no way he would see his wife alive again and that by his tacit complicity he was a willing accessory to her murder, Dermot felt like an executioner. In the ante-room at the far end of a seemingly endless corridor, great walls of glinting steel and a galaxy of space-age lights were visible through a glass porthole. The anaesthetist, who was bent over a table filling a syringe, greeted Sidney by name. Producing a weak smile, Sidney placed her arm with its plastic identity bracelet on top of the thin cotton blanket as instructed. Advised by the nurse that it was time for him to leave, Dermot had gazed down at his wife, so vulnerable, so peaceful in her ethereal gown, and softly touched her cheek.

'You'll look after her, won't you?' he asked the nurse anxiously.

'Yes,' the accent was New Zealand and the tender smile she gave Sidney as she gently replaced a strand of hair which had escaped from the white cap, reassuring. 'I'm your wife's special and I'll be with her all the time.'

Unable to utter anything, except for a strangulated 'good luck' – as if it was an exam Sidney was about to sit rather than putting her life on the line – Dermot hugged his wife briefly, and cruelly extricating his fingers from hers stumbled like a blind man through the swing-doors.

Only so much coffee could be swallowed in a day: only so many shrink-wrapped sandwiches like sawdust in the mouth. He could have gone home. In view of the many hours it took to 'explant' a heart and lungs and attach the replacement organs, Professor Cortes had suggested that he should. The thought that he would be alone in the house – Sebastian was at Rupert's – with its echoes of Sidney, that Sidney might need him, was a deterrent. On one of his visits to the cafeteria, he had noticed Martin Bond sitting grimly by himself. Glad of someone to talk to, Dermot had taken his unsteady coffee cup over to their usual table. Bond had scarcely glanced up. He seemed unwilling to talk.

'Is Anna all right?' Perhaps there had been a setback.

'No change.'

'Can I get you something?'

Bond shook his head.

Sitting down uninvited, Dermot drank his coffee in silence. He wondered if he had he done anything to offend.

'Sidney's in theatre.'

Bond nodded.

Dermot shook his watch.

'I keep thinking it's stopped.'

Barely indicating that he had heard, Bond seemed unaware that Dermot was seeking comfort, that he desperately needed reassurance that Sidney, whom he had delivered into the hands of the butchers in the sixth floor abattoir, would come out alive.

'I should never have allowed it. It was against my better judgement.'

It was as if he had not spoken. Martin seemed distracted. Pushing back his chair, he stood up.

'If you'll excuse me.'

Without a backward glance, he returned his cup to the counter, and walked towards the lift. Dermot was left to sort out his jangled thoughts, to try to re-establish his grip on what was happening. His practical experience had supported the unity and congruity of his everyday life, which he had taken for granted. He had been happy to remain within confines that had the stamp of reality. The inner transformation of the last few hours was beyond his existential grasp (as if he had been watching the curtain rise on a play) seemed to have propelled him into another realm in which he would not have been at all surprised to find flying carpets and winged horses. He could no more make the leap of faith demanded by the situation in which he found himself, than Sidney, who was impervious to the existence or authority of God, and because she had not elected to enter into the specifically religious province of meaning could accept the presence of the Saviour. Struggling with the curious and essentially unsettling phenomenon of organ transplantation, he attempted to cross the threshold, to step into the emotions, values and beliefs of another world – the superficial acceptance of which he found anathema.

* * * * *

While Dermot battled with the philosophical issues that lay like a cloud over his life, Eduardo Cortes, untroubled by the phenomenological understanding of reality, was coolly and calmly dividing Sidney's sternum with an oscillating saw, prior to diverting the blood from her heart. While heart-lung transplantations had assumed exaggerated importance in the eyes of the media and the general public, in the hands of a competent surgeon the operation, although intricate and time consuming, was technically no big deal.

The shadow of a shadow of self-doubt had passed fleetingly through his mind after, as he struggled to exclude any vestige of bias he had made the decision that Sidney, rather than Anna, was the rightful recipient of the heart bloc. The fact that the patient, painted with iodine, covered with green drapes and speared with intravenous and arterial monitoring lines was a colleague with whom he had once danced the tango and attempted to entice into bed had zero effect on his performance. In the sterile cosmos of the operating theatre, people's idiosyncrasies, human beings' individual dispositions, had little place. Eduardo was tuned into clotting mechanisms and pump oxygenators, tubes and reservoirs, membranes and tissues, veins and arteries, bone and muscle, flesh and blood. Had his own grandmother been on the table he would have neither hesitated nor faltered. He could not allow himself to feel sorry for Anna. He permitted no qualms at consigning her once more to the waiting-list on which, if suitable organs did not shortly materialise, she would languish and die. Had he allowed his emotions to cloud his clinical judgement, he could not have done what he was doing, what he had been trained to do.

Extending his hand from time to time for an instrument which would be thrust firmly into his palm by the Malaysian theatre sister, who had worked at his side for so long that she could anticipate his actions, Eduardo made an incision in Sidney's right atrium, and threaded large tubes into each of the venae cavae before connecting them to the pump oxygenator. For the duration of the transplant, this deceptively simple triumph of engineering, now taken for granted, would take over the functions of the heart itself. After an injection to prevent the blood from clotting and coagulating in the pump mechanism, tubes were placed, clamps adjusted, and the bypass proper, for which everyone round the table had been waiting, as for the first act of an opera, began. Giving the order for the thermostat on the pump oxygenator to be turned down and the patient's body temperature lowered, Eduardo divided the aorta and the main pulmonary artery. When Sidney's heart had given its last anaemic beat, he excised the vital organ from her chest, and signalled for it to be taken away for transplant.

Standing back from the table, a compact figure surrounded by masked acolytes, he looked down for a moment at the empty cavern. The sight of a technically living, ostensibly breathing human body with a deep hollow where its heart should have been, never failed to fill him with awe. Rousing himself from his momentary reverie, he nodded to his senior registrar to bring the new heart and lungs from the nutrient bath. Handling the replacement organs with exquisite delicacy, Eduardo trimmed the aorta and pulmonary artery to the correct size. When he was satisfied, without the least ceremony, with no rite of passage, he lowered the new heart and lungs into the abyss and with the minimum of short, sharp, softly spoken instructions, devoid of either encouragement or criticism, stood by while his senior registrar, slowly and painstakingly, with the dedication of one who knew his job, accurately sewed them into their new home. When once or twice he hesitated, a brief word from his chief ensured that what had been a very good stitch became a perfect one. Occasionally there was warning of potential danger, now and again a terse admonition. The mood was one of low-key optimism illumined by the expectation of success.

While the transplant procedure was now routine, it had not always been so. Transplantation legends had been handed down from as long ago as the fourth century when two brothers, Cosmas and Damien, were said to have been canonised for achieving a number of miraculous cures. One of these was the grafting of the healthy limb of an Ethiopian donor on to the body of a bell-tower custodian whose leg had been amputated. Such myths, retold down the ages, appealed to that part of the mind which clung to the hope that human life could be made eternal. If it were possible to replace worn-out or sick body parts with new and vigorous ones, there would be no need to die.

Since Cosmas and Damien, since the fourth century, progress had been made. In an age of scientific astonishments, patients were leaving hospital every day bearing hearts and lungs, kidneys and pancreases which had begun life elsewhere. Heart transplants – unimaginable only fifty years ago – had gone swiftly from the realms of fantasy to becoming standard surgical procedure.

It was now four hours since Sidney had been wheeled into theatre and her replacement heart was in place. As he secured the last suture line, the Senior Registrar removed the clamp to allow freshly oxygenated blood to irrigate the coronary arteries of the replacement heart, which had now been deprived of blood for two hours and forty-five minutes. With the donor pulmonary arteries united with Sidney's own, the transplant was complete and already, in the adjacent operating suite, her discarded heart was being sutured into its new home.

Leaning forward, Eduardo studied the result of his assistant's handiwork. Although the vessels had filled with blood, the new heart seemed uncertain of its surroundings and balked at assuming its own rhythm. It was the first anxious moment. When it unexpectedly started fibrillating furiously, beating irregularly like a tom-tom, and twice as fast as it should, the team was galvanised into action. Shouting for the defibrillator, Eduardo applied the paddle-shaped electrodes to the ventricles, but the myocardium remained resistant. For the first time since he had entered the operating theatre, Eduardo thought fleetingly of Sidney, briefly superimposing her image on to the patient on the table, but there was little time to dwell on it as, moving swiftly and nimbly, he stitched wires to the heart's surface and connected them to a pacemaker which, with a bit of luck, would force the new heart to beat until it gathered its own momentum. While he did not allow his misgivings to show, the reluctance of the graft to palpitate regularly disturbed him. When it displayed no signs of strengthening, of asserting its independence, the situation began to look grave and he detected a change of mood in the operating theatre. More coolly than he felt, and aware that around him and across the table his team were exchanging uneasy glances, he called for increasing doses of stimulants, first one, then another. The team had been on its feet for five hours. The next forty-five minutes would be crucial. Having selected Sidney for transplant, Eduardo was unwilling to have her come so far, to put her life on the line and her trust in him, only to lose her now.

*   *   *   *   *

Afterwards, Dermot was unable to recall exactly what he did during the six-and-a-half hours that Sidney was in theatre. Six-and-a-half hours excised from his life. He didn't know how long he had been in the Day Room watching waterbucks mate in the African Bush, and *Animal Hospital*, and an asinine chat show in which members of the audience seemed to get an incomprehensible kick out of revealing their innermost secrets for the benefit of viewers at home.

He had reached an all time low. He could never remember feeling so utterly, utterly hopeless, in the literal sense of the word, so absolutely convinced of the futility of living, notwithstanding his religious convictions. At that moment the door of the day-room opened and Sebastian had put a tentative head round the door.

'Dad?'

'I thought you were supposed to be at Rupert's?'

'Rupert's Dad brought me. He's waiting downstairs.'

With Sebastian on the chair next to him, with Sebastian's comforting hand in his, there was no need to talk. Suffocated by a tidal wave of unfamiliar feeling, of being at one with his beloved son, of having him by his side when he was most needed, when Dermot had reached the very depths of despair. Dermot could not have spoken had he wanted to. He was not sure how long they sat there, each of them praying for Sidney in his own way. Only when the TV programme changed did Dermot look at his watch.

'You'd better go, son. Rupert's father will be waiting.'

'I'll stay if you want.'

'You go and have your dinner. I'll ring you straightaway...'

'Promise?'

'Promise.'

'Cheers then, Dad.'

'Cheers then.' Putting his arms round the boy Dermot hugged him tightly, feeling the warmth of Sebastian's body as he collapsed for a moment in his arms.

'See you later.' With a wan attempt at a smile, the boy was gone.

*   *   *   *   *

It was already dark when Eduardo, dishevelled and still in his greens, came into the Day Room to the accompaniment of horses' hooves down a cobbled street which came softly from the costume drama now being enacted on the TV.

Although people, both patients and relatives, had come and gone during the day, leaving the single ashtray overflowing with cigarette stubs and the out-of-date and tattered magazines in disarray, both they and Sebastian had long gone and Dermot was now alone. He could not have moved from the moulded plastic chair had he wanted to. He guessed that the worst had happened. That Sidney had not survived. 'It's all over.' Eduardo said, in weary confirmation.

Dermot's ashen face paled. His misgivings were justified. He should not have let Sidney go ahead with the transplant. He felt angry with Eduardo for what he believed was an experiment on a living human being in the interests of science. He was glad he had persuaded Sebastian to spend the night with Rupert. How was he going to break the news to the boy?

'It was touch and go for a time.'

One hour after the last suture, to the relief of everyone, Sidney's new heart had reluctantly started to beat. Strengthening to the point where it took on a vigorous, healthy tone, it began to assert its independence of the pacemaker wires. Six hours after the heart and diseased lungs had been removed, and the remaining tiny leaks in the suture lines had been repaired, the heart-lung machine was stopped and the bypass tubes withdrawn. The breast bone was brought together with thick, stainless steel wires and the skin stapled. When the closure was complete, Sidney had been taken to the isolation room in the cardiac surgery intensive care unit.

'All over?' Stunned, Dermot parroted the surgeon's words.

The smile, which melted the hearts of women, broke over Eduardo's face as, allowing himself a brief moment of jubilation, of satisfaction at a job well done, he returned from the outer space of the operating theatre to the real world. He put a hand on Dermot's shoulder.

'All finished. Your wife's in ICU.'

SEVENTEEN

What persuaded Bernice Partridge to change her mind was the fact that the crime of which Wayne was suspected had turned out to be murder. It was the policeman who had sat outside ICU day after day waiting for Wayne to wake up (and who had been instructed, in view of the severity of the offence, to extend his vigil for an extra week), who had told her. With no one to talk to as she sat at Wayne's bedside – the nurses were too busy to chat for long – Bernice had got friendly with the constable whose assignment was equally tedious. At first she hadn't believed it. Liberating car radios, Okay. Drugs, well nobody was perfect. She drew the line at murder, which according to PC Dave Watkins was not only of a particularly brutal nature involving an elderly woman in her own home, but an open and shut case. Remembering Wayne in his salad days, when he had been a high-spirited schoolboy capable of nothing more mischievous than kicking his football through the odd window, Bernice had needed some persuading. When Dave, taking out his notebook and getting as much mileage out of the saga as possible, related how the force had not only found that the marks left on the victim's face correlated with the soles of Wayne's boot, but that the pensioner's blood had been found on his clothes, Bernice, sick to the stomach, capitulated.

Requesting to see Mr Ahmed, who was 'looking after' Wayne, she told him that she had had a change of heart – a pertinent turn of phrase – and that anyone who wanted them was welcome to his bits and pieces. Donating his organs would not bring Wayne back, but putting them to good use was the least she could do to make amends for what she considered was her son's dastardly deed. She wanted nothing more to do with him, and was hard put to remain sitting by his side.

She had discussed the matter with her employer.

139

'You poor darling,' Fiona had said when Bernice had confessed about the murder, and sitting her down at the kitchen table had poured her cleaning lady a large G & T, and one for herself while she was about it. Her response to the news that Bernice was going to donate Wayne's organs had precipitated a theatrical hug.

'Honestly Bernice,' Fiona said. 'I can't say that I'm in favour of all those ghastly animal experiments, all those dogs and chimpanzees they practice on, all those poor little rats and mice, all that dashing after the Holy Grail. But I do think it's truly unselfish of you. Truly wonderful. What an epitaph for Wayne! To expiate the murder, to actually give someone the "gift of life".'

Bernice had been so carried away with her own generosity, that the high it generated had incited her to nick one of Fiona's suspender belts and a pair of black silk stockings. She wore them under her figure-hugging cherry-red skirt to cheer herself up, the next time she went to the hospital.

Constrained to make sure that Bernice understood exactly what she was giving her permission for, and precisely what was entailed, Mr Ahmed explained to her that while to many people transplantation seemed futuristic, thousands of patients actually died while they were waiting for a suitable donor; thousands of donors, likewise, were allowed to die each year with their organs unused and therefore wasted, either because no one was willing to approach the family of a lost loved one, or because potential donors had not made a bequest when they were able to do so. Once he had convinced Bernice of the service she would be doing by donating Wayne's organs, reinforcing Fiona's belief, Mr Ahmed went on to explain the procedure by which the said organs would be 'harvested'.

After Wayne had been given doses of steroids and antibiotics, he would be transferred from ICU to the operating theatre where his bloodstream would be injected with an anticoagulant to prevent clotting. The heartbeat would then be stopped with potassium solution, before the heart, and any other organs for which Bernice gave her permission, was surgically removed, upon which it would be put on ice and rushed to its new recipient. Reluctant to hear any more of the details, and much of what the surgeon had said had gone over her head, Bernice declared her willingness to sign the consent form not only for

Wayne's heart and lungs but, while they were about it, for any other bits and bobs they could put to good use.

All the paperwork was satisfactorily completed, and Mr Ahmed assured her that when they had finished with Wayne's body it would be carefully stitched up and the eyes closed in a dignified manner. She went back to see her son. Looking at his angelic face that seemed as if butter wouldn't melt in his mouth, at his chest moving up and down rhythmically as if he were in a deep sleep, she paradoxically felt like a murderer herself. Her resolution faltered and she wondered if, having given her consent to donate his organs, she could take it away again. Dave Watkins, who followed her into the room where Wayne, attached to his network of tubes, lay on his catafalque, put her straight.

'Suppose he was to wake up?' Bernice was looking for reassurance.

'He can't wake up. He's dead.'

'What you sitting outside for then?'

'Regulations.'

'Funny things happen. You read about them.'

'All right. Suppose he did. What's he got to look forward to? Doing life for murder? You ever been inside?'

'Not personally I haven't'

'Well then. Anyway he isn't going to wake up. Brain-dead is dead.'

'He don't look like a murderer.'

'They never do. I seen enough of them. You can't tell. People do funny things. He was doing drugs.'

'Yeah, I know.'

'Him and his mate. It was the drugs that did it.' Feeling sorry for her, he tried to soften the blow.

'You reckon?'

'Probably high. You all right, Mrs Partridge?'

She nodded. 'Bernice. I'll say goodbye to him.' Having made her decision, she wasn't going to come back again.

'I'll wait outside.'

Waiting until he had gone, and knowing that Wayne couldn't hear her, Bernice said:

'Wayne?' And when he failed to answer. 'What you want to do it for? Blink if you can hear me.'

Her son's blue eyes remained fixed.

'Squeeze me hand.'

There was no response to her touch.

141

Despite herself, she felt her throat muscles tighten and her womb contract.

'Forgive me.' It was a whisper.

As if loathe to disturb him, she crept out of the room and into the green corridor where Dave Watkins was once more sitting on a chair. Given the circumstances, she was ashamed to admit she quite fancied him. Looking up at Bernice's tear-stained face, at the shredded tissue in her fist, he glanced at his watch. 'I'm off duty in a minute, Bernice. Buy you a drink.'

*   *   *   *   *

There were no words which could accurately describe Dermot's feelings when he learned from Eduardo that Sidney's operation had been successful, and that he would be for ever in debt to the family of some unknown donor for giving his wife a chance. His immediate reaction was 'thank God she's alive', but his second, after he had been to ICU to see Sidney, was 'how can anyone do this to a human being?'

On his knees in the hospital chapel, his first port of call after his brief conversation with Eduardo, Dermot recalled his ongoing dialogue with Sidney. While she would have understood his reaction, she was at a loss to comprehend his faith, and supported Freud's 'scientific' approach to Christianity. As far as she was concerned, God – not necessarily Dermot's God, but anybody's – was wish-fulfilment. He wasn't really there but believers imagined he was because they wanted him to be.

Dermot's reply, asserting that this was not proof that God did not exist, but simply an assertion that he did not, was to dismiss Freud's analysis as one which had been prejudged rather than scientifically studied, and that it was based on hopelessly outdated nineteenth century rationalist propositions. 'Wish-fulfilment' was not only a two-way argument but a basic logical error. While maintaining that atheists didn't want God to exist, therefore they invented his non-existence to support their wishes, he conceded that it was not particularly difficult to think of people – such as the perpetrators of the Holocaust – who had every good reason for wishing He did not: they were unlikely to view His future judgement with much enthusiasm. At the most basic level, if human feelings of need (hunger and thirst) pointed to the means by which they could be satisfied (food and drink), why should the same thing not be true of our spiritual hunger and thirst? Sidney's alleged 'disproof' of God's existence seemed to work on the assumption that the existence of God could guarantee you some sort of easy ride, some sort of spiritual consolation which made life more bearable. It was an interesting hypothesis but far from the truth. Many Christians had been martyred for their faith and had given their lives in the name of 'consolation'. Sometimes Dermot believed that Sidney felt threatened by his belief, and when she challenged it – often, he thought, by way of provocation, she liked to wind him up – he felt no need to defend his Christianity.

Sidney's reservations notwithstanding, he put his hands together, bowed his head, and inwardly and silently thanked God for bringing her safely through the transplant operation that in his darkest moments he had been convinced she would not survive. By the same token he prayed for her speedy recovery and that henceforth He would keep her safe and well under His protection. He didn't know what he had expected. While Nicholas had explained that after the operation Sidney would be on a ventilator, unable to speak, and would be deeply asleep for some considerable time, Dermot had been unprepared for the effect on him of the jumble of tubes, the drips, drains and monitors, which sprung Medusa-like from her body.

He had been advised by the hospital to take some compassionate leave from the college to participate in Sidney's care. As the days went by at her bedside he learned from the nurses in their special gloves and aprons whose job it was to monitor her condition and keep her free from pain and anxiety, that the drip going into a vein in her neck via an infusion pump, contained drugs to stimulate the contraction of the new heart and stabilise its rate of rhythm. He learned that the three fine wires emerging from the skin beneath her breastbone and in contact with the outer surface of the heart, were connected to a small pacemaker box attached to the bed; that the electrodes attached to the skin of her chest and abdomen conveyed information to the computer screen, which showed a continuous display of the electrical activity of the heart; that the urinary catheter was connected to a collection bag, and that the several large tubes which led from her chest wall to bottles stored beneath the bed were chest drains which provided an outlet for any blood which accumulated after the chest had been closed and served to prevent the lungs from collapsing.

It was difficult to believe that it was Sidney beneath the spaghetti junction of plastic. Had it not been for the support of Sebastian, who had been brought up with IT and was less daunted than Dermot by the space-age paraphernalia with which his mother was surrounded, Dermot would have been hard put to get through the agony of the first few days which were unlike anything within his remit. Although he had already been briefed about the bewildering array of drugs Sidney would have to take in the short term, and the immunosuppressants which she would have to take for the rest of her life to prevent the body from rejecting the transplanted organs, he luckily had no inkling of what was yet to come.

When Sidney woke up with the ventilator still in her mouth, she was unable to speak.

'Sidney?' Unaware of whether she was able to see, able to hear, Dermot breathed a sigh of relief. So far, so good. Progress was being made.

'It's all over, Mum.' Sebastian, whom the last forty-eight hours seemed to have propelled into adulthood, had become the parent and Sidney the child.

'You've come through, darling.' Dermot gripped her hand. 'Everything's going to be all right...'

Before he had finished speaking, Sidney had drifted off again. The New Zealand nurse – whose name was Kirsty and who spent her day writing, watching, organising, reorganising and watching again – fluently understood the technology. She knew how to read the monitor, how to suppress the immune system, how to reduce the volume of fluid, how to keep the kidneys functioning. Having, for the umpteenth time, filled in the observation chart at the end of the bed, she dipped a swab into a plastic bowl and wiped it round Sidney's mouth.

'Don't expect too much. We'll get Professor Cortes to check the ventilator. She isn't fighting it. He'll probably take her off it in the morning.'

Confidently leaving Sebastian, who had been allowed a couple of days off school, by his mother's bed, Dermot, who was yet to have a proper meal, made his way to the canteen. Feeling isolated and anxious, and unable to attach any semblance of reality to the past two days, he desperately needed someone to talk to. The last person he had in mind was Martin Bond who, for reasons best known to himself, seemed anxious to avoid conversation.

When Martin brought his tray over to Dermot's table and sat down uninvited, Dermot was surprised.

'I owe you an apology...'

Helping himself to the mustard, Dermot did not reply.

'I understand from Nicholas that Sidney has had her transplant. That she's recovering in ICU.'

'She's not out of the woods.'

'It's early days. You probably don't know this, no reason why you should. But when Sidney's name came up on the transplant list, Anna's was beside it. The donor organs were suitable for them both.'

Dermot suddenly understood Martin's behaviour. It was his turn to apologise. He would have been equally angry himself.

'I'm so sorry. I had no idea. I don't know what to say.'

'It's not your fault. The Prof made the decision.'

He had waylaid Eduardo Cortes in the corridor, put himself at his mercy, abased himself for Anna, it was his last chance.

'Before you make your decision, Professor Cortes...'

'The decision is made.'

'I beg you to take into consideration my daughter's condition...'

'What makes you think I haven't?'

Eduardo's decision to give the available organs to Sidney rather than to Anna Bond had been based on the fact that although Sidney was, by a long way, the older of the two and had already lived half her life, other than for her pulmonary hypertension and its complications, she was comparatively fit and healthy. Anna on the other hand, who had been ill with repeated infections since childhood and had, amongst other things, severe lumbar scoliosis and osteoporosis due to pancreatic insufficiency, had not come well out of the assessment. Even if she were to survive a transplant, a procedure still not undertaken lightly, he had taken a pessimistic view of Anna's survival and thought that in view of her condition she might be little better off. Had there been no other patient on the transplant list who was more likely to benefit from the donor organs, had Anna been entered on the computer print-out he had studied as a 'QUALY' – someone able to enjoy a better quality of life – he might just have taken a chance.

'I beg you to think about Anna's age...' Martin Bond's voice broke into his thoughts.

'I'm afraid this conversation is out of order, Martin.'

'Fuck order. I'm asking you, pleading with you. Let Anna have her transplant. She can't survive more than a week or so without one. Ask Nicholas. Nicholas will tell you. My daughter's life, her *life* Professor, is in your hands.'

Eduardo Cortes stared at him. Expecting a speech about how he didn't talk to relatives, that he lived in some rarefied atmosphere of his own in which the day-to-day condition of patients had no place, Martin was surprised when the Professor put an arm around his shoulders.

'Why don't I come and take a look at your daughter,' his voice was gentle, sympathetic. 'As soon as I've got a few moments I'll come up to the ward.'

'The Prof agreed with Nicholas about Anna,' Martin told Dermot, 'That she's going rapidly downhill. He seemed genuinely concerned.'

'You sound surprised.'

'Not that he did much. Just stood by the bed and stared at her. It was the expression on his face made me change my mind about the guy. It took the wind out of my sails.'

*   *   *   *   *   *

'My name's Carol, Sidney. Sidney, can you hear me?'

Somebody was calling her. Somebody was speaking to her. How dare anybody wake her up? She was aware that something terrible had happened, or was about to happen to her. She couldn't remember what. She opened her eyes, but was surprised that she could keep them open. She saw a room. People. Heard voices but was unable to make out what they were saying. Felt a familiar hand in hers. She tried to convey that she was thirsty, but there was some obstruction, something in her mouth. She was unable to speak. Before her eyelids fell again she saw a flashing monitor by the door.

'Sidney!'

For God's sake! Why not let her sleep?

'My name is Carol, I'm Prof Cortes' SHO and I'm going to remove the ventilator for you. You'll be more comfortable. All I have to do is undo this tape and pull.'

Suddenly the obstruction was out. It had gone. With what appeared to be so little effort. She was shocked and relieved. She started to cough, wanted to ask Dermot – for it was he holding her hand although she saw only the red blur of his sweater – if she had actually had a transplant or it had been some nightmare? Each time she tried to speak, she choked. There was so much she wanted to say. Was she alive? And if so, how long had it been since the operation? For how many hours had she been under the anaesthetic, where was Sebastian? She wanted to see Sebastian. Had the transplant been successful? Somebody gave her an oxygen mask.

She couldn't have had a transplant after all. If she had she wouldn't be needing oxygen. Managing to look down at herself, trying hard to focus, she saw, to her surprise, that there were black stitches and dried blood on her chest.

*　　*　　*　　*　　*

After keeping himself awake for forty-eight hours, a tidal wave of fatigue and relief washed over Dermot which did not go unnoticed in ICU.

'Why don't you get some rest, Dr Tanney?' Kirsty was busy with her charts again, and watching Sidney's breathing at the same time. 'We'll call you if we need you.' She had eyes everywhere. 'The physio will be along soon.'

He had been given a relative's room near the ward so that he could stay by Sidney's side. He was expected to learn about Sidney's new lifestyle, how and when to administer her medication and monitor her breathing, so that when she was discharged he would feel confident about what to do and what problems to look out for. For the moment all he could think about was sleep. He detached his hand from Sidney's. He was only the helper, the main thrust of battle would be hers.

He badly needed some coffee before going to his room. The regular canteen lady sugared it without asking. Birth, death, hope, despair, the little agonies of our little lives alleviated by her shrink-wrapped sandwiches, her thick cups of comforting tea.

He hadn't noticed Martin Bond behind him. He was in a state of agitation.

'Coffee?'

Bond shook his head.

Putting his money on the counter, Dermot picked up his cup.

Bond followed him to what had become 'their' table. He had never seen the American so distraught.

'Why don't you sit down?' Dermot pulled out a chair.

Bond remained standing.

'I was hoping you'd be here.'

'Is everything all right?'

Bond gripped the back of the chair.

'You want the good news or the bad?'

Dermot felt his heart sink. He hoped against hope that nothing had happened to Anna.

'The good news is that Nicholas thinks Anna's going to get her transplant…'

Dermot waited. Bond took a deep breath. There were tears in his eyes.

'And the bad news?' Dermot stirred his coffee which was already stirred.

'Colin just died.'

EIGHTEEN

There had been a nuclear explosion. She was in hospital. In ICU. She wondered if she were the only one left alive. She searched for the bell. It had fallen on to the floor. She tried to reach it but the bed was too high. There were tubes and wires everywhere. They held her prisoner. She had to call somebody. She didn't want to be alone. She pulled at the sticker holding one of the electrodes to her chest. The ECG machine bleeped. No one came. She pulled off a lead. Then another. The monitor was going crazy. According to the screen she was dead. She shouted. Her voice wasn't strong enough. She tried again to reach the bell. This time she slipped. The leads pulled tight. She was being strangled. She panicked. She was bathed in sweat. She told herself to be sensible, that soon someone would come. She didn't believe it. She heard her name called. Opened her eyes.

'Bacon sausage, darlin', or soff boil egg?'

The ward-maid, with the breakfast trolley, grinned at her.

'Thought you was never going to wake up!'

'I have these nightmares,' Sidney told Nicholas later. Her voice was scarcely recognisable and he had to strain to hear what she said. One of the hazards of the operation was damage to the nerve of the vocal cords, which in the fullness of time would resolve.

'All post-op patients report nightmares,' Nicholas made notes on her chart. 'It could be the anaesthetic, or the drugs we give you after the transplant. It could be the operation itself. We don't really know.'

They had taken her back to Top Floor Surgical, after her chest drains had been removed, where the deadly routine of life on the ward, which started at six a.m. for no apparent reason, had set in. She was encouraged to be as mobile as possible. She progressed in what seemed a cruelly short space of time from walking the length of the ward to pedalling on a wooden board and finally to the exercise bicycle. Worse than the bewildering array of drugs (some of which she had difficulty in swallowing and most of which made her unbearably nauseous) worse than the physiotherapy, the struggling to breathe from her stomach rather than her chest, the postural drainage and coughing techniques (she was unable to cough unaided) that were to be only part of a punishing daily regime for life, was the knowledge that within her body, keeping her alive, were a heart and lungs which belonged to someone else. That what she had won, someone else had lost. The scientist in her had given way to the metaphysician: the donor tissue had assumed personality, and having transgressed boundaries, flown in the face of a basic notion of order, she had lost the sense of her own identity and wondered if she had within her the heart of a murderer or of a life-enhancer, whether she had become the devil incarnate or a saint.

There was a second nightmare. In it she was a cannibal, a nineteenth-century pioneer trapped by a winter snowstorm in the Sierra Nevada, a Uruguayan rugby player stranded in the Andes mountains, who overcame her sense of repugnance at violating a strict social taboo to take in the flesh of another as a means of preserving her own life. Sometimes she played a game with Dermot, trying to guess the sex or personality of the donor, the ethnic group to which he or she belonged. She made a joke of it. She did not express directly the feeling of terror that sometimes gripped her new heart. She did her best not to think about it, to dismiss what she guessed was paranoia, but she felt the changes in her body. She discussed it with other transplant patients who had been readmitted to the ward, some of them in their fifth year. They said it still happened to them, that even now they had fantasies in which they had had not only organ but character transplants, they had taken on the personality of the donor in subterranean moments of fear.

In the short intervals between the physio and the drug therapy that kept her busy all day, Sidney had an ongoing dialogue with Dermot, who for so long had been her strength and who left her side only to eat. They debated the tragic and often violent death of others, the taking in of another's flesh to live, the confusion of boundaries, the mutilation of the dead, the acceptance by society of new practices which evoked powerful fears and taboos; they talked of how it had taken England four centuries of dissection before voluntary donation had triumphed.

Ironically the boot had now shifted to the other foot. Although waves of relief flooded over her every time she thought how lucky she had been and how relatively short a time she had had to wait for her transplant, Dermot had become the rationalist, and it was she who had the recurring thought that someone had to die for her to live. The fact that her donor would have died even had she not required a heart bloc did not make it any easier and when she dwelled on it she was consumed with overwhelming guilt and intense sadness. She suffered nightmares in which – weak and weeping from her inability to cough properly – she wondered whether or not the transplant had been a big mistake, and whether it might have been easier to have slipped quietly away.

She didn't have much capacity for concentration; it was a strain talking to anyone and she had a vision of an empty space where her mind had been. She had been encouraged by visits from her colleagues in the department and felt it vital for them to see what a wonderful operation a heart-lung transplant could be. While their cards, their good wishes and their touching declarations of how much they were looking forward to having her back were appreciated, she felt fraudulent for accepting the gifts of champagne and chocolates, and the lavishly beribboned basket from her mother who, overwhelmed with relief, had extravagantly filled it with exotic fruits. It was Dermot who deserved everything; Dermot upon whom some of the physio and almost all the drug therapy had now devolved; Dermot who did most of the work.

Three days after the transplant, before the gruelling régime began to take its toll, she had been out of bed, sitting in the armchair, able to breathe freely and feeling better than she had felt for years, when he had arrived with a jeweller's box.

'It's not my birthday!'

But it was. A renaissance. She felt as if she had been reborn.

Inside the box was an eternity ring, of sapphires, her birthstone. She was moved by the symbolism, touched by the unspoken message. 'What have I done to deserve it?'

She put the ring on her finger.

Dermot jingled the change in his pocket.

'I wanted you to know how much I care.'

151

A week before her discharge from the hospital her mood of elation had altered as the punishing régime took its toll. Face down on the bed, her head and shoulders hanging over the end, she was having a shouting match with Dermot. They were sparring with each other like boxers in the ring.

'Dermot you're murdering me!' Her voice was still husky.

Dermot, who had her by the shoulders and was shaking her violently, took no notice of her pleas for mercy.

'Cough, woman, cough!'

'I can't, Dermot, I can't.'

'Sure you can cough.'

'Dermot, please. Let's leave it for today.'

'You're not going to give up now.'

'I'll wait for the physio.'

'The physio said you had to cough.'

'You're killing me, Dermot.'

'Sure I will if you don't cough.'

Managing to produce a cough, her daily enemy, Sidney collapsed exhausted. Letting her go for a moment, Dermot moved to the locker. Taking a syringe he drew up a measured amount of the evil-looking cyclosporin and squirted it into a glass which he held out. Sidney turned her head.

'I can't. I feel sick.'

Dermot stood his ground

'Twice a day for the rest of your life.'

Taking the glass from him, Sidney made no attempt to drink.

'Take tiny sips.'

Sidney put the glass to her lips. She tried and gagged.

'I can't. It's foul.'

It was as if she had not spoken.

'Have a little rest then try again.'

Dermot had schooled himself not to feel sorry for her. It was the only way. Pretending not to notice as she sipped and gagged, sipped and gagged, thanking God he was not on the receiving end of what he knew to be a putrid brew, he lined up a regiment of bottles and, referring to the chart drawn up by Nicholas, dispensed a dozen pills, some of them obscenely large, into a container. He filled a second glass with water as

Sidney finally drained the contents of the first, and held it out to her, standing by as she swallowed to make sure she did not cheat.

'You have no idea...' She shuddered.

'It's hard.'

'...No idea at all,' draining the glass of water she tried to crawl back into bed.

Dermot barred her way.

'Bicycle!'

'Please Dermot. I'm not up to it.'

'Cycling?'

'Living.'

She had been pedalling for some time when Eduardo, attended by a nurse, swept, without knocking, into the room.

'Don't you dare give up!' Dermot was saying.

'Stop fighting with me, Dermot.'

'I'll fight like hell.'

'Tour de France?' Eduardo intervened.

Sidney glared at him.

'That's not funny.'

Eduardo took her notes from the end of the bed.

'I never promised you a rose garden. How are you?'

Exhausted, Sidney leaned over the handlebars.

'You should know. You made me.'

'Don't ever say that.' Eduardo's voice was angry.

'She did half a mile yesterday,' Dermot said quickly.

'If it wasn't for Dermot...' Sidney said.

'You're a lucky woman.' Eduardo looked long and hard at Sidney. 'Dermot's a lucky man. I want to do a cardiac biopsy. Make sure the heart isn't rejecting. Three o'clock,' he addressed the nurse before making swiftly for the door, adding his Parthian shot.

'It's nothing.'

'Nothing for you.' Sidney addressed his retreating back.

Dermot checked the dial on the bicycle. 'Another five minutes.' Sidney started to cry.

'Have I said something?' He took out his handkerchief. 'What is it?' His voice was sympathetic.

'I don't know. I don't know anything. Perhaps Baron Frankenstein has inserted a lunatic's brain into my skull.'

'You're back in the land of the normal living, Sidney. We'll get through this together.'

'For what?' she blew her nose on Dermot's handkerchief. 'More X-rays, more biopsies, more ECGs, more bloods, more frusemide, more amiloride, more Maxolon, more Mucaine,' she looked towards the locker. 'More of that unspeakable cyclo? It's too much…'

'Think of going home again. Don't you want to go home? You'll be out of here in a week.'

It was not an inducement. Her mother was coming to stay. To look after her. She hated being dependent. She had got used to the hospital. She was afraid, both for herself and for Anna who, unexpectedly, and to the delight of the entire ward, had at long last had her transplant. Anna's progress was slow. Her debilitated condition meant that every anxious step on the road to recovery took twice as long as Sidney's. Despite their differences in age, the two had become close. Sidney had taken the girl under her wing. She didn't want to leave Anna, who was poignantly aware of the stranger in the next bed and grieving for Colin.

Martin Bond was a different man. The despair in his eyes had given way to hope. Dermot had stayed with him while Anna was in the operating theatre. Martin told him about Colin to take his mind off Anna. The boy's death had affected him too. Colin had been plugged into his Walkman as usual. Martin had taken him a Liverpool strip. He had modelled it for Anna, grinning with delight. Even the smallest size was too big for his wizened frame. In a spontaneous gesture of pleasure, there had been few presents in his life, he had flung his skinny arms round Martin's neck. As soon as he had removed them, Martin knew that something was wrong. Colin had fallen back on to the pillow. Still smiling. His eyes fixed.

'Colin? Colin!'

There was no reply.

The crash team had been summoned. They arrived in seconds. There were mysterious sounds, agitated voices from behind the curtains. Then it was quiet. The nurses who had cared for Colin, who had got to know him, wept softly. A sudden infarct in his damaged heart had killed him. Mercifully it had been quick. His parents travelled down from Liverpool and they cremated Colin in his Liverpool strip. Martin liked to think that it was what the boy would have wanted. That he had made his last moments happy.

Anna had survived the transplant. News of the available organs, from the Smithfield hospital, had come suddenly. Convinced that he would not see his daughter again, Martin had said goodbye to her with a heavy heart. Now that the moment for which he had been waiting for so long had come, he had felt, like Dermot, as if he were a murderer, as if, in signing the consent form, he was consigning Anna to certain death. Anna had been in no state to worry about the transplant. Too weak to speak, clutching her father's hand, she had communicated with her eyes.

Uncertain of his ability to get through the night on his own, Martin had knocked on Dermot's door. Apologising for disturbing his friend, for dumping his problems on to someone who had worries of his own, Dermot had replied that everyone was 'involved in mankind'.

They had spent the night in discussion, touching lightly on matters of philosophy, art, religion, folklore, anthropology and surgery. By the time Eduardo came to tell Martin that Anna had survived the transplant and was in ICU, so absorbed had they been in conversation that neither of them had noticed it was already light.

Describing to Dermot his first visit to Anna in ICU, it was as if Martin had witnessed a miracle.

'Her lips were pink, Dermot, as if they had been painted. When the Prof came in, he lifted the blanket and I felt her toes. They were warm as toast. Anna's feet haven't been warm for years.'

Despite the fact that he had had no sleep, they had been unable to eject Martin from ICU until they had removed her ventilator and Anna had opened her eyes.

'They were like washed stones,' Martin said. 'The whites of her eyes were clear for the first time. She tried to speak. I couldn't make out what she was saying. Sounded like 'orange, orange'. I guessed she was thirsty. I guessed she wanted a drink. Then I realised. She was asking for Colin. Once they've taught her how to breathe, it'll be back to the ward and on to the bicycle. Bicycle! Ten years ago Anna couldn't step outside in a stiff breeze. Three months ago she couldn't even dress herself.'

By the time Anna came out of ICU, Sidney was climbing nineteen stairs. Sidney monitored Anna's progress, spurring her on when she flagged, encouraging her when she wanted to give up, just as she had been encouraged by Dermot.

Sidney had finished her stint on the bicycle and climbed back thankfully into bed, when the door of the side-room opened once again. This time it was Nicholas holding a blue exercise book and a minispirometer. He handed the spirometer to Dermot.

'This is to take home. It's to test the volume and flow of air through Sidney's lungs...'

'Excuse me,' Sidney addressed Nicholas from the bed, 'But I am the patient.' Stifling a yawn, Nicholas ignored the interruption. This time it was not the patients in Top Floor Surgical who had kept him awake. Max had colic and Mary a nasty dose of mastitis which made feeding the baby difficult and painful. Much of his night had been spent ministering to his wife and son, changing Max's nappies and walking up and down the flat singing in an effort to console him and jiggling him up and down in his arms.

He continued to address Dermot. '...The spirometer must be used every single day. For life. Without fail.' He gave Dermot the exercise book. 'The Fulham Blue Book'. To record the results of the 'blows'. Any failure to keep a conscientious record can result in chronic rejection going undetected. Small airways of the lungs can become blocked by fibrous tissue. This could lead to a deterioration...'

'Excuse me...' Sidney said.

'...a deterioration in function which causes progressive and irreversible lung damage.'

'I thought I was supposed to be the...' Sidney's voice was muffled by sobs.

'What's the matter darling?' Dermot rushed to her side.

'I'm...supposed...to be the expert.' Tears were coursing down her face. 'Chronic rejection is my specialty. I object to you two talking over my head.'

'I'm afraid she's a bit down today...' Dermot apologised to Nicholas.

'There you go again!' Sidney was getting hysterical, making it difficult for her to breathe.

Nicholas indicated to Dermot to leave the room. Sitting on the bed as he waited for Sidney to compose herself, he handed her a tissue to dry her eyes.

'Sorry about that,' she said eventually.

'There's no need to apologise.' Nicholas' voice was gentle.

'I don't know what came over me. I feel so…so…I don't know what I feel.'

'Battle fatigue.' Taking the tissue from her Nicholas threw it into the bin. 'The war is over and it's a shock to be alive.'

Sidney noticed the physician's bleary eyes, his stubbled chin.

'You look pretty battle fatigued yourself.'

He told her about Mary and the baby. To give her something else to think about. To take her mind off herself. For the first time since she had been ill Sidney saw the young man as a husband and father with not only a full workload but with problems of his own. She realised that although Nicholas did much of the work, it was Eduardo, who performed the transplant operations and breezed in and out with his retinue who somehow got all the acclaim.

'I've never really thanked you…'

'Nothing to thank me for…' Covering up his embarrassment, Nicholas reached for the chart from the end of the bed. 'On the contrary. I'm writing you up for the torture chamber tomorrow.'

'The torture chamber?'

'The gym.'

'I honestly don't think I can take any more punishment.'

Replacing his pen in his pocket, Nicholas made for the door.

'You're doing great, Sidney.' It was the nearest he could get to sympathy. 'Give it time.'

When Nicholas had left, a bouquet of flowers, almost obliterating the nurse who carried them, was brought in. Dermot, who had followed her in, removed the card.

'Gavin Wyatt? Isn't he on TV?'

'Let me see.' Taking the card Sidney turned it over.

'What does it say?'

'Thank you for saving my life.'

' "For saving my life"?'

'Someone must have let the cat out of the bag. Gavin Wyatt has *my* old heart.'

157

NINETEEN

By the time Bernice Partridge realised she was pregnant, Sidney had been home for eight weeks. At first Bernice hadn't believed the doctor, how could she be having a baby when she hadn't been having sex? Then she remembered. It was the night they had taken Wayne off the life-support machine – that was a laugh to start with – the night they had removed his organs, decimated her son's body to give someone else, someone she didn't give a shit about, the chance to live. Angry with Wayne for committing what Police Constable Watkins had told her was a particularly heinous crime (his words) he had divulged the details of the murder to her over a lager in the Rat & Parrot. She hadn't thought that she would mind when that crap the hospital called 'brain-death' – and which was outside her understanding – became death (as she knew it) and Wayne had been cremated in the hospital chapel, minus his youthful heart and strong lungs and goodness only knew what else. While Wayne was in the operating theatre, where in the normal run of things they tried to save people, to put them back together rather than taking them apart, PC Watkins, whose role as vigilante was over, had walked her back to the flat to check on the kids. Finding that Alice had taken them to the park, she had put the kettle on and found a drop of brandy for her nerves and they had sat on the sofa. Dave had put a comforting arm round her shivering shoulders and before they knew it one thing had led to another and he was divesting her of Fiona's suspender belt and black silk stockings which provoked no objection on her part and which seemed mightily to turn him on. By the time he had accompanied her back to the Smithfield hospital – he refused to let her go alone – the procedure was over. A doctor took her to the mortuary where she had said a final goodbye to Wayne whose mutilated body was discretely covered. She remembered walking slowly away from the hospital into the city night, glad that she had the strong arm of Dave Watkins to lean on and wondering, in view of what Wayne had done, why she had cried and cried. It was strange, when you came to think about it, how one life had ended – never mind all that 'brain-dead' stuff – and another, had begun, although goodness knows how she was going to cope.

It was Fiona who had pointed out that not one life but two would have been delivered that night when they violated Wayne's body, sawed through his ribcage and robbed him of his vital parts, that there was not only the new baby to consider but the recipient of Wayne's heart.

'I hope he don't murder anybody,' Bernice said.

Fiona had reassured her that such evil proclivities were not relocated with the organs. Bernice was not so sure. Each time she walked down the street pushing the baby in his buggy, the twins dragging their feet by her side, she wondered if one of the people whose eyes she caught, that taxi driver, that dreadlocked roller-blader, that woman weighed down with the supermarket bags, that smug traffic warden, that pudding-faced adolescent selling *The Big Issue,* was harbouring Wayne's heart. Sometimes she had nightmares about it. She dreamed that she had been pressured into donating Wayne's organs (although this was not strictly true), and that she would be punished for her treatment of her son in hell. Dave Watkins, whom she still met for a drink now and again – although she hadn't told him about the baby, what was the point? he had no intention of leaving his wife and kids – said it was a load of cobblers, it wasn't a bad deed she had done, but a good one, she had benefited mankind. After she'd seen Dave she regarded herself as some kind of heroine, and as far as mankind was concerned she was glad to have done her bit. All the same, when she really thought about it, the grisly act for which she had given her permission began to niggle her; then a picture came into her mind of the poor old girl Wayne had murdered and it all got too complicated and she decided not to dwell on it, to concentrate on the new life within her and how she was going to manage with four kids and forget about Wayne.

Bernice was not the only one who was troubled. Although Sidney had entered the land of the living and was back at her computer and catching up with her reading, she found it hard to concentrate as she thought about her old heart and how it was managing without her.

'I wonder how Gavin Wyatt is doing?'

'Gavin Wyatt?' Dermot put down his book.

159

'The TV actor. He sent me those flowers, remember? Thanked me for saving his life.'

Dermot picked up the book again.

'I'm sure he's fine.'

'You're not into all this recycling business are you, Dermot? It makes you twitchy. Goes against the grain. I've only just realised. Perhaps I realised all along. I don't have any problem with it, people's bodies are their own 'private property' to dispose of as they see fit.'

She was her old self again, not the vapid Sidney of before the operation but the Sidney she had been before she became sick. Feeling better than she had for a long time, she no longer questioned whether it had all been worthwhile. Despite Dermot's fussing over her, looking for signs of rejection or infection, and his injunctions, to avoid twisting, to avoid lifting heavy weights, not to overdo it, to rest when she became tired, she relished her new freedom. She had already walked as far as the local newsagent's and even done some gardening, and although she was not yet back at the hospital she was in daily touch with the department and had thrown herself into her work. In an act of expiation, because it made her feel better, she had written a letter to her donor family – although Debbie had not promised that they would get it – in which she had tried to express her overwhelming gratitude to them while sympathising with them in their loss. Since confidentiality was respected, she had no idea whom she was addressing and although she felt ready to do it, it was a hard letter to write, but it was a symbolic load off her chest.

She was especially grateful to her mother. Now that she had something positive to do, Diana Sands was a changed person. She had arrived bearing home-made cakes and a great many appetising meals for the freezer, cooked in the great surge of relief with which she greeted the news that Sidney had survived the transplant and that Diana was no longer required to stand by able to do nothing while her daughter's condition worsened. Even given Sebastian's prodigious appetite they would have a hard time getting through it all. Sleeping in the top floor spare bedroom next to Sebastian, her mother had seen them through the early days, to give Dermot a chance to supervise Sidney's physio and medication – which took up most of his time. This arrangement suited Sebastian. He got on well with Grandma, who spoiled him as Sidney never had time to and played cards with him for a penny a point.

On Sidney's return from the hospital with Dermot, she had found a 'WELCOME HOME MUM' banner stretched across the front door and an outsize jar of licorice allsorts by her bed. Sebastian's relief that she had returned, that she had not died on him, as he had been convinced she was going to, was manifested daily in a dozen different ways. He brought her cups of tea when she didn't want them (had Sebastian had his way she would have drowned in tea) fetched and carried, waited on her hand and foot. She worried lest the attention he was paying her was at the expense of his school work. He assured her, airily, that it was not. When she actually broached the subject of her recovery, and that from now on everything was going to be all right, he withdrew once more into his carapace.

Once he said to her:

'It's a bit creepy isn't it?'

'What?'

'You know. Having someone else's…whatsits inside you.'

'Not really.'

It rarely bothered her any more. She had too much to think about. Certainly did not dream.

'I'm still your mother.'

When she tried to put her arms around Sebastian and he had slithered from her grasp, she realised that she had hit the nail on the head.

'It's still me, Sebastian. I haven't changed.'

But she had. Life, which she had thus far perhaps not appreciated, had become precious: the air she breathed freely after so long gasping for it; the ability to lie flat, which she had not been able to do for a very long time; the fact that despite the scar on her chest and the stretch marks and her face puffy from the drugs, she could prepare a simple meal, put her own dishes away, appreciate a single drop of dew on a garden flower. She no longer took life for granted. She knew that if she were not meticulous about her medication, the currency in which she was required to pay for her every day on the planet, it would not be a question of passing away painlessly, peacefully in the night, but dying of massive internal bleeding, of infection, of heart failure. There seemed so little time.

She had come home from the hospital not only with new organs but also with new ideas. Apart from the research she was working on and the conference she was organising, in which she would present her own pathology, she had decided to set up the Sidney Sands Lung Transplant Fund both to raise the profile of transplantation with the general public, so that more families might agree to becoming possible donors, and to finance the research that would take the project forward. She was busy sounding out prospective donors and patrons; investigating ways to raise money which would further the understanding and prevention of the complications of rejection, in the hope that lung function in post-transplant patients could be optimised to enable them to live many full years of life. She was already planning a Christmas concert, for which she had reserved the largest lecture theatre in the hospital and had provisionally booked an oboe band to play a programme of Baroque and festive music to be followed by seasonal refreshments. Her mother had promised to make the mince pies.

That was the funny thing about her mother. Before her transplant, when Sidney had been at death's door, Diana Sands refused to believe that she was ill, and now that she was back in the land of the living insisted upon treating her like an invalid. She rang at least once a day to see if Sidney was manifesting the slightest sign of rejection or infection. Her mother's misgivings about organ transplantation, which she had divulged to Sidney one night as she played a game of gin rummy with Sebastian, were not based on religious or moral considerations, but were a result of her visits to the geriatric ward of the local hospital, where twice a week she undertook voluntary work. What was the use of organ transplants, kidney machines, pacemakers, defibrillators, test-tube babies, all of which high-tech procedures were high-profile and income-generating, while feeding and caring for patients was not?

'All that stuff makes people live a lot longer,' joining in the conversation, Sebastian shuffled the cards.

'A lot of old people don't want to live longer, Sebastian. What they do want is a little tender loving care. Old people are not allowed to be ill today. Not allowed to recover at their own pace. Nobody bothers if they're hungry or thirsty, nobody bothers to make them comfortable.'

'They've got nurses.' Sebastian took a card.

'Very few. They're short-staffed. That's why they have volunteers. Anyway the nurses haven't got the training. There is so much bureaucracy, so many guidelines they have to follow, so much gobbledegook and technology to cope with, it's as much as they can do to slap some pre-plated food in front of the poor souls three times a day. There's no time to help them eat and drink – that's what I do – no time to get to know them as individuals, no time to find out about their backgrounds, to take an interest in their problems. All they know is to call them by their first names – quite elderly people! – stuff them with antibiotics, radiate them, operate on them, then expect them to jump out of bed to make way for the next acute 'customer'.

'Doesn't anyone complain?' Sidney asked. 'I thought there was supposed to be a patients' charter?'

'They complain all right, darling. Nobody listens. Patients want to know why they are being resuscitated, ventilated, having tubes stuck into them left, right and centre. They're left alone for hours at a time and there's no one around to make their lives tolerable. I had one old lady who'd been sitting out since before breakfast. She suffered from bouts of dizziness and pressure pain in her buttocks, and kept sliding on to the floor. Every time someone picked her up and propped her back in her chair, she'd beg to be allowed to lie on the bed. Elsewhere it would be called torture. I'd hate to think what Florence Nightingale would make of it if she were to come back today.'

While her mother's solicitousness eventually got on Sidney's nerves, at least she had gone home. Dermot's attentiveness was driving her crazy. Last night they had had a bust-up.

Dermot had been to the supermarket and was unpacking the groceries, filling the fridge and the freezer and doing what passed for singing.

She thought if he repeated just once more *Night and day, You are the One, Night and day, You are the One, Night and day, You are the One…*(in his off-key voice) like a needle stuck in a groove while she was trying to work, she would go mad.

'For God's sake!'

'Sorry!'

He started whistling through his teeth as he held up a tray of chicken drumsticks.

'How does a nice curry grab you? Or a risotto? I could make a risotto.'

He took a handful of mushrooms and a bunch of coriander from a brown paper bag.

'Mushrooms. Fresh coriander...'

She was not blind.

'Would you rather the risotto?'

'I'm not very hungry.'

'Sebastian will be hungry.'

'Sebastian is staying at school. Rehearsal for the end of term concert.'

At least he had a better voice than Dermot.

'Thanks for telling me.'

Glancing up at the sarcasm in his voice she noticed that Dermot was wearing a red lambswool sweater.

'New sweater?'

'I've been wearing it since your op. You've got to eat something Sidney. What will it be now, the curry or the risotto?'

'I'll get myself some cornflakes later.'

'What nutriment is there in cornflakes?' he moved the spirometer from the table. 'How were your blows today?'

Sidney pushed over the Fulham Blue Book.

Dermot turned over the pages.

' "Forced Expiratory Volume in one second. Monday: 2.75 litres..." It's gone down! Monday! That was yesterday Sidney. Today is Tuesday. If your lung function drops more than ten per cent it can indicate infection. It can indicate rejection...'

Sidney snatched the book from him.

'You don't want to have another bronchoscopy. You don't want to have to go into hospital again.'

'I'm quite capable of using the spirometer. I'm quite capable of measuring my lung function...'

'Nicholas said to be sure to write your blows down *every day*. He said it was extremely important. I don't see today's written down!'

'...without you interfering.'

As she returned to her computer she was aware that Dermot had retreated into one of his familiar silences, that he was hurt and stunned. She watched him from the corner of her eye as he started to prepare the meal.

'Will we wrap up and take a walk around the block later?' He was making an effort for her sake, he didn't want her upset.

'I have to finish this paper.'

'Was there any need to start working so soon? The Prof said you should take things easy, that you should take things slowly, that you mustn't *over*-rehabilitate...'

Eduardo had been angry with her in the hospital. Still attached to a drip she had sneaked into the bathroom for the first time since her transplant. Her body, embroidered with stitches from the base of her neck to her ribcage, pacing wires sticking out from beneath her left breast and four drain wounds which were just beginning to heal, felt sore and in need of relaxation, and her hair needed washing. She had just slid gratefully into a hot bath, taking care not to let the water touch the pacing dressing, when Eduardo, deciding to do a ward-round and finding her bed empty, had flung open the bathroom door. Holding out the skimpy bath-towel he had demanded that she get out of the bath immediately. Dripping and shamefaced, with the towel barely covering her and apologising to the nurses she had eluded, she had followed the furious surgeon and the students who surrounded him back to the ward.

'The transplant unit depends on me,' Sidney told Dermot. 'I'm behind as it is.'

Dermot put a hand on the lid of her laptop.

'Why don't you put it away now?'

'Dermot, you will have to stop telling me what to do.'

'It's for your own benefit.'

'Paternalism is the worst form of tyranny.'

'What's that again?'

'Nothing. It doesn't matter.'

'It matters. You jump down my throat. I don't know what's got into you. I can't say a word.'

'Just leave me alone.'

'That's a fine thing to say.'

'I can manage.'

Dermot held up the Blue Book.

'Manage! You can't even...'

Losing her cool, Sidney searched through her briefcase.

'I wrote it on a piece of paper...'

'You've to write it in the book.'

'Stop treating me like an idiot. Stop treating me like a child.'

'I don't know what's the matter with you. You upset everyone. You upset your mother. You refused her carrot cake.'

'I ate her chocolate cake and her coffee cake and her fruit cake... I draw the line at carrots!'

'You told her to eat it herself.'

'No point in wasting it.'

'Sebastian wanted to make you some flapjacks...'

'When Sebastian cooks the place is a tip.'

'Everything the boy tries to do for you...'

'If you'd all just leave me alone.'

'If that's what you want.'

'Look, I'm sorry.' Sidney said eventually, in the long silence which followed.

'There's no need to apologise.' Dermot said, his lips a thin line.

'I'm fed up...'

'It's still early days.' Dermot went back to his nanny voice, went back to being concerned.

'I'm fed up with you being a martyr Dermot. With you treating me as if I'm old china. As if I'm liable to break.'

'That's not what you said three months ago.'

'Things change. I've changed.'

'You can say that again. There's times I don't recognise you.'

'I don't recognise myself. Do you think there's a psychological price to pay,' Sidney said, 'for flying in the face of our myths?'

'What myths would they be?'

'The Island of Dr Moreau, Dr Jekyll and Mr Hyde, Dracula...' she pointed to her chest. 'Perhaps she was irritable and bad tempered?'

'She?'

'He then.'

'I think you're imagining things.'

' "Once upon a time, in a Czech village, a young man, blind from birth, begged the doctor to give him a new pair of eyes. Instead of giving him the eyes of a young girl, as he'd promised, the doctor secretly gave him the eyes of animals. When he was given the eyes of a fish, the blind man – who was now no longer blind – saw fins and scales; when he was given the eyes of birds, he saw the sky and the clouds; when he was given the eyes of a lion he saw jackals and wildebeest…" '

'It's not a personality transplant you've had…'

'You obviously think it is.'

'It's the drugs make you bad-tempered.'

'I am not bad-tempered…!' Sidney lost her rag. 'I'd just like to be left alone. I'd like you to give me some space. I need some space. Why don't you get on with your own work? What happened to the book you were writing, your broadcasts, your articles for *Nature*? You haven't been out for months. You haven't been to the cinema, you haven't been to a single meeting…'

'I didn't want to leave you.'

'Why don't you get on with your own life?'

She could see she that she had upset Dermot again.

'You mustn't think I don't appreciate what you've done for me. Without you Dermot, I would never have come through. It's just that there's so much to do…'   .

'Give it time.'

'Time! Time! That's all I ever hear. You know very well that even the most successful transplant patient hasn't lived for more than fifteen years. Most of them don't get past year one.' She took out her handkerchief. 'Oh God!, Dermot. I don't know what's the matter with me. I'm not much good at being dependent, I suppose. You've done so much for me. I'd like to do something for you.'

'You could set the table for starters.'

'You don't have to jolly me along any more!'

The message wasn't getting through.

'It's all right. I'll do it. You know what I really want, Sidney? What I'd really like? More than anything else in the world. What I have dreamed of for the last six months…'

'How would I know? I didn't even notice your new sweater. I've been so wrapped up in myself.'

Coming up behind her, Dermot kissed the back of her pale neck before drawing her into his arms.

'I've dreamed of making love to my wife.'

TWENTY

The next morning Sidney was running a temperature. There was no reason why she and Dermot should not have made love, something that each had thought privately, like going for long walks together, they would never do again. It was there in black and white under Lifestyle in the Transplant Clinic's *Information for Patients.* After an eight-week period of post-operative abstinence, and provided the patient was feeling fit enough, sexual activity was recommended as beneficial to the lungs.

Despite the authorisation, had Dermot not had the foresight to bring a bottle of champagne to bed with him, both of them would have been inhibited by the fear that unaccustomed exertion would be too much of a strain for Sidney's new heart. Afterwards, for the first time in months they lay contentedly and at ease in each other's arms.

'How was it for her?' Dermot allowed himself a joke.

'She thought it was great.' At peace for the first time in months, Sidney answered in kind.

At six a.m., as usual, at the first sound of the alarm, they were both awake. There was a schedule to get through, a meticulous rehabilitation programme which encompassed regular medicines and exercise, fresh air, early nights and plenty of good food. Lying in bed, even at weekends, was a thing of the past.

Postural drainage was the first item on the punishing programme which must be completed every day, even when Sidney was back at work, and to which they were struggling to become accustomed. While Sidney lay across the bed, Dermot's task was to shake her until she had managed to clear her lungs of the sputum that had accumulated during the night. After this there was lung function to be checked. A low reading on the spirometer indicated the presence of infection, which had to be taken extremely seriously. After checking her weight (for fluid retention) and swallowing the dreaded immunosuppressant, there were several different pills to get down and her temperature to be checked before Sidney put on her trainers for a jog around the block, leaving Dermot to prepare breakfast. The distance she covered each day would gradually be increased until she was able to run two or three miles. Several lengths of the local swimming pool would then be added to the curriculum. This time-consuming routine – pills, postural drainage, spirometer, temperature and weight checks – had to be repeated each evening and carried out in perpetuity, with no excuses, no time off for good behaviour and never a day missed. Any failure on Sidney's part to adhere to the schedule, in particular the spirometer values, even when she was feeling perfectly well, might result in rejection going undetected and progressive, irreversible lung damage.

When she got out of bed feeling inexplicably tired and short of breath – she had thought fatigue and breathlessness things of the past – Sidney blamed the exertions of the night. When the spirometer registered low and her temperature well above normal, her heart sank and she looked at Dermot in horror. She had been doing so well. She was determined to do well. She was not some wishy-washy patient. She was Professor Sidney Sands.

Knowing that it was too soon for the chronic rejection, which usually occurred only several months after the transplantation, she guessed that her infection was due to the suppression of her immune system by the cyclosporin. The consequences of this could be serious and must be treated in hospital straight away. It was a great disappointment.

'Everything's been going so well!' Dermot was even more disappointed.

'It's par for the course.'

Sidney was more downhearted than she sounded. Although she had kidded herself that she was different, her clinical instinct told her that this would be the first disappointment of many. Infection in transplant patients was unavoidable but she was unable to rid herself of the feeling that, although she had taken the utmost care, avoided public transport and crowded places and people with obvious infections, she had somehow brought the setback upon herself.

Back again in Top Floor Surgical she felt like a recidivist, as if she had committed some crime. Stories of rejection and septicaemia, deteriorating chest X-rays, and respiratory function bandied about by more experienced recidivists in the ward and destined to make her feel better, failed to reassure her at all. Nodding politely to a young woman in a pink track-suit who sat cross-legged on the adjoining bed, she sunk into unaccustomed apathy and nursed her hurt pride.

'Sidney?'

'Anna!'

The rosy-cheeked girl, with her once dark hair now streaked defiantly blonde and tied in a pony-tail, was a far cry from the blue-lipped waif who had been at death's door when she had last seen her. She had failed to recognise Anna who throwing caution to the winds had jumped down from the bed and embraced her like a young puppy.

'I am so pleased to see you. I am bored out of my mind. Guess you had such a great time on Top Floor Surgical you couldn't keep away...' Catching sight of Nicholas, Anna's voice tailed off. The more she saw of the transplant physician, the more she yearned for him. She kept her feelings from her father and tried not to think of Mary and the baby.

'Hi, Nicholas! He doesn't even know I exist. Watch this.'

'Hi, Anna,' the physician's voice was non-committal. How are you today?'

Without waiting for an answer, Nicholas made for Sidney's bed, closing it from view in a practised gesture.

'And what have you been up to?'

Sitting beside Sidney and unfazed by the unrequited love which filtered palpably through the poppy-strewn curtains, he fastened the cuff of the sphygmomanometer round her arm and checked for the sound of the systolic pressure. Asking Sidney to cough, he listened to her chest. It was like old times.

'Am I rejecting?'

She hadn't gone through hell on earth only to die now.

'Two steps forward and one step back...'

'Cut the crap, Nicholas.'

Such talk was for patients. Not for Sidney Sands. She was going to beat this thing, going to make history, if it was the last thing she did. But she was back on the conveyor belt, back in the system. Chest X-rays, blood tests and medication, Fibre Optic Transbronchial Biopsy, oxygen as necessary, twenty-four hour care...

When they brought her back to the ward after the investigations, Anna was engrossed in a book.

'Did you know that "cancer cripples vitality, makes eating an ordeal and deadens sexual desire while TB is an aphrodisiac conferring on the patient extraordinary powers of seduction." It doesn't say anything about lung transplants.'

'What on earth are you reading?' Sidney's eyes were not focusing.

'*The Magic Mountain.* According to Thomas Mann the "Symptoms of disease are nothing but a disguised manifestation of the power of love; all disease is only love transformed…" '

Sidney was unwilling to destroy the girl's illusions. There was nothing decorative or lyrical about disease. The human body was the human body.

' "Love transformed". Do you think that's why I'm madly, deeply, passionately, incurably, irrevocably in love with Nicholas who is devoted to Mary and whose only concern is monitoring my blows?'

'There are plenty of other men out there…' Sidney realised that she sounded like her mother. 'They'll be like bees round a honey-pot, once you get out of this place.'

'My father's not going to be too pleased. He's used to having me to himself. Nicky said I could go home next week,' Anna said. 'He's cool…'

Sidney let her chatter. She could not believe this was the same Anna.

'Do you ever have fantasies,' Anna said, 'about your new heart? Emily Pankhurst, Joan of Arc, Florence Nightingale?…I know that the Smithfield organs must have belonged to somebody good, somebody beautiful. I feel so beautiful inside. My donor must have been a really gentle person. You know what I'm going to do when I go home? I'm going to read for an English degree. I want to write. Meanwhile I'm going to set up a help-line. For transplantees. To provide support and friendship. To help you cope. I'm going to call it BASH. Body Shop Helpline. BASH will put patients and their families in touch with other patients and families who've been through, or are going through, a similar experience. It will keep people's spirits up while they're waiting for assessment and give help when it's needed. I spent so much time crying. So much time alone. This way we'll all get to talk to one another, belong to one big exclusive club.'

If Sidney hadn't recognised Anna, she hardly recognised Martin Bond who came almost running through the swing-doors.

'Great to see you but sorry you're back,' he greeted Sidney affectionately.

'It's nothing,' Sidney hastened to reassure him. 'A few breathing problems, slight fever...'

Putting a gift-wrapped box on Anna's bed, Martin nodded. 'I met Dermot downstairs. We're going for a drink.'

Anna unwrapped a pair of pink trainers.

Martin was unable to keep the pride from his voice. 'What do you think of my Anna? Anna's never worn out a pair of shoes in her life.'

In the pub opposite the hospital, Martin raised his glass to Anna. 'You know what she said to me yesterday, Dermot. "If I only live for six months it will all have been worth it. For the first time in my life I know what it's like to feel normal." '

'Sidney was feeling normal. Until today.'

'It must be tough for you.'

'They don't tell you how tough.'

'Sharks and piranha fish.'

'These infections are par for the course.'

'You're always so bloody sanguine.'

'A week or two of steroids...'

'So bloody optimistic.'

'Sidney hated my optimism. She used to shout at me. Wanted me to put myself in her place. Imagine it was my life under threat. She wanted me to stop being positive. To stop pretending everything was all right. She wanted me to admit that I was afraid.'

'Were you afraid?'

'I had to make it through for her. Let me tell you something Martin. I used to think living with dying was hard. Living with living is harder.'

'Anna's going to set up a help-line. To provide support for people having to cope with transplantation. To put patients and carers in touch with other patients and carers.'

'Brilliant idea.'

'Okay, the hospital gives you a lousy booklet. They give you information. It's not a question of information. This will help the people who are turned down. People who go away without hope. People who are given a transplant only to have it snatched away...'

'Reassurance is what's needed.'

'Exactly. Anna's subscribers will have a common interest, be able to keep each other's spirits up. Help and advice will be a telephone call or an e-mail away. I haven't really had a chance to talk to you, Dermot, since Sidney's transplant. You were too occupied, and I was too worried about Anna. What happened to your misgivings?'

'It's hard to say. You know when Sidney first became ill, even in the face of my own uncertainties, I used to pray that a donor would be found before it was too late.'

'Correct me if I'm wrong, but it seems to me you conveniently reversed your opinions and forgot your reservations the moment your own wife's life was at stake.'

'You could put it like that. What I had neglected to consider however – and what I have since come to realise – is the role that the caring, the generosity, the compassion and the love have to play…not only in the donors' decision to donate their organs, but more importantly, in human existence. When push comes to shove 'gifts' are about human relationships.'

'Isn't that what transplantation is about?'

'I'm still not certain. Sometimes I think we've crossed the Rubicon, opened Pandora's Box, entered into some Faustian pact. Did you know that in Japan there's no such thing as a heart-lung transplant? They refuse to accept that brain death is the end of life. Maybe the Japanese know a thing or two…'

'Hang on a minute. My father spent a good chunk of World War Two in Changi prison. Not to put too fine a point on it, they didn't seem all that bothered then about evaluating the precise moment of death.'

'To my way of thinking – and it will take more than Sidney's transplant to change it – the rational mind has a way of making its opinions felt, the crucial issue is not so much the definition of brain death, but the status of the body itself. Pig transplants, mechanical hearts, genetic manipulation. Aren't we encouraging a new wave of body snatchers? Isn't it irresponsible to do experiments – transplanting heads on live monkeys, which is not only another questionable animal experiment but bad science too – when the downside is the possibility of creating greater suffering through the spread of retroviruses and finishing up with nothing but a whole heap of dead monkeys?'

'You know as well as I do that animal experimentation is essential for scientific progress and the development of new medicines.'

'Monkeys are sacrificed for no other purpose than to give the impression that these are properly conducted 'scientific' experiments.'

'The difficulty is not whether animal experiments are scientifically necessary, but are the experiments themselves bad science? Are they looking at questions to which they need to know the answer or acting so crudely that the results are meaningless? What does Sidney have to say about it?'

'I don't discuss the moral issue with Sidney. In the circumstances it would hardly be fair. I've enough to do to get her through the day, to get her from one day to the next. Take a look at this.' Dermot put his newspaper on the bar. 'I hope Sidney doesn't see it.'

Martin Bond followed Dermot's finger to a headline. *Soap star Gavin Wyatt takes own life after heart transplant.*

'They gave him Sidney's old heart.'

'Seems it didn't work out.'

'I can understand how he felt.'

'You're a miserable bugger. Did you ever hear the story about the guy with the artificial heart who asked the surgeon if he'd still be able to make love? Don't worry about it, the surgeon tells him, that's another organ!'

'Gavin Wyatt sent Sidney flowers...' Dermot's mind was still on the actor's death. 'Thanked her for saving his life. I hope to God she doesn't see the evening paper. She'd be devastated if she knew.'

'Same again?' Martin refilled the glasses. 'I've been thinking,' he said when he came back from the bar. 'Why don't we throw a party for the girls?'

'A party! Anna hasn't even been discharged.'

'Not right now. I was thinking of *next* year...'

Neither of them spoke. Next year seemed far away.

'On Sidney and Anna's 'first' birthday'.

'We can have it at our house,' Dismissing thoughts of the dead actor, Dermot humoured Martin.

'We'll invite the Prof...'

'And Nicholas.'

'Debbie and Alison...'

'The staff of Top Floor Surgical...'

'I'll bring the biggest cake you've ever seen.' Martin raised his glass. 'To the four of us!'

'The four of us. Thank God for small mercies,' Dermot said.

TWENTY-ONE

Bernice sat on a bench in the park rocking the shabby buggy in which the infant David Wayne Partridge slept, his head lolling on one side, while his older brother and the twins played amongst the dog-shit on the meagre grass. The yellow forsythia and the pink almond blossom were in bloom, and the few desultory daffodils that hadn't been vandalised as offerings for Mother's Day proclaimed the coming of a late spring and the approach of summer which for some meant long days, balmy nights, and renewal of hope.

For Bernice, one day was much the same as the next, an endless round of shopping, cooking, cleaning, nappy-changing, journeys to and from the launderette and waiting in line at the Post Office to collect her allowances. The seasons merged unostentatiously one into the other, and there was little hope to be renewed. Although a year had passed since Wayne had died, she still thought about him every day, and the more she thought about him the more she thought of herself as a murderer. It was as if she rather than Wayne had, in some convoluted way, done the foul deed, and by giving his organs away in a rash moment, she had her son's blood on her hands. Finding the few snapshots she had of him – Wayne as a baby, Wayne as a bleached headed toddler, Wayne grinning behind a football almost larger than himself, a self-conscious Wayne on the beach at Scunthorpe – she had stuck them up with blue-tack on the door of the fridge and looked at them every time she got out the Easy-spread or the kids' milk. Time had led enchantment to her idea of him and viewed from a distance she had talked herself into believing that he had not in fact done the murder of which he had been accused, that there had been some miscarriage of justice, that he had been joy-riding and it was the pursual by the police that had led to the fatal crash. She would have liked to discuss the matter with Dave Watkins, but Dave had been up-

176

graded to Sergeant and had been transferred to Edinburgh, so they had completely lost touch. Looking at Dave's baby, who slept all day and cried all night – once, crazy with tiredness she had seriously considered hurling him from the thirteenth-floor window – she wondered which side of the law he would be on when he grew up and whether he would have criminal tendencies like the big brother whose name he bore, or join the police force like his father. Glancing up from the baby-buggy to see what the other three were up to, she got a sudden fright. A youth, he must have been about nineteen or twenty, wearing skin-tight cycling shorts and who with his almost white hair and his knowing face could have been Wayne, was wheeling his mountain bike by its swan-necked handlebars along the path towards her. When he propped up the bike, and sat down, knees wide apart above muscular calves, at the far end of the bench, she could almost smell his masculinity and felt herself go hot and cold.

'Nice day.' He put his helmet on the bench between them.

'Yeah.'

He nodded towards the baby-buggy.

'She yours?'

'He. Yeah.'

Bernice uncrossed her legs. She was glad she had put on a pair of Fiona's fishnet stockings with her white stilettos.

'Got a ciggie?'

He took a crumpled fag from his pocket and handed it to her.

'Come here often?' Taking out a lighter he sidled towards her, his eyes blue, like Wayne's.

'Yeah.' Lowering her lashes, Bernice inclined her head towards him as he cupped his hands over the fag. Perhaps the summer wasn't going to be so bad after all.

*　　*　　*　　*　　*

Sidney had become a celebrity. She kept a file of her newspaper cuttings:

'A Dose of her Own Medicine: By an odd trick of fate which attracted the attention of the national and international press, Professor Sidney Sands, Professor of Histochemistry and a driving force spearheading major areas of research at the Fulham Hospital, and cardiac surgeon Professor Eduardo Cortes, had been collaborating as research partners for many years. They were jointly researching pulmonary hypertension when Professor Sands' own heart and lungs became so badly damaged that a heart-lung transplant was the only possible treatment. One year after the successful operation, Sidney Sands, who is back in the Department of Histochemistry sometimes working twenty hours a day, has raised nearly half a million pounds for the Sidney Sands Lung Transplant Research Fund...'

The growing stack of newspaper cuttings and the 2,000-odd letters of good wishes she had received from friends, colleagues, fellow sufferers and a world-wide public were not all. On a landmark occasion she had had the unprecedented experience of presenting her own case at one of the famous Fulham Hospital Staff Rounds. Her pre-transplant days had been presented by Nicholas Lilleywhite, the transplant itself by Eduardo Cortes, and Sidney Sands, the patient under discussion, had had the surreal experience of introducing her own pathology to a packed and emotional lecture theatre, which had greeted her exposition, in which she showed slides of her own damaged lungs, with a prolonged ovation not usually associated with such meetings. This unique event marked her first day back at work – when typically she had carried out a long overdue spot check on the labs – and was the point at which the Fund was launched in earnest.

Sidney hadn't felt so well in years and couldn't recall a time when she had felt better or had more energy. She was immensely active, never tired and was full of plans for the future. The drugged days after the transplant, when Dermot had kept vigil by her bedside, had faded into hazy memory, as had the months which had superceded them and which had been decidedly dodgy. Apart from the first blip which had taken her back to Top Floor Surgical, she had had no more infections. There had been one scary and luckily short-lived chronic rejection episode, knocked on the head with steroids, after which she had developed adverse side-effects from taking the hated cyclosporin. Now she was established on the immunosuppressant drug FK506, Prograf Tacrolimus, which so far had given her no further trouble, and was in regular touch with Eduardo Cortes who carried out her regular MOTs.

Driven by the urge to succeed which had carried her to the top in her career, she had achieved goals realised by no heart-lung transplant patients before, and all in all, although it had not been easy and had required reserves of willpower at which even Dermot had been amazed, it had been quite a year. Apart from the regular schedule of postural drainage, exercise, and drug therapy carried out before and after work, she was not only swimming fifty metres daily at the local pool, but had completed a one mile sponsored walk, done a challenging climb in the Lake District (where they had taken Sebastian for half-term), and braved a long-haul flight by herself to attend a conference in San Francisco. As far as heart-lung transplants were concerned she was not only a paradigm for others but she was making history.

The Christmas concert was a sell-out. The Transplant Fund, for which she had somehow been able to find the stamina, and to which she had applied the same determination, courage, and single-mindedness that she had shown throughout her recovery, had gone from strength to strength, and a fund-raising committee had already been established at the hospital. So far she had set her sights on a Gala performance of a new play (for which she was twisting the arm of the producer, who was finding it hard to refuse), and an evening of lieder to be performed by members of the Royal Opera Company who were sympathetic to her cause. Both she and Eduardo were totally committed to developing treatment for people with lung disease for whom transplantation was the only option until man-made lungs implanted inside the chest cavity came a step closer. The plan was to understand exactly why complications and the effects of rejection occurred and to devise means for preventing them in the hope that lung function in affected individuals could be optimised, enabling them to live a full life.

One such affected individual was Anna. In the year since her transplant she had been readmitted to Top Floor Surgical no less than five times with episodes of rejection. She not only found the daily regimen tough going – there were many occasions on which she had almost given up – but still suffered from a host of minor symptoms, ranging from night-sweats to deafness, which made her profoundly depressed. Unlike Sidney, she was finding it hard to put the transplant behind her. Although the bouts of rejection had not so far indicated graft failure, each episode had left a significant reduction in her lung function. Medically she was considered 'fit'. Emotionally it was not so simple. Once the post-operative euphoria had worn off, Anna not only had repeated nightmares about Colin, for whom she continued to grieve, but became obsessed by the fact that although technically she was still alive she had lost her old self. The Anna Bond with whom she had grown up no longer existed. Despite the support of Sidney – she was a frequent visitor to the house in Islington – long talks with the hospital transplant counsellor who had assured her that these uncomfortable feelings were shared by other patients, and frequent sessions with the psychologist, she still had persistent feelings of remorse which she confided to Nicholas, for whom she still secretly pined, on one of her stays in Top Floor Surgical.

'I feel guilty that I'm doing so well. Guilty that someone had to die to give me a chance to live. Guilty that I survived the operation. Guilty because I'm not a whole bunch of laughs. Guilty because I'm letting everyone down. Why can't I be like Sidney?'

'Don't worry about it. More patients react like you than like Sidney. Sidney's a special case.'

Nicholas handed her the mirror from her locker in which her rosy cheeks, sparkling eyes, and blonde highlights were reflected.

'A year ago you were dying. We thought you weren't going to get through the day. Now everything you do, everything you want to do is new for you. It's a shock to the system. You have to give yourself time. All beginnings are hard.'

Martin was at a loss to understand why Anna, who a year ago had been on oxygen twenty-four hours a day, was unable to do a thing for herself and scarcely able to keep alive, and who was now capable of virtually everything, was unhappy. He discussed his bewilderment with Dermot.

'I didn't think it would be like this,' he said, as they took what had become a regular Saturday morning walk in Hyde Park. 'I imagined that from here on in everything would be wonderful. Anna was so determined to have control over her life, so determined to live. She had such faith in her transplant. Each time she has a chronic rejection episode she feels that her lungs are betraying her. That they're letting her down.'

'It's bloody hard work for the girls,' Dermot said.

'Sure it is,' Martin kicked a stone, 'But we get the shitty end of the stick.'

'Bursting into tears for no reason…'

'Temper tantrums. One time Anna nearly kicked down the door.'

'She couldn't do that a year ago! Sidney's up and down like a yo-yo. They can't help the mood swings. It's out of their control.'

'Still bloody sanguine.'

It was not true. Although Dermot knew that even when Sidney threw an unopened bag of licorice allsorts at him in a moment of rage, it was the drugs speaking, he took the verbal abuse personally. Unable to remain buoyant in the face of Sidney's illogical behaviour, he felt hurt and offended. Usually he went out, to a lecture or a meeting until he had got his act together, and Sidney, full of contrition for behaviour over which she had little control, had calmed down.

On the afternoon of her 'first' birthday, demonstrating the lung function she fought so hard to maintain, Sidney helped Sebastian blow up the heart-shaped balloons and put up a banner which she and Anna had made: 'Life is Wonderful the Second Time Around.' The fact that she had not only survived for a whole year, without too many setbacks, but also managed to get the Sidney Sands Transplant Fund off the ground was a miracle. Tears of gratitude and excitement were never far from her eyes and never more so than when Dermot had announced, as he zipped her into her party dress, that he had a very special birthday present for her. Seeing that he had nothing in his hands, no beribboned package, no jewellery box, she had looked questioningly at him in the mirror.

Dermot took a deep breath.

'I've applied for a donor card. I'm going to donate my organs. When I die.'

Given his reservations, Sidney knew that the decision to give another human being the gift of life had not been made lightly. She realised the struggle Dermot must have had in coming to it and the sacrifice of conscience that it meant. His generosity was a gift in the true sense of the word. It was the best present she could have had.

When Martha telephoned to wish her a happy birthday and enquire how she was feeling, Sidney confessed that she felt lucky to be alive. If there was one lesson the past year had taught her it was to live from day to day and to savour each one as if it were her last.

'I used to regard organ replacement as something purely physical. Like putting a new battery in the car. Nobody tells you how you get a whole new take on things, how it changes you emotionally.'

181

Detecting a break in Sidney's voice and not wanting her to crack up on her 'birthday', Martha changed the subject.

'What's the latest on the work front?'

'I'm doing a study on tissue typing with the Prof.'

'How long before you publish the results?'

Grounded for a brief moment, Sidney hesitated.

'A couple of years.'

There was a brief pause – Sidney didn't think it was the satellite connection – before Martha said:

'Terrific!' Then 'Sidney, are you still there?'

'Somebody is!'

'Hey, hey! I bet the Prof doesn't like you to talk like that.'

'I only talk to you like that. I keep stumm with Dermot. It passes.'

'That's my Sidney! I'm really sorry I can't celebrate with you…'

'I know you'd be here if you could.'

'Give my love to Dermot, and Mom.'

Sidney looked over her shoulder.

'My mother is buttonholing one of my Senior Lecturers. She has the poor guy up against the sideboard. I expect she's telling him how clever I am. If I don't go and rescue him soon she'll be showing him my homework!'

'You go ahead. I just wanted to say many, many happy returns and to tell you how proud I am of you…'

'I couldn't have got this far without you.'

'Ms High Achiever? Ms Mega Ambition? Don't you believe it. Talk to you soon, honey. 'Bye for now.'

'Thanks for calling. It's good to hear your voice.'

It was good to hear everybody's voices. She heard the familiar sound of Martin's and guessed that while she had been speaking to Martha he had arrived with the birthday cake. It was on the table. Pink. With one candle. In the shape of a heart. Sidney leaned forward to read the inscription. 'Sidney and Anna. Happy Birthday.'

'Where is Anna?'

'In ICU.'

Sidney couldn't believe it. 'We can't have the party without Anna!'

'Another of her chronic rejection episodes. She said to sing Happy Birthday for her.'

Although she was shocked to hear that Anna was in Intensive Care, Sidney tried to make light of it. 'Chronic is such an ominous word. All it means is that there is scar tissue in your lungs. It's something we all have to live with.'

'Martin brought you a present.' Deflecting the conversation, Dermot indicated a human-size pink bunny-rabbit with floppy ears, ensconced in an armchair.

Martin hugged Sidney emotionally. 'According to the salesperson it's suitable for one-year-olds!'

'Everyone's been fantastic.'

The most fantastic of all had been Sebastian, who in the past six months had grown, both mentally and physically out of the grunting of his chrysalis phase and at five foot eleven inches was almost as tall as Dermot. The advent of his manhood had revealed not only reserves of maturity and good nature on which Sidney now relied, but a penchant for his school work, and in particular mathematics, which while cementing his fractured relationship with his father had widened the intellectual gap between himself and his grandmother. Her birthday present for Sidney had been for some mysterious reason (Sidney suspected a tombola) a tapestry set when it was still as much as she could do to sew on a button.

Now, very much the young man in his trendy shirt, Sebastian was answering the doorbell, greeting the guests, relieving them of their gift-wrapped parcels and bottles and courteously directing them to the living-room which had been decorated with balloons and which was becoming increasingly noisy and crowded.

When it was time to cut the cake, Sidney, reborn, ran down to the kitchen for a sharp knife. Eduardo was at the sink, getting himself a glass of water.

'Well, young lady, how does it feel?'

Leaning against the wooden table Sidney, wearing a slim black sheath dress with one seductively bared shoulder, that stopped short of her tell-tale scars, dropped her party façade.

'You'll think I'm very wicked...'

'I wish you were.'

Eduardo never missed an opportunity. Sidney ignored the remark.

'A year is not enough, Eduardo. I need ten, I need fifteen years...'

'You mustn't be greedy.'

'What's wrong with being greedy? With wanting what you have? What other people have? A life expectancy that is normal? I would like to grow old, with Dermot. I would like to see my grandchildren...'

'Who knows, by the time you've finished your research...'

'I would like to live long enough to finish my work.'

'Wouldn't we all? Think how you were a year ago...'

'Don't give me all that crap about how grateful I should be.'

'You have to trust the transplant team, Sidney. We've got you this far. We're all in this together.'

'The shit we are, Eduardo! I'm the one who's had the transplant. I'm the one on the receiving end. I'm the one who has to take the drugs. How would you like it?'

Eduardo shrugged his shoulders.

'I wouldn't have agreed.'

Sidney was shocked. 'You wouldn't have agreed to a transplant? Am I hearing you correctly..?'

Putting his glass on the draining-board, Eduardo took her in his arms.

'You see, Sidney, I'm not so brave.'

Upstairs the party was getting rowdy. They awaited the return of Sidney with the knife. She offered it to Nicholas, who had a glass of beer in his hand. He covered his eyes in mock horror. 'Don't give it to me. I'm a physician. I can't stand the sight of blood!'

She handed the knife to Eduardo who brandished it in front of Nicholas.

'Maybe you need a brain transplant.'

Backing off and taking a piece of paper from his pocket, Nicholas unfolded it to the accompaniment of inebriated cheers.

'Professor Cortes, staff of the Fulham, ladies and gentlemen.

It is my privilege to organise tonight's proceedings...'

A voice from the back of the room called 'You couldn't organise a piss-up in a brewery!'

Nicholas ignored the interruption.

'...And to act as toast master for this wonderful celebration, to which people have come from all corners of the globe. I would like to call upon Professor Eduardo Cortes to propose the first toast of the evening. Professor Cortes.'

Putting one hand in his pocket and rocking back and forth on his feet, Eduardo spoke softly and without notes.

'Just over a year ago, an extremely sick Sidney came to see me. Not only was she uncertain whether or not she should have a transplant, but she wanted to know what sort of a man it was who went round – 'chopping people up' I believe was her expression – when there was only a fifty-fifty chance of survival. Having checked my credentials with the Guild of Master Plumbers...' He waited for the laughter to subside. '...Sidney decided to put her faith in me. Bravely she stepped forward into the tunnel, stepped forward into the darkness. As you can all see from her happy and radiant...'

'And sexy!'

'Her happy and radiant, and sexy appearance tonight, the rest is history. In the Department of Histochemistry at the Fulham, world centre of excellence...' This time there were cheers. 'World centre of excellence, Sidney is once again running rings round her team and once again they have trouble keeping up with her. Her energy is boundless; her capacity for work is legendary, as is her immense dedication. I'm sure you will all agree that without Sidney's expertise, without her efforts, without her inspiration, our research could not go forward and a great many lives would be lost. I ask you to look at this beautiful lady, at this lovely phoenix who has risen from the ashes and somehow managed to find the strength to apply the same courage and single-mindedness which she has shown throughout her remarkable career, not only to her recovery but to her efforts to raise funds for further research into the cause of her illness. Forget those early days, those dark days. Forget about the past. Forget about the further hurdles that no doubt lie ahead, and drink to the future. I would like you all to join me in wishing "Happy Birthday Sidney!"'

Overcome with emotion, Sidney did not hear the sound of Nicholas' bleep. She was unaware that after making a short call on his mobile, he had whispered something, grave faced, to Martin after which the two of them had slipped out of the room.

'Eduardo, Nicholas, Dermot, Sebastian, colleagues and friends,' Sidney said into the expectant hush. 'I am sure you all know what a deeply moving occasion this is for me. Please don't take any notice if I cry...'

The silence was tangible as she struggled to continue.

'Thank you Eduardo... Sorry! Thank you Eduardo, for leading me through the tunnel – which at times was very frightening. Thank you Nicholas for your pre-operative and post-operative care and for continuing to monitor my 'blows'. Thank you to the nurses and staff at the Fulham for an exceptional standard of care. And – I don't know how to say this – a great big thank you to my unknown donor and his or her family, who gave me a priceless gift, which I solemnly intend to put it to the best possible use. Last, but not least, thank you Dermot, not only for loving and supporting me, but for nursing me back to health. I don't want to embarrass him further but I know it hasn't always been easy. This was to have been a joint birthday party. Anna Bond, who – thanks once more to Eduardo – will also be 'one year old' in a couple of weeks, was supposed to share it with me. Owing to a blip, Anna has unfortunately had to go back into the Fulham and cannot be here tonight. I am sure she is here in spirit. I'd like to ask everyone to drink, not only to Anna but to all the other transplant patients for whom Anna has set up BASH. Anna!'

Looking round the room, Sidney raised her glass. 'Where's Martin?'

She could not have known, as she plunged the knife into the birthday cake amid cheers and laughter, as she removed the weeping candle, that Martin was at the Fulham Hospital where Anna was in heart failure. Could not have known, as Dermot slipped a CD into the record player and the evocative sound of tango filled the room, that at that moment Martin Bond, who was not a religious man, was on his knees praying. Could not have known, as Eduardo took her in his arms and they moved in tandem to the evocative beat of the tango, as they had done so long ago in Rio, that in the intensive care unit of the Fulham Hospital, the heart and lungs for which her 'transplant twin' had waited so long, and on which so much hope had been placed, were fighting a losing battle.

Professor Julia Polak: the inspiration behind *Intensive Care*

Professor Julia Polak is the inspiration behind Rosemary Friedman's book. As Professor of Endocrine Pathology at the Royal Post-Graduate Medical School based at Hammersmith Hospital and an expert in lung disease, she was diagnosed with pulmonary hypertension and underwent a heart and lung transplant at Harefield Hospital at the hands of Professor Sir Magdi Yacoub in 1995.

As a result of her experience Julia went on to set up the Julia Polak Lung Transplant Fund to support research into improving the longevity of lung transplant patients and treatment of lung disease. Her research pointed to the direction of the engineering of tissue as the way forward and in 1999 she founded the Imperial College Tissue Engineering Centre, which researches growing human tissue for the repair and replacement of organs. She is Director of the Tissue Engineering Centre and is based at Imperial College School of Medicine at Chelsea and Westminster Hospital.

The Julia Polak Lung Transplant Fund raises money to fund the work of the Tissue Engineering Centre into developing lung tissue. Donations can be sent to:

The Julia Polak Lung Transplant Fund, Imperial College Tissue Engineering Centre, 3rd Floor, Chelsea and Westminster Hospital, 369 Fulham Road, London, SW10 9NH.

HOUSE OF STRATUS

Internet: **www.houseofstratus.com** including author interviews, reviews, features.

Email: **sales@houseofstratus.com** please quote author, title and credit card details.

Hotline: UK ONLY: **0800 169 1780**, please quote author, title and credit card details.
INTERNATIONAL: **+44 (0) 20 7494 6400**, please quote author, title and credit card details.

Send to: House of Stratus
24c Old Burlington Street
London
W1X 1RL
UK